The Purpose of Erie
Curve Ball

Jane Neagley

The Purpose of Erie - Curve Ball

Copyright 2025 by JaneNeagWrites

www.janeneagwrites.com

ISBN: 979-8-9990352-0-2

Cover Art by RD Creative Strategy

Interior Design by MWilbur Designs | www.mwilburdesigns.com

Editing by Elyssa Warkentin | www.elyssawarkentin.com

The Purpose of Erie
Curve Ball

Jane Neagley

The Purpose of Erie - Curve Ball

Copyright 2025 by JaneNeagWrites

www.janeneagwrites.com

ISBN: 979-8-9990352-0-2

Cover Art by RD Creative Strategy

Interior Design by MWilbur Designs | www.mwilburdesigns.com

Editing by Elyssa Warkentin | www.elyssawarkentin.com

"Great Scott!"
"I know, this is heavy,"

- *Doc Brown and Marty McFly*

Chapter 1

June 1987

Cassidy Banker pulled her blue Toyota Corolla into a second-row spot in her apartment complex's parking lot. She turned off the ignition and sighed, leaning her head back against the headrest. Her long, wavy, dirty blonde hair pressed into the fabric behind her. She gazed out into the clear, June night sky.

After sitting for a long moment, she took a deep breath, collected her keys and dark grey purse, and climbed out of the car. She quickly locked the car door with her key before turning and walking into her complex.

Cassidy swiftly scaled the stairs to her second-floor apartment and let herself in.

"I'm back," she called out, hanging her purse and key lanyard on the coat tree to the right of the door.

"Hey," her roommate, Marissa, called out from the direction of the kitchen. Cassidy made her way down the entry hall and into the large living room which connected to the rectangular galley kitchen. Marissa was standing at the counter chopping

1

a block of cheese into snack-sized slices. Marissa was petite and thin with dark brown hair that was almost always set in two French braids along the sides of her head.

Cassidy kicked off her white Nikes and padded over to the kitchen to help herself to some of Marissa's cheese. Cassidy was about three inches taller than her friend. And while Cassidy was nowhere near overweight, she had an athletic build – twelve years of competitive softball will do that to you. She always felt large next to Marissa, twinging a bit of jealousy, especially on their nights out to meet guys. However, Marissa herself never made Cassidy feel insecure, and Cassidy comfortably grabbed a handful of cheese slices from the cutting board before walking back into the living room and plopping down on the sofa, stretching her legs out to the middle cushion.

"Stress eating?" Marissa asked as she cut the final two slices and put the knife in the sink.

"Mmmm," Cassidy agreed, taking a bite out of a slice of cheese. Marissa collected her cheese slices into a bowl and made her way to the living room. She took a seat on the opposite side of the sofa and stretched her legs out in front of her, her ankles resting atop Cassidy's feet.

"How'd it go tonight?" she asked, casually popping a piece of cheese in her mouth. It was the first Friday of June, and in the Banker family, the first Friday of the month meant family dinner night. Cassidy and her four brothers all returned home to their parents' house for a family meal.

Cassidy's parents, Art and Lynne, had started this tradition when their eldest left for college. The monthly dinner had been routine for nine years now. Both Art and Lynne were nearing retirement, and with all five children out of the house, they looked forward to it more than ever. Their children, on the other hand, had mixed feelings. Some months they loved it, some months, they would have rather stayed home.

Cassidy's brother Alex was the eldest of the Banker children. Twenty-eight, now, with medium height and a slightly stocky build, his dark blond hair rested just atop his ears. He dreamed of being a novelist, and spent most of his free time scribbling away on his notepads. However, wannabe writer doesn't pay the bills, so Alex put his creative writing skills to work at his job with the Erie Times Newspaper where he wrote the "Household Hints" and personal advice columns. Cassidy always found it amusing how much stock people put in the paper's advice. If all those women that wrote in only knew they were getting their relationship tips from a chain-smoking, day-sleeping, twenty-eight-year-old man, they'd die of embarrassment. She had to admit, Alex gave surprisingly good advice, though.

Next was twenty-seven-year-old Matty. Tall and thin with short, light brown hair, Matty was a math teacher at the high school in Cambridge Springs, just two towns over from Erie, where they all grew up. Matty was loud, sarcastic, and funny. He made friends wherever he went, yet he had a knack for putting his foot in his mouth. Lucky for him, he could win people back pretty quickly, or at least defuse the situation with a well-timed joke.

Technically, Cassidy was next born. However, she only held that place by a twelve minute margin. Cassidy was a twin. She and her brother Eric were twenty-five. Both had wavy, dark blonde hair and stocky builds. While they were obviously not identical, there were striking similarities between the two of them – much to their mutual dismay.

Twins were expected to be best friends, close companions: two peas in a pod. Cassidy and Eric were not. They didn't hate one another, but they definitely weren't close. They'd never shared a friend or even a secret. When spending time with family, they always gravitated to their other brothers, all of whom they were much closer with than each other. This was an unfortunate fact of their lives. Neither were thrilled about it, but neither wanted to put in any effort to fix it.

They'd both graduated college three years ago – class of 1984. Eric from the University of Pittsburgh and Cassidy from Edinboro University. Eric was back in Erie now, working as an HR assistant for a computer training facility. He'd always been into computers. Cassidy was a Certified Public Accountant at a small accounting firm downtown. She'd always loved numbers and was very organized. Accounting was her dream career.

Finally, there was Ben, the youngest Banker at twenty-one. Ben had the lightest blond hair of the five kids, and he always wore it long, to his chin – much to the intense disdain of their mother. Ben was currently on summer break before his senior year at Mercyhurst University in Erie, studying to be a therapist. Cassidy couldn't understand how he'd selected psychology as a major. Ben couldn't listen to a shopping list before going to the store; how on earth was he going to listen to his clients? Yet Ben remained on the Dean's List every semester and played varsity soccer for the school.

But Ben was not Cassidy's concern at the moment. She was thinking about how to answer Marissa's question.

"Hmm? How did it go?" Marissa prodded, gently tapping her heel on Cassidy's foot.

"Well," Cassidy began, letting out a loud breath. "Eric's

engaged."

"What?" Marissa squawked, completely bug-eyed.

"Yeah," Cassidy said in a low, long drawl.

"That Laura girl?"

Cassidy shook her head as she munched on her final piece of cheese.

"Laura is Alex's girlfriend," she corrected. Alex and Laura had been together for eight years, since their sophomore year at college. She was an art teacher at the vo-tech school and worked part-time painting and designing sets at the Erie Playhouse. The two of them lived in bohemian bliss in a loft downtown.

"Oh, that's right."

"Eric is with Ellie," Cassidy clarified.

"Eric and Ellie," Marissa said in a mocking tone. Cassidy smiled.

"I've met her a few times, she's not bad."

"Sure about that?" Marissa raised an eyebrow. "You're not super convincing."

"Honestly, she's fine. You know, it's just... it's Eric. It's hard for me to be happy for him. Especially for him getting married before me. You realize the entire planning, preparing, showers, and wedding itself will just be people asking, 'When are you getting married?' 'Your twin got married before you, how do you feel about that?'" Cassidy ended with a huff.

"Ugh, yeah, people suck."

"They do," Cassidy agreed, resting her head on the back of the sofa.

"You just have to remember, it's Eric's day."

"It's not Eric's day, it's Ellie's day. Eric's just along for the ride," Cassidy replied bluntly. Marissa laughed out loud.

"How long have they been dating?" Marissa asked, once she had stopped laughing.

"A little over a year, I think."

"Did your mom flip?"

Cassidy rolled her eyes hard. "Oh, my gosh, yes. She went absolutely crazy."

"Well, at least it'll only be pure chaos until the big day. Have they set a date?" Marissa asked.

"Eric mentioned that Ellie wants a snow-free wedding, so they need to hurry up and do it now, or it'll be next May, probably," Cassidy said with a shrug.

"Ahhh, the joys of Erie weather," Marissa mused.

"Yeah, it's fantastic." Cassidy replied, though she honestly did love the area.

"You're really upset, aren't you?" Marissa asked gently after a long moment of silence. Cassidy shrugged.

"I guess I always just assumed that I would be the first to get married, because I'm the girl. Or, I don't know, maybe Alex would have been first, but no matter what, it definitely wouldn't have been Eric."

"Well, Eric marrying before you may not be the worst thing…." Marissa suggested. Cassidy lifted her head and raised an eyebrow. "Your mom can get all her crazy out on him, and then when it's your turn, she'll be calmer."

"Calm is not one of my mother's functions," Cassidy retorted.

"Well, it'll give you a preview of what she gets upset about, then. You can learn how to avoid it."

Cassidy rolled her eyes. "If you say so,"

The girls changed the topic to their workdays, movies, celebrities, and everything in between. They chatted away happily for over an hour.

Cassidy had met Marissa their freshman year at Edinboro University, a small state university outside of Erie. They lived in the same residence hall, and both were plagued by horrible roommates in their freshman year. The two girls bonded quickly and ended up rooming together the next three years of school. After graduating, they both got jobs in Erie and happily jumped at the chance to get an apartment together on the edge of the city.

The girls departed to their respective bedrooms to go to bed a little before eleven. Cassidy flopped back on her bed, feeling a bit more relaxed than she had when she first got back from dinner at her parents'.

A loud, shrill ring roused Cassidy from a deep sleep. Again, the noise rang out. Cassidy gave a disoriented sigh and rolled over onto her back. A few seconds later, the sound echoed once more. Cassidy had the groggy realization it was the telephone in the living room. She strained to open her eyes and glance at the digital alarm clock on her bedside table. 1:33 glowed back in large red numbers. Cassidy swore. Suddenly she heard the sound of a door opening and determined steps down the hallway. Marissa had gotten up to end the ringing.

"What?" Marissa answered the phone sounding equally annoyed and exhausted. Cassidy lay motionless, waiting to hear Marissa slam the phone down and stomp back to her room. Unfortunately, that's not what happened. A few unintelligible grumbles later, and Marissa let out a bellow.

"CASSIDY!"

Cassidy leapt out of bed faster than she thought possible and dashed to the living room where Marissa stood looking disheveled, exhausted, and very irritated.

"It's your stupid brother." She set the receiver down on the table and stomped back to her room, slamming the door.

"Sorry," Cassidy called as she tried to think who could be on the phone.

'Stupid brother' could easily apply to any of the four of them.

"Hello?" Cassidy put the receiver to her ear and plopped down on the oversized chair in the corner of the room, crossing her legs underneath her.

"Hey." The breathy, unmistakable voice of her eldest brother, Alex, answered. He had clearly just taken a drag off his cigarette.

"What do you need?" Cassidy asked, stifling a yawn.

"You don't want to talk to me?" Alex asked, sounding slightly offended.

"Do you know what time it is right now?"

"Of course. It's 1:34," Alex replied coolly. Cassidy rolled her eyes and decided not to explain to him that some people sleep at this time of night. It was pointless, and she wasn't awake enough for that conversation.

"Okay. What's up?"

"Just wanted to check in," Alex replied sweetly. Cassidy bit her tongue to keep herself from telling him to call her at normal hours. She knew he was honestly trying to be nice.

"Um, well, I just saw you a few hours ago," Cassidy chuckled.

"I know, but I thought Eric's engagement might have thrown you. You looked like a ghost when he told mom and dad." Cassidy smiled to herself as she heard him take another drag. Her eldest brother was always the most observant of all of them. And while he and Cassidy led very different lifestyles, they loved one another fiercely. Cassidy never felt she had a favorite brother, but Alex was forever her champion.

"I didn't mean to make it obvious, but I was surprised," Cassidy admitted.

"It surprised the hell out of all of us," Alex said with a chuckle.

"Really? Eric didn't tell you guys anything?" Cassidy knew Eric talked to their brothers more than her. Granted, the bar of communication was pretty low between the twins…

"Naw," Alex said. "He never mentioned anything about engagement. He told us when they started dating, when they started sleeping together, meeting her friends and family. So, I guess it was coming, but he really never said anything. Not to me, at least."

"I guess that makes me feel better," Cassidy said with a shrug.

"Are you sad? Or pissed?"

"I don't know. Still processing, I guess."

"Processing what?"

"The whole thing."

"Do you hate Ellie?" Alex asked abruptly.

"I don't really know Ellie," she said honestly. "I guess I don't really know Eric, either."

"Cassidy," Alex said in a warning tone. She heard him let out a smokey breath.

"What?" she asked, irritated.

"You know Eric, you guys just don't get along. You need to stop feeling sorry for yourself that you're not best friends with him. That ship sailed a long time ago and you've both already milked it for all it's worth. Pick another battle."

Cassidy felt her jaw tighten. His words were annoyingly true, which only made them sting harder.

"Fine," she said quietly.

"Cassie—"

"What do you want me to say?" Cassidy asked.

"I want you to say what you're feeling!"

"I'm – I'm feeling… terrible," she admitted.

"Why don't you tell me about it?"

But Cassidy couldn't explain. She suddenly felt a rage boil up in her. Every thought and feeling, fear, shock, and annoyance, all seemed to bubble up into one big lump inside of her. She was going to explode. She could feel it. But she didn't want to. She wasn't prepared to face her emotions yet.

"I don't want to talk about it! It's the middle of the night! I'm done!" she snapped.

"Cassidy," Alex protested.

"Go to bed, Alex!" She slammed the phone down with a satisfying click. But she was instantly filled with regret and guilt. She bit her bottom lip as she leaned forward over her crossed legs and let out a low groan. She swore under her breath at her ridiculous childishness before getting to her feet and stomping back to her bedroom, closing the door behind her, and face-planting onto her mattress. She willed herself to fall asleep before the tears came.

Chapter 2

Cassidy ran her eyeliner pencil gently under her left eye and blinked twice as she leaned closer to the mirror to make sure her left eye matched her right. She set the pencil down and grabbed her dark pink lipstick, applied it liberally before smacking her lips and smiling back at her reflection.

She and Marissa were going out that night. They'd decided they both needed to let loose. They used to go out often in college, but since graduation they only seemed to go out once a month at the very most. They were due a night of fun – especially after last week's family dinner. After sliding her make-up back in her top dresser drawer, Cassidy walked over to the full-length mirror on the back of her bedroom door. Her teal strapless party dress fit her toned body perfectly. The flared hem rested about an inch above her knees. Her long, dark blonde hair had been curled and teased, making it look stylishly feathered, but not overly big. She couldn't understand why that was the style now. Seemed like way too much work. Cassidy smiled at herself, feeling pleased with her appearance. She thought she'd get at least one free drink that night. Perfect.

Marissa was in the galley kitchen pouring a pre-game shot for each of them. Her dark brown hair was tied up in a perfect bun and her petite frame was covered in a light pink dress, cut similarly to Cassidy's except Marissa's had thick shoulder straps. Only someone Marissa's size could pull that off and still look sexy.

"Heyyyy!" Marissa said as she walked the shot glass over to Cassidy. The girls were eye to eye tonight since Marissa wore three-inch white heels. Cassidy had no idea how she could walk, let alone dance in those things. But Marissa wore high heels every chance she got. Cassidy stuck to her flat black strappy sandals.

"You look great!" Cassidy remarked as she took the glass. She really did – but then, she always did.

"You, too!" Marissa said, raising her shot glass. Cassidy clinked hers against it and they both downed the strong liquid.

"Phew!" Cassidy gasped. Marissa shook her head and laughed.

"I just called the taxi; should be here in a few minutes," Marissa said.

"Great!" Cassidy picked up her purse to make sure she had everything. Wallet, ID, house key, two condoms, and a box of Tic-Tacs. She was ready.

"How much cash are you bringing?" Marissa asked. She was digging through her little black purse, as well.

"I have $28. That should cover two drinks and the taxi. That means I need to find some guy to buy me one or two,"

Cassidy explained with a smirk. Marissa chuckled.

"I'm taking $15 and it's all for the taxi. I want men to buy all my drinks. It's been a long few weeks. I deserve it."

Cassidy rolled her eyes. She had no doubt all of Marissa's drinks would be bought for her. Marissa was petite and pretty, and filled with confidence. Her bold manner is what drew Cassidy to befriend her all those years ago – she was confident, yet not conceited. A fine line to walk, but Marissa danced across it beautifully.

Two loud honks rang out from the parking lot outside the apartment window.

"That's us!" Marissa gushed. The girls quickly grabbed their bags, turned off the lights and departed the apartment, locking the big red door behind them.

They headed down the complex stairs, through the small, nondescript lobby and out the door to the waiting yellow taxi out front.

"Hello!" Marissa called as the girls approached the taxi. The driver rolled the window down. A large puff of grey smoke from his cigar billowed out.

"Yeah?" the gruff middle-aged man asked.

"Taxi for Marissa Solomon?"

"That's me; get in." The driver coughed and rolled his window back up. Marissa and Cassidy climbed into the dark back seat.

"Where to?"

"Revolution – the club downtown," Marissa instructed. The gruff man simply nodded, pressed the button to start the toll, and the taxi lurched forward. The girls talked as they weaved through the streets of Erie. Before they knew it, they were being dropped off on the narrow sidewalk in front of the large, tan building. A neon red sign glowed above the entryway. Two large men stood framing the doorway.

"Thanks," Marissa and Cassidy said to their driver. They handed him the $8 cash, clambered out of the yellow car and walked over to the bouncers.

"ID, ladies," the black-shirted man on the right side of the door said in a surly tone. Both girls handed him their licenses. He eyed both IDs and both girls for about fifteen seconds, really making a meal out of it, before handing the licenses back to the girls with a curt nod. The bouncer on the left side opened the door to let them in.

Two steps inside and the door thumped closed behind them. All of their senses were stimulated in an instant. The inside of the club was as dark as it was outside, but without the benefit of street lights or car headlights. The music rang through the air. An old Pat Benatar song was being spun by the DJ on the other side of the large room. Their nostrils were filled with an overwhelming mixture of cigarette smoke, spilled beer, and gallons of perfumes. Cassidy and Marissa gave each other a quick side glance before bursting into large grins. Memories of fun nights out as college students were flooding back. They were both very much looking forward to tonight.

Cassidy led the way to the long, dark wooden bar along the right side of room. They weaved through the high tables that were almost all occupied, past the row of circular booths along the wall until they reached the corner of the bar.

While it was a Saturday night, it was also the beginning of summer and ninety-five percent of Erie's college students had gone home for the summer. Erie had four universities right in the city center, and several others in the surrounding suburbs, including Edinboro University, where Cassidy and Marissa had attended. During the winter, this club would have been completely packed at this hour, with a long line out the door. But it was summer and there were less than a hundred people there that night. Oh, well. The lines were shorter!

"Hi, ladies," The bartender, a tall man with short black hair, greeted them as they rested their forearms on the bartop.

"Hey," Marissa replied with a sultry smile. Cassidy bit her lip to hold in a smile.

"What can I get yinz?" the bartender asked.

"What are you offering?" Marissa asked, leaning forward. Cassidy couldn't help but let out a small giggle. The bartender smiled back at Marissa knowingly.

"Drinks," he replied with a smirk. This was definitely not the first time a pretty girl had flirted with him.

"We'll take two shots of B52," Cassidy interjected. She had no doubt that Marissa could get flirt long enough to get them free shots, but she was ready to dance.

"Sure thing, sweetie," the bartender nodded as he quickly got to work. Marissa leaned to her right and brought her lips to Cassidy's ear.

"I had this!" Marissa whispered, sounding slightly discouraged.

"I want to dance. We'll get free drinks later," Cassidy insisted.

"We'll get them now," Marissa insisted. Cassidy chuckled at her friend.

"Here you go, girls," the bartender said, pushing two filled shot glasses in front of them.

"Thanks," Cassidy said.

"That'll be $6." Cassidy reached for her purse.

"Come on, really?" Marissa asked, reaching out and resting

her hand on his forearm.

"I think so," the bartender replied, clearly enjoying the attention of a beautiful young woman in a tight pink dress. Marissa slid her hand down his arm to entwine their fingers before pulling his hand towards her and placing a soft kiss on his knuckles.

"Please? I'll save you a dance," Marissa pleaded, kissing his fingers once more. The bartender let out a sigh.

"Fine. $2. But I'm getting my dance. My shift ends in forty-five minutes."

"I'll be waiting," Marissa replied with a smile, slowly pulling her hand from his. Cassidy watched and shook her head. The girls reached into their purses and each took out $1.

"Your tip comes later," Marissa said with a wink before picking up both shot glasses and walking to the nearest high table.

"You're unbelievable," Cassidy told her, taking one of the shot glasses from her hands.

Marissa shrugged. "I don't know what you're complaining about. I just saved you two bucks! And I'm the one that has to dance with that weirdo later."

"I thought you liked him?" Cassidy asked with a laugh. Marissa frantically shook her head.

"Ew, no! He's way too full of himself, and I can already tell that he's going to be grabby."

"Well, shit…" Cassidy said with a sigh.

"Here's to more free drinks and getting too drunk to be aware of the disaster dance that awaits me!" Marissa proposed, raising her glass.

"I'll drink to that!" Cassidy agreed. The girls clinked their glasses and downed their shots in one gulp.

They both gasped as the alcohol hit their systems. They set their empty glasses down on the table.

"We need to dance!" Cassidy told Marissa.

"Absolutely!" Marissa agreed. The girls linked arms and weaved their way onto the small dance floor in the back of the club. During the school year, you could barely move on the dance floor with all of the packed bodies – which sometimes had advantages. However, with maybe sixty other people on the dance floor, the ratio was near perfect. It didn't feel empty by any means, yet there was room to actually move.

Duran Duran cried out from the speakers and Marissa and Cassidy began dancing and jumping along with the beat as they made their way to the center of the crowd.

Cassidy felt her entire body loosen up as she danced, her mind focused only on the music blaring around her. It was one of her favorite feelings. Nothing else in the world mattered at that moment. Nothing but dance.

They jumped, danced, swayed, and twirled to four more songs without missing a single beat. As a Tiffany song started, Marissa grabbed Cassidy's arm and pulled her close so she could talk in her ear, the only way to be heard over the speakers.

"Those guys over there have been watching us," Marissa pointed. Cassidy glanced over. She was right. There were two 20-something guys leaning against the DJ booth smirking at the two of them.

"Hmmm," Cassidy mused as she smiled back. They were both good looking. One was thin framed with curly brown hair while the other was a bit more muscular with very short hair, just longer than a buzz cut.

"Should we wave them over?" Marissa asked.

Cassidy shrugged. "Why not?"

The girls smiled at each other before each raising an arm and waving a "come here" motion. The guys smiled and began weaving through the dancers as they made their way to the center where Cassidy and Marissa stood.

"Hi there," the muscular guy with very short hair said as he reached the girls. He was a good six inches taller than Cassidy in her flat sandals and Marissa in her heels.

"Hello," Marissa said happily.

"What are your names?" he asked.

"I'm Cassidy."

"And I'm Marissa." The guys nodded at them.

"Who are you two?" Cassidy asked them.

"I'm Pete," the short haired guy replied, "and this is my buddy, Brandon." The thin, curly haired man waved and smiled sheepishly.

"Hey," Marissa said, her focus solely on Brandon. Cassidy quickly realized that Pete was going to be hers, which honestly did not bother her in the least. Pete was a very good-looking guy.

"You guys wanna dance?" Cassidy asked eagerly.

"Yeah," Pete and Brandon agreed in unison.

Without hesitation, Cassidy took Pete's hand in hers and pulled him a few feet away, while Marissa took a step closer to Brandon. A Michael Jackson song was now blaring out of the speakers and the four of them began moving to the beat.

Pete pulled Cassidy close to him as they danced. The scent of his aftershave was thick, but Cassidy found it alluring. She brought her arms up to rest her hands on his shoulders while his large hands came to rest on her hips. She felt a tingle shoot up her spine. She had not had a boyfriend, or any romantic contact, in almost a year. Strong, firm, male hands grasping

18

her hips, with fingertips resting on her butt, felt like a jolt. A good jolt.

Cassidy and Pete's eyes locked as they moved to the beat. They were lost in their own little bubble, unaware of how long they danced. Cassidy was vaguely aware of people jostling around them, and the sounds of many different artists playing through the many speakers, but her focus was on Pete. His touch, his smile, his smell. Cassidy felt elated.

"Want a drink?" Pete asked, his lips right next to Cassidy's ear. She shivered involuntarily.

"Yeah," Cassidy said with a big nod. Pete took Cassidy's hand in his and led her through the crowd and over to the bar. They quickly ordered their drinks, a Budweiser for Pete and a Midori Sour for Cassidy, and they found their way to one of the high tables.

"Tell me about yourself," Pete asked over the music with a smile as he took a swig of his beer.

"What do you want to know?" Cassidy asked with a giggle, chewing on the tip of the black straw in her drink.

"Where are you from?" Pete asked.

"Meadville, but I've been living right in Erie since graduating college," Cassidy explained.

"Where did you go?"

"Edinboro, so I've always been in the area."

"You've never left Western Pennsylvania?" Pete asked.

"Oh, we've gone on vacations around the country, and I did a semester abroad my junior year."

"Edinburgh, I'm guessing?" Pete teased.

"Yep," Cassidy chuckled. "Edinboro has an exchange program with Edinburgh in Scotland. EU students can go to other places, but most of us go to Scotland, as the application is easier."

"Did you like it?"

"I loved it! I went fall of junior year and came home for Christmas. It was perfect," Cassidy told him, smiling as she thought of her time in Scotland.

"That's really cool."

"What about you? Where are you from?" Cassidy asked, taking a large sip from her straw.

"Lorain, just outside of Cleveland," Pete told her. Cassidy nodded. She could have easily guessed northern Ohio or further in the mid-west. His accent was much thicker than hers. Erieites had a mix of a diluted Pittsburgh and a diluted mid-west accent, creating a dialect of their own.

"What brings you to Erie?" Cassidy asked him curiously.

"I'm looking to get a coaching job. Didn't have any luck in Cleveland, so I'm going to try Erie," Pete explained.

"What do you coach?"

"Baseball. I played for Ohio State. I love it. I know I won't make it in the majors but would love to coach," he told her.

Cassidy's face lit up. "Ahh! I played softball!"

"Oh, yeah?" Pete asked, looking amused.

"Yes. Started in third grade and played all through college. Travel teams, tournaments, the works. I loved it! Actually, the only time I didn't play was when I was in Scotland for three months."

"I was the same with baseball! Started young and played the whole way through," Pete said, taking a large gulp of his beer.

"Where are you looking to coach?" Cassidy asked.

"I've put my resume out to a few of the universities in the area. If I don't hear anything I'm going to hit the New England area. I do have a cousin up at UCONN, which would give me an in. I'd be happy to coach for them, but I thought I'd try something closer to home first," Pete explained.

"Wow, well, good luck!" Cassidy said, raising her glass in his direction. Pete smiled and clinked his bottle on her glass. They both drained the contents of their respective drinks.

"Wait here, let me get us a treat," Pete said with a wink. Cassidy giggled, a large smile spreading over her face. She was on cloud nine. She watched him walk back to the bar before starting to look around. The club was filling up a bit more. She gazed around the dance floor for a long moment before spotting Marissa's pink dress. She was energetically dancing with Brandon, and both seemed to be having the best time. They were starting to spin and Cassidy watched, in awe of Marissa's dancing skills in high heels. There was a clink on the table and she saw that Pete had returned.

"What do we have here?" Cassidy asked playfully, looking down where Pete had set a number of shot glasses full of clear liquid.

"I thought we could use some shots before we go back out on the dance floor," Pete smirked.

"Oh, yeah?"

"Come on, I just got three for each of us," Pete said as he divided the glasses and pushed three towards Cassidy.

"Fine," Cassidy agreed. While she had spent the majority of her weekends in college partying, she had slowed down considerably since graduating. These would be shots three, four, and five in the last two hours. Plus her mixed drink. She made a mental note to cut herself off after downing these shots. Her tolerance was not what it used to be.

"Ya ready?" Pete asked, raising the first glass in the air.

"Ready," Cassidy agreed, picking up the glass on her right.

"And, go!" Pete said. Both Pete and Cassidy downed the contents of the first glass and immediately moved on to shots two and three, slamming the glasses down on the table after completing each.

"Ahhhh!" they cried in unison, Cassidy laughing hysterically. Her head was already buzzing.

"Wanna dance?" Pete asked.

"Yeah!" Cassidy extended her hand to him. Pete took it and quickly pulled her through to the dance floor. They immediately started jumping along to the Devo song and Cassidy felt her heart race with exhilaration. By the end of the song, she could feel the alcohol had hit her system. The room was getting a tad blurry and her dancing had become a little wobbly and off kilter, but still in a fun, whimsical way. She was at the point of drunkenness where you believe anything is possible – also, that everything is funny. The sweet spot.

Cassidy and Pete were happily swaying in each other's arms when Cassidy looked up and saw Pete looking down at her. Her heart skipped as their eyes locked. Suddenly the air felt thick. The music faded into a loud hum, and Cassidy felt like the crowd around them had disappeared. Pete slowly lowered his head. Cassidy fluttered her eyes closed in anticipation just before his lips pressed against hers.

A spark shot up Cassidy's spine at the touch of his kiss. His lips were soft yet firm. She gripped his broad shoulders tightly as she felt him wrap his arms around her waist.

Pete's lips moved firmly against hers for a long moment before slowly pulling back. Cassidy involuntarily let out a gasp as they pulled apart. They looked at one another and smiled.

"Wow," Pete said breathily.

"Yeah," Cassidy agreed with a grin. Pete leaned down once more to place a quick peck on her lips before they resumed dancing to Billy Idol.

Chapter 3

The next hour was a bit of a blur for Cassidy. There was loud music, dancing, and more kissing; however, later she wouldn't be able to remember any specifics. Finally, she started to feel her feet ache from dancing, and the whimsical room-spins of drunkenness morphed into exhaustion. She was ready to leave.

"Hey," Cassidy called to Pete over the music. "I think I need to tap out."

"You okay?" Pete asked, still grooving to the beat from the speakers.

"Yeah, I'm just wearing thin. Time for me to go." Cassidy had spent years at EU exceeding her limits and learning the consequences. She knew when she needed to stop.

"Oh! Well, my place is just around the corner. Seriously, a five-minute walk, tops. I'll get you some coffee," Pete offered, sliding his arms around her waist. Cassidy bit her bottom lip as she thought. She knew exactly what would happen if she agreed to go back with Pete. After a quick moment of internal debate, she decided that was exactly what she wanted to happen.

She gave a small shrug. "Sure," she said.

Pete's face lit up before he quickly composed himself. Cassidy almost wanted to laugh.

"Ready to head out, then?" Pete asked, leaning down so his lips were right next to her ear. Cassidy felt a tingle shoot through her body.

"Let me find Marissa and say goodbye." Cassidy told him.

"Oh yeah, I wonder if she and Brandon hit it off?" Pete took Cassidy's hand and led her off the dancefloor. Cassidy chewed her lip once more. She really hoped Marissa was having as good a night as she was. She would feel like a terrible friend if she found out Marissa had been miserable.

Pete and Cassidy weaved their way through the high tables and people drinking and laughing all around them, their eyes peeled for their respective friends. After a couple minutes of searching, Cassidy spotted Marissa's pink dress out of the corner of her eye.

"Over there," Cassidy said, tugging on Pete's hand and pulling him towards the row of circular booths on the far wall.

Marissa and Brandon were cozied up in the second booth from the left, drinks on the table in front of them. They were talking with their faces very close together. Cassidy smiled. Her friend looked happy. Perfect.

"Hey!" Cassidy called happily as they got to the booth. She dropped Pete's hand and climbed in, snuggling up next to Marissa.

"Oh, hi!" Marissa said excitedly.

"What's up, man?" Pete asked Brandon. Brandon simply nodded back at him with a smile.

Cassidy leaned in close to whisper in Marissa's ear. "I'm going to go home with Pete," she admitted with a sheepish grin.

"Who's Pete?" Marissa asked seriously.

Cassidy stared at her. "Him!" she said nodding behind her.

"Ohhh!" Marisa's eyes widened with excitement.

Cassidy smiled at her before glancing up at the guys, making sure they weren't listening – but they had scooted over to the other side of the U-shaped booth and were having quiet discussion of their own. Good.

"How's it going for you?" Cassidy asked.

"Oh, so good! Brandon – is that his name?" Marissa paused, thinking. Cassidy could tell she was even further gone than she was.

"Yes."

"Yeah, Brandon is really nice. I think he's the one," Marissa said in the overly-serious tone that very inebriated people use when trying to make a point.

"'The one' what?" Cassidy asked, starting to giggle.

"The ONE one!" Marissa insisted. Cassidy let out a laugh.

"Uh huh."

"On my wedding day, I'm going to remind you that you laughed at me," Marissa said.

"Okay, you do that." Both girls laughed. Pete and Brandon glanced over at them, causing them to laugh harder.

"Oh, oh, wait!" Cassidy said, trying to settle her giggles.

"What?" Marissa asked, still chuckling.

"Did that bartender ever come by for his dance?" Cassidy

asked. Marissa tipped her head back in exasperation.

"He totally did. Well, we walked up to the bar, and Brandon… that's his name, right?"

"You really need to work on remembering that," Cassidy advised.

"It's a confusing name!"

"It's not."

"Anyway," Marissa continued, "Brandon and I went to get drinks and of course that bartender was there. He starts going 'oh hey, where's my dance?' and I just tried to ignore him, ya know? But he just kept asking. And Brandon is like 'I think she's hanging out with me, mate' which is so sweet, but the bartender dude was not getting the picture." Marissa sighed.

"And?"

"And he ended up charging us like double for the drinks. It was so dumb," Marissa whined. Cassidy rolled her eyes.

"Bartender dude is a douche."

"Major!" Marissa agreed.

"But are you good here with Brandon?" Cassidy asked.

"Oh, yes. You go have lots of fun!" Marissa teased. Cassidy smirked at her.

"Okay, I'll be back home tomorrow."

"And you'll tell me everything?"

"Always!" Cassidy assured her, before giving her a playful kiss on the cheek and scooting out of the booth. Pete glanced over when he saw her get up and stood and wrapped up his conversation as well.

"See ya, man," Pete said to Brandon. The two shook hands and grinned at one another.

"Ready?" Cassidy asked Pete.

"Let's go," he said, taking her hand and leading Cassidy

out of the club and onto the street. The fresh air felt wonderful on Cassidy's face. The club was so very warm and stuffy; the warm summer breeze was a welcome change.

"I love summer," Cassidy mused as she followed Pete down the street.

"Yeah, it's fuckin' A," Pete agreed.

While Cassidy was very happy to be outside at the moment, her feet were really starting to hurt as they walked another block through the city. She was grateful she was wearing flats, at least. She had no idea how Marissa and other girls did this stuff in heels.

"Just up here," Pete said, pointing to the grey apartment building on the block in front of them. Cassidy scrunched up her face slightly. She knew this building, but she had no idea why. More than generally knowing her way downtown, there was something very familiar about this place, but she couldn't quite place it at the moment. She blamed the alcohol. Her head was still buzzing.

"Great," Cassidy said, lost in thought.

"You alright?" Pete asked as they crossed the street to his block.

"Yeah, sorry. I just feel like I've been here before," Cassidy said. Pete shrugged, seeming less concerned about the coincidence than she was.

"Maybe it was some other guy you met," Pete suggested, holding the building door open and letting Cassidy inside. She sighed inwardly. Great, Pete took her for a slut. While she knew he had reason to think so, given that she was going home with him, she'd rather not have had the confirmation.

Cassidy and Pete got into the elevator. Pete pressed the button for the third floor and they started to ascend. It was one of those creepy, black metal, cagy-looking elevators. Cassidy hated them. But it was once again, annoyingly familiar. The elevator car lurched and creaked upward as Cassidy frowned at the open wall and pipes. Then the car stopped, and the door groaned as it opened onto a grey hallway.

Pete led Cassidy to the second door on the left and unlocked the door. Inside was a large, open studio apartment with exposed brick along the exterior wall. Black metal beams across the ceiling gave it an industrial feel.

Adding to the masculine industrial design of the apartment, the whole place felt like a total bachelor pad. Two full cases of beer sat next to the fridge. The sink was filled with dishes. The only pieces of furniture, aside from the bed and a small dresser in the far end of the studio, were in the center living area – a sofa and a chair, both black leather, and a dark wood coffee table covered in girlie magazines, multiple half-filled glasses, and an open pack of cigarettes.

Cassidy felt like she was back in college visiting her then-boyfriend at his frat house.

"Welcome!" Pete said proudly. Cassidy glanced back and gave him a small smile. While she found the apartment filthy, she'd grown up with four brothers. Slovenly males did not faze her in the least.

"Great space," Cassidy lied. Pete walked over to the small, L-shaped counter in the kitchen area.

"Want a drink?" Pete offered.

"Sure, thanks," Cassidy said. "Can I use your bathroom quick?"

"Yeah, just over there." Pete pointed towards the sleeping area. Cassidy nodded and found her way. The bathroom was a decent size and covered in dark green tile. While it was slightly untidy, it was at least clean and free of gross stains or concerning smells. However, the aftershave scent remained thick. She quickly used the bathroom and returned to the kitchen area to find Pete waiting for her with a shot glass. She set her purse on the floor of the living room before joining him in the kitchen.

"What is this?" Cassidy asked playfully, raising an eyebrow at him.

"One more," Pete insisted.

"I'm already in your apartment, you don't need to drug me," Cassidy remarked sarcastically.

"I wouldn't!" Pete said, looking mildly offended. Cassidy ignored him and took the shot glass from his outstretched hand with a sigh. She really had been hoping for some coffee or water. Oh, well.

"Cheers!" Cassidy and Pete said in unison before downing the contents and setting the empty glasses on the counter.

"Come here," Pete whispered. Cassidy couldn't help but smile up at him. He was very handsome, and he had been good to her all night. She took a large step forward and placed her hands on his shoulders. Pete gave her a quick smile before leaning down and connecting his lips to hers.

The kiss deepened, and Cassidy felt a flutter in her belly. She gripped his shoulders a little tighter as his arms snaked around her waist, pulling their bodies together. Cassidy slid her right hand up to the side of his head; his incredibly short hair tickled her fingertips slightly. She liked the feeling.

They kissed until they were breathless, their mouths moving

in perfect synch. Cassidy felt a warmth begin to spread from her core out to her limbs. It had been far too long since she had felt this way.

Pete's left hand slid down from her lower back onto her butt and gave a firm squeeze. Cassidy gasped loudly at the touch. She felt Pete smile against her mouth.

"Come with me," Pete whispered pulling his lips a centimeter off of hers before reattaching them in slow, gentle pecks. Using his hold on her backside, he slowly led her across the apartment towards his bed. Cassidy found herself struggling to walk, and stumbled every few steps. Between Pete's touch, the constant kisses, the alcohol, and walking mostly backwards, she was at his mercy to get there without crashing to the floor.

Cassidy finally felt the mattress against the back of her knees. Pete wrapped his arms tightly around her once more and they resumed their deep passionate kisses. Cassidy again felt sparks shooting up her spine as their mouths moved together. She was on fire.

Without warning, Pete quickly spun them around so he was the one at the mattress and he took a seat, pulling Cassidy close so she was standing between his knees. She pulled back for a moment to look at him once more. In this position, she was almost an inch taller than him. They smiled at one another, and Pete reached up to gently rub his thumb along her cheek. Cassidy bit her lip at his soft touch. She felt like putty.

Cassidy rested her left hand on his shoulder and her right on his cheek. His jaw was strong and firm, clean-shaven. He must have shaved right before coming to the club.

She leaned forward and connected her lips to his. As he kissed her back, she could feel his hands slide up her back to the top of her dress and begin to fumble with the zipper. Cassidy felt a strong tingle of anticipation. Within seconds she felt air on her bare back as the zipper lowered. Pete wasted no time in sliding her dress down her body until it lay pooled around her ankles. Cassidy gave a slight shiver. She was left in nothing but her light pink panties. She felt quite exposed, especially as Pete was still fully clothed.

He pulled back to look at her. Cassidy bit her lip as she felt his eyes on her.

"Holy shit, you're fit," Pete breathed, his eyes locked on her stomach. Cassidy chuckled.

"What can I say? After years of competitive sports, I developed a love of exercise," she said truthfully.

"You're so hot," Pete said, finally looking her in the eye. Cassidy blushed and kissed him again.

Pete immediately deepened the kiss, which Cassidy happily reciprocated. They had only been kissing for a long seconds when Cassidy felt Pete's fingertips on the hem of her panties. She quickly pushed on his chest and firmly shook her head.

"What?" Pete asked, looking confused.

"We're going to even things up first," Cassidy told him. She stepped out of her dress and kicked it a couple feet behind her, kicking off her sandals in the process, as well. Cassidy reached down and pulled at Pete's red shirt.

"Oh!" Pete reached up to help pull off his shirt. He stood and quickly removed his shoes and jeans, tossing them all aside, before reaching down and removing his socks, as well. He returned to his seat on the bed in just his dark blue boxer shorts. Cassidy smiled at his obvious eagerness.

She took a moment to drink him in with her eyes. He was extremely muscular and toned. He had a large tattoo on the front of his right shoulder and top of his chest. Cassidy couldn't quite place what it was, but it looked like something Japanese.

"Ya commin'?" Pete asked with a smirk. Cassidy simply nodded and climbed up on the mattress so her knees were on either side of Pete. He rested his hands on her hips while hers rested on his firm chest and she pressed her lips down on his. They shared three long kisses before Pete tightened his grip on Cassidy's hips and flipped them over so she was flat on her back on the center of the mattress with Pete stretched out on top of her.

"Ooof." Cassidy grunted involuntarily at the sudden movements and the feeling of Pete's weight on her.

Pete tenderly brushed a few strands of her long hair behind her ear before kissing her once more. Cassidy felt a sudden hardness push into her thigh as they kissed. The feeling sent the tingling from her spine down to her toes. She nipped at his bottom lip a couple of times before he crashed his mouth back onto hers and deepened the kiss. Pete's hands freely roamed Cassidy's mostly bare body, her back, sides, stomach and breasts, occasionally slipping down to her thighs.

Cassidy, in turn, ran her hands up and down his back and sides. His entire body was firm and muscular. She had never been in bed with someone as fit as he was. She couldn't decide if she was excited about that or not. What she was excited about was Pete's continued touch on her body with his hands and mouth.

Slowly, both of Pete's hands found their way to her hips and his fingers looped into the hem of her panties. He started to slide them down her legs. Cassidy pulled her mouth off of Pete's to help him remove her final covering and toss them on the floor, before returning the favor and helping Pete remove his boxers.

Within seconds they were both completely naked. Cassidy felt her heart give a weird thud. There was something terrifying, liberating, exciting, and yet overwhelming about being completely naked in front of a new guy. But she didn't have long to process her current situation; Pete quickly leaned back over her and kissed her neck enthusiastically. His need for her pressed firmly into her lower stomach, and she shivered again. They were so close.

"Pete," Cassidy said with a gasp, trying to focus as his tongue slid just below her left ear.

"Hmmm," Pete grunted.

"You have a condom, right?" Cassidy asked.

"Fuck," Pete said as he pulled his mouth off of her and sat up. Cassidy bit her lip nervously. Was that a fuck yes or a fuck no?

He awkwardly crawled over to his nightstand and slid the drawer open, digging frantically inside. Cassidy watched shamelessly. His whole body looked strong – especially his large, protruding member that looked ready to go. Cassidy let a low, deep breath as she stared at it. She quickly shook her head and turned away. She had never been one of those girls that was obsessed with dicks. She liked them, but never went out of her way to see them or got all giddy about them. However, at this current moment, her body wanted his. Perhaps it really had been too long since her last time. 'Get it together, Banker,' Cassidy scolded herself mentally.

"Got one!" Pete said happily, holding up the square package in his fingers.

"Good," Cassidy said, watching him tear open the plastic

with his teeth. He settled down to lie on his side next to her. "Here, let me do that," she offered, taking the condom out of his hands and slowly rolling it onto his dick. She felt him watching her as she gently trailed her fingertips along his length.

"You ready?" Pete asked with a grin. Cassidy simply nodded. Pete pressed his lips to hers and leaned her back onto the mattress as he climbed on top. He used his knee to push her legs apart and settled himself right at her opening.

Without any hesitation, Pete pushed forward and entered. Cassidy gasped, pulling her mouth back from his. Pete quickly found a rhythm and Cassidy dug her nails into his shoulder blades to hold on. He completely filled her, pushing her whole body deep down into the mattress. The faster he moved, the more her breathing began to pick up. She got warmer and warmer, heat spreading from her core. Cassidy started to gasp; Pete placed a sloppy kiss on her lips before letting out a loud groan and giving a hearty shudder.

It was over already. Cassidy gritted her teeth as she felt Pete slide out of her. He collapsed at her side. She glanced over at him; he was clearly lost in post-coital bliss.

"Babe," he whispered, kissing her on the cheek quickly before slowly getting his breathing back in order. Cassidy chewed on her lip a bit longer with a weird feeling in her belly. The moment had gone from hot to cold far too quickly. What an anti-climactic night. After a few long minutes of lying in silence, Cassidy glanced over to her side once more to find Pete's eyes were closed. Was he asleep?

She sat up and gave his shoulder a hard shove. He let out a groan and rolled over onto his stomach. Back to sleep he went. Cassidy rolled her eyes. She hopped up off the bed and went to collect her clothes. She redressed quickly before heading to the bathroom and relieved herself once more before leaving. As she was washed her hands, she glanced at herself in the mirror. She looked rough. Her make-up was starting to smear and her eyeliner had definitely spread, giving her the start of a racoon look. Her hair was frizzy and tangled. She tried to run her fingers through it to fix it, but that only made it looks slightly fluffier. She frowned at herself for a moment.

"Pete," Cassidy called as she walked back to the bed. Pete was still passed out on his stomach, completely naked atop his comforter. She took a seat on the edge of the mattress.

"Hey, I'm going to go," Cassidy said, a little louder as she patted his shoulder.

"Hmmm," Pete grunted.

"I'm going to go," Cassidy repeated.

"Kay. You're hot. Want me to call you, write your name and number by the phone in the kitchen," Pete instructed sleepily without moving or even turning his head to look at her.

"Okay, bye," Cassidy said in a mocking sing-song voice as she got off the bed. She quickly grabbed her purse from the living area. She paused a moment as she looked over at the phone and large pad next to it. After a quick internal debate, she decided to not leave her number. Cassidy let out one last sigh before departing the apartment and closing the door behind her.

Chapter 4

"I'm an idiot," Cassidy whispered to herself as she walked down the hallway, back to the creepy elevator. It seemed even more ominous now that she was riding it alone. It finally rattled to the ground floor and the door opened onto the lobby. Cassidy glanced at the clock over the closed front desk. 1:45AM. She sighed. It had been an eventful evening. She wandered past the mailboxes to the large payphone hanging on the wall and rummaged in her purse. She found a quarter, then picked up the Yellow Pages to find the phone number for a taxi.

Cassidy had just flipped to the Ts when she was startled by sound of the front door opening.

"What the hell are you doing here?" a familiar voice said in very surprised tone. Cassidy jumped. Her eldest brother, Alex, was standing just inside the door.

"What the hell are you doing here?" Cassidy retorted, shocked.

"I live here!"

Cassidy froze. Everything clicked. This was Alex's building.

She had been here before. That's why she'd recognized it when Pete first brought her there. "Oh, yeah," Cassidy said with a smile.

"What are you doing here?" Alex asked, sounding calmer.

Cassidy blanked. She was not in the mood to tell her brother that she'd just had a one-night stand. Ew. "Oh, just a night out in the city. I knew there was a phone here, so I'm calling for a cab," Cassidy lied. She shrugged up at Alex, never losing her smile.

Alex simply stared at her. He clearly didn't believe her. "Mmmhmmm," he hummed, running a hand through his wavy dark blond hair before crossing his arms over his chest.

"I'm just calling a cab! Everything's fine," Cassidy insisted.

"You don't look fine," Alex said with a grimace.

"What's wrong with how I look?" Cassidy asked, though she fully knew the answer.

"You look like a hooker!"

Cassidy scowled. "I do not," she spat - though he honestly wasn't too far off.

"Oh god, is that what you do now?" Alex asked, mock-horrified.

Cassie sighed. "Really?"

"I don't know what you do with your time," Alex said with a shrug.

Cassidy smacked his arm and he chuckled proudly. "You're an idiot," she grumbled.

"Yeah, but I'm your favorite of the idiots," Alex beamed.

Cassidy thought about it. He was kind of right. While she did love all of her brothers, there was something special about her relationship with Alex.

"I guess," she admitted reluctantly.

"Come on upstairs," Alex offered.

"I'm going to call a cab; I'm ready to go home and crash."

"Come on up and sober up a bit first," he suggested.

"Alex, I'm tired."

"I know, and you can crash here if you want – but just come on up and get some water and food in you. Please," he insisted. "I know you think you still feel okay now, but you get in that taxi and you're going to barf before you get back to your place."

Cassidy thought about it. She did want to go back to her own apartment and bed, but she really could use some food and water sooner rather than.

"Okay," she agreed, closing the Yellow Pages and returning the quarter to her purse. Alex smiled.

"Great! Laura will be happy to see you," he said, walking backwards through the lobby. Cassidy nodded and followed him. She was excited to see Laura, too. And quite grateful that she and her brother were both night owls right now. Alex led them back, once again, to the elevator.

"Oh, no," Cassidy whined. "I don't want to ride the death lift again. Isn't there another way up?"

"There are stairs, but there's no way in hell you'd make it up four flights in your condition," he said.

Cassidy groaned. He was right. The elevator dinged as the door opened and the two Banker siblings entered the cart. Alex pressed the button for the fourth floor and the ascent began.

"Bleh, I hate this," Cassidy sighed.

"Sick already?"

"No! Well, kinda. But I just hate this thing. It's so creepy."

"It's part of the aesthetic," Alex replied haughtily. Cassidy couldn't help but laugh.

The elevator lurched to the fourth floor, the door dinged and opened once more. This grey hallway looked exactly like the floor below it, where Pete lived. Cassidy followed her brother to the last door at the very end of the hall. Alex quickly unlocked the door and led them inside. The apartment was much larger than Pete's. While it had the same industrial loft features, it was a completely different layout with a large kitchen at the entrance of the loft and the living room nestled against the far wall. On the other side of the kitchen was a hallway to two bedrooms and a shared bathroom. Cassidy found it much homier than Pete's apartment.

"Laura, we have a visitor," Alex called, closing the door behind them.

"A visitor?" Laura asked, rushing into the kitchen. She beamed when she saw Cassidy, and Cassidy returned the smile. Laura was tall and thin, about the same height as Alex. She had shoulder-length, dark brown hair with a few streaks of a cool royal blue dyed throughout. She wore a baggy yellow tank top and ratty grey sweatpants covered in paint stains. Only she could make it look good. Laura had an effortless cool that no one could match – especially since it was paired with genuine niceness. Cassidy had always liked Laura. Their lifestyles were incredibly different, but Cassidy still found a kindred spirit in her.

"Hi," Cassidy said happily.

"Cassidy!" Laura gushed as she walked over and gave her a big hug.

"Found this working girl loitering in our lobby," Alex teased. He grabbed a large glass from the cupboard and went to the sink to fill it.

"Shut up," Cassidy sassed.

"I think you'd do a good business. Make some nice money," Laura said with a wink.

"Thanks – I'll update my business cards," Cassidy smiled. Alex groaned.

"Please do not encourage her to be a street walker," he pleaded, handing Cassidy the glass of water.

"You started it," Laura pointed out. Cassidy wanted to make a remark, but she was distracted by the glass of water. It looked glorious. She quickly brought it to her lips and started drinking, draining the contents in less than a minute. It was heavenly. She hadn't realized how dehydrated she was until that moment.

"Can I get another?" Cassidy asked her brother.

"Of course! Help yourself," he said with smile. Cassidy refilled her glass once more while Alex lit a cigarette before reaching into the pantry for a snack.

"Come on over to the living room and take a seat – you look like you need a break," Laura said. Cassidy followed her to the large living room. The far wall was exposed brick, and the room was filled with cozy, mismatched sofas and chairs that all worked together with an eclectic charm. A small TV sat in the corner on an old A/V cart Laura had rescued from a school dumpster the year before. It had lost a wheel, so they used a small block of wood to steady it. The center shelves were filled with Laura's art supplies. Next to the TV cart in front of the large window was an enormous easel with a half-painted canvas resting on it.

Cassidy plopped down on the closest sofa and curled her legs up underneath her.

"What are you working on?" she asked, taking another large gulp of water.

"Sunset over the water," Laura said with a smile. She walked over to her easel and picked up her brush once more, dabbing it in some paint and applying a stroke to the canvas.

"Nice," Cassidy mused. Alex walked past her and plopped down on her right.

"Here," he said, tilting the box of Cheez-Its towards his sister.

"Ooo, thanks." She reached in and grabbed a handful, ungracefully funneling them into her mouth. Alex watched her with a bemused smile.

"So, what are you doing downtown at this hour?" Laura asked casually, her eyes focused on her canvas. She gingerly dabbed her brush in one spot.

"I went to a club," Cassidy replied, her mouth full of crackers.

"And now you're here? Oh, shit! You went home with someone in our building?" Laura cried, spinning around, her eyes wide with intrigue.

Cassidy shrugged her shoulders playfully and took another drink to wash down the crackers. She felt Alex glaring at her and did her best to ignore him.

"Maybe," she admitted with a smirk. Alex made a disgusted groan before taking a long drag from his cigarette.

"Ignore him. I'm happy for you! It's been almost a year since you and Kevin broke up. You needed this."

Cassidy blushed and dropped her head. Her almost-sister-in-law had an opinion on her sex life. Great. "Don't get all weird. It was just tonight. I wanted to go out and blow off some steam, and I did. This is not a new beau."

She reached over to the box Alex was holding. He playfully pulled the box a few inches back, just out of his sister's reach.

Cassidy let out a small sigh. Alex held the box out towards her and just as Cassidy reached out he yanked it back again, causing Cassidy to teeter slightly.

"Give me the damn box!" Cassidy said loudly. Alex chuckled and brought the box back towards her. Cassidy grabbed the entire thing and moved it to her lap as she helped herself to another handful.

"So bitchy for a working girl who just got paid," Alex teased.

Cassidy shot him an annoyed glare. "How's the novel coming, Dear Abby?" she jabbed back.

"Alright, guys," Laura cut in, still focused on her painting. Alex and Cassidy glanced at each other and gave a quick shrug. An unspoken truce.

"Where do you guys go when you go out?" Cassidy asked.

"There's a great bar next to the playhouse. It's so much fun. Lots of artists there. Someone's always playing live music, the walls are covered in murals…"

"And they make one hell of a Brandy Old Fashioned," Alex interrupted.

"Ah, priorities," Cassidy said sarcastically.

"What is it with you and that drink?" Laura asked, turning and setting her hands on her hips.

"They're good!" Alex said.

"It's an old man drink," Laura scoffed.

"No, it's not. It's classy."

"Pop Pop drank Brandy Old Fashioneds," Cassidy pointed out.

"Pop Pop was pure class!"

"Pop Pop was old."

"And classy." Alex cocked his head to the side as he looked

at his sister.

"Fine, but the vital fact here is that you drink old people drinks," Cassidy smirked.

"Told you!" Laura chimed in. Alex rolled his eyes and groaned in defeat.

"Oh, hey, we have to remember to pick up the stuff to make curry tomorrow," Alex remarked, perking up.

"Already got it," Laura said, returning her attention to her easel.

"You're making curry?" Cassidy raised an eyebrow suspiciously at Alex.

"Yes!" he replied. "We've made it a few times."

"My old college roommate, Jennifer, and her boyfriend are coming over tomorrow," Laura told her.

"And she loves curry?" Cassidy asked.

"She introduced me to it. I literally had never had it until I roomed with her."

"And Laura got hooked and got me into it," Alex explained, flicking his cigarette into the ashtray beside him. "We decided to try and make it ourselves last year. Seems to get better each time."

"We finally know what we're doing," Laura added. Cassidy chuckled. Cooking had never been Alex's forte; this culinary adventure must have been completely supervised by Laura.

"When did we first have a curry?" Cassidy asked Alex.

"I think I was in late high school… at one of dad's work parties, I think."

"Oh, yeah, what was that Indian holiday? Dibadi?"

"Diwali," Laura corrected.

"Ahh, yes."

"Yeah, and mom was annoyed that people kept trying to put

leis and scarves on her because she wore that blue suit that she loved, and hated not showing it off," Alex said with a chuckle.

"Oh, my god, yes. And Ben almost threw a tantrum because there weren't any French fries and that was all he wanted." Cassidy started to laugh at the memory.

"Meanwhile, Matty ate four plates of food and then barfed in the fountain outside in the front courtyard," Alex laughed, shaking his head. Cassidy laughed loudly.

"How have I never heard about this before?" Laura asked through giggles, setting her paintbrush down.

"I don't know! I haven't thought of that night in years," Alex shrugged, his laughter beginning to slow.

"We were in true form, that night. Dad was so embarrassed." Cassidy grinned sheepishly.

"Eh, you, Eric, and I had fun," Alex noted.

"True." Cassidy smiled at her brother, enjoying the forgotten memory.

A comfortable silence fell over the room as the laughter came to an end. Cassidy felt a wave of exhaustion wash over her.

"Can I use your phone?" Cassidy asked with a yawn. She was tired.

"What for?" Alex asked. He made a grab for the box of Cheez-Its, but Cassidy saw him coming and knocked his thigh with her curled up leg. Alex rolled his eyes.

"To call a cab. I'm really tired and I do want to crash. I appreciate the water and snacks; definitely needed them more than I realized, but I'm ready to go."

"Alex, don't let your little sister take a taxi in the middle of the night," Laura said, returning to her canvas. Cassidy scrunched her nose. "Little sister?"

"Wasn't planning on it," Alex said. He stood up from the couch and extinguished his cigarette in the ashtray.

"Are you holding me hostage?"

"Ideally, but you'd be an absolute nightmare to keep locked up," Alex said as he stretched his arms above him. Cassidy smiled.

"So?" she asked.

"So, I'm going to drive you home. Come on, get your shit," Alex said as he walked past Cassidy.

"Really? Thanks!" she said happily. She was honestly thrilled that she didn't have to call for a cab. The late-night drivers were always creeps. She quickly finished the last few sips of her water and stood herself up.

"I'll be back in a jiff," Alex said to Laura, walking over and giving her a quick peck on the lips.

"'Kay," Laura replied cheerily. "Cassidy, it was nice seeing you. We'll have to do dinner sometime, you and me."

"I would love that." Cassidy followed Alex back to the kitchen. She set her empty glass on the counter and picked up her purse.

"Ready?" Alex asked, twirling his key ring on his finger as he waited by the front door.

"Yep."

Despite making a fairly good argument for the stairs, Cassidy found herself bullied back into the creepy elevator for the fourth time that night, which she frankly felt was cruel. The siblings made their way to Alex's white Honda Accord parked in the three-story parking garage next door. Once in the car, they weaved out to the main entrance and onto the street.

"Thanks for the ride," Cassidy said as she looked through the cassette caddy that had been on the floor of the passenger seat.

"No problem."

"Ooo, Billy Ocean!" Cassidy said with a smile, pulling out the cassette and popping it in the tape deck. A few bars 'Caribbean Queen' played before Alex spoke.

"Cassie, are you okay?" he asked seriously as they came to stop at a red light.

"Yeah, why? Do I look green? I promise I won't barf in your car."

"I appreciate that," Alex chuckled.

"Why do you ask?"

"I don't know – you aren't really the type to get shitfaced and sleep with a random guy," he said, accelerating as the light turned green.

"How do you know?" Cassidy asked with a large smirk.

Alex shot her a quick side eye glare. "I know you."

"Alex, I partied all the time in college. You do know I'm not a virgin, right?"

"Ugh, yeah," Alex sighed. "But, you've had boyfriends, relationships. Who the hell was this guy tonight?"

"Are you really asking me this? You wouldn't be happy if I asked you who you're sleeping with."

"The answer would be easy: Laura." Suddenly both Alex and Cassidy started to chuckle. It felt good.

"Are you mad at me?" Cassidy asked finally.

"Why would I be mad?"

"You shouldn't be, but I thought maybe you would be because I hung up on you last night – but honestly, it was late and you woke me up, and –"

"I'm not mad, Cassie," Alex interrupted.

"Oh," Cassidy said.

"I'm just concerned. I don't want you acting stupid just because you're mad at Eric."

"I have no idea what you're talking about," Cassidy replied firmly. "I went out tonight because I haven't gone out in weeks. What happened with Pete was not planned."

"Pete? Is that tonight's mystery man?" Alex teased. There was a hint of venom in his voice.

"Ugh, are we back at my apartment yet?" Cassidy sighed, tipping her head back onto the head rest.

"Pete who?" Alex asked. Cassidy suddenly felt a rock at the pit of her stomach. She had no idea what Pete's last name was. She'd just had sex without knowing the guy's full name. She had never done that before. She couldn't tell if she felt ashamed or liberated. She wanted to feel liberated, but Alex was right – random one-night stands had never been her style. She felt shame start to creep in.

"Do you not know?" Alex pushed. Cassidy could not admit it to him.

"Of course I know!" she lied. "I'm just not telling you. I don't want you chasing the poor bastard down."

"Bastard, huh?"

Cassidy groaned in annoyance and Alex chuckled. She reached forward to turn the stereo up and put her mind to Billy Ocean's lyrics.

The car made two more turns and went down a long street before they reached the parking lot of Cassidy's apartment complex on the southern edge of the city. Alex drove up to the entryway and parked the car, letting it idle. He reached over and lowered the volume on the stereo.

"You're home," he said plainly.

"Thank you, I do appreciate you," she said with a smile.

"Anytime." Cassidy leaned over and gave him a hug, which he happily reciprocated.

"Goodnight, Alex," she said as she pulled out of the embrace and opened the car door.

"Goodnight, working girl," Alex replied, looking smug.

"You're such a dick," Cassidy said, rolling her eyes. She would let him have his fun tonight – but she planned to hit him when she was sober.

"See ya!" Alex said as Cassidy climbed out of the car.

Cassidy yawned as she slowly climbed the stairs. Even though she was exhausted, she was thrilled to not be in the horrible elevator of doom once more. She unlocked her apartment door and closed it quietly behind her. The apartment was dark. It was almost 3 AM; why wouldn't it be?

Cassidy tip-toed to her room. She spent all of ten seconds debating whether she should make the extra effort to properly prepare for bed.

"Screw it," she whispered to herself before tossing her purse on the floor, kicking off her shoes, and flopping down face-first onto her mattress. She was asleep within less than a minute.

Chapter 5

The incessant beeps from the bedside alarm clock brought Cassidy back to consciousness. She blindly reached around until her hand found the clock and smacked the OFF button. The room was draped in silence once more. She yawned widely and slowly blinked her eyes open. The sun was beaming through the window. She took a few minutes to stretch and roll before heaving herself out of bed. Standing, she looked down and saw that she was still in her party dress from last night. She groaned.

Thirty minutes later, Cassidy was showered and dressed in fresh clothes – a grey T-shirt and dark blue gym shorts – and had brushed her teeth and braided her hair. She made a bee-line for the kitchen for some food. It was 9:30 in the morning, which was late for Cassidy, who was generally an early riser. It had thrown off her usual meal schedule. She was a morning eater. She could happily skip dinner, but breakfast and morning snacks were her lifeblood.

Coffee was brewing, bread was in the toaster, and she was

pouring Corn Flakes into a bowl when Marissa's bedroom door opened.

"Hey!" Cassidy called, but it was not her roommate's voice that replied.

"Uh, hi," a deeper voice said. Cassidy's head snapped up. She was surprised to see Brandon standing at the door.

"Good morning!" Cassidy tried hard to control her expression.

"Morning!" Marissa called, running out from her bedroom and pushing around Brandon. "I'm just walking him out," she added, taking his hand and leading him down the hallway towards the door. She was still in her usual light pink nightdress, while Brandon was in the same outfit he'd worn last night.

"Okay," Cassidy said, returning her attention to her breakfast.

Cassidy was returning the margarine to the fridge when Marissa came back into view, looking sheepish.

"That was a little surprise," Cassidy teased, carrying her breakfast to the living room.

"Uh, yeah." Marissa giggled and poured herself a cup of coffee, joining Cassidy on the couch.

"Was it a good night?" Cassidy asked, taking a large bite of her toast.

"Really good. We stayed at the club for another hour after you guys left, then took a cab back here. I invited him up for coffee. We ended up talking for over an hour, about everything under the sun, then he kissed me, and well… one thing led to another." Marissa grinned.

"Nice!" Cassidy cheered. "Was he good?"

"Oh, yeah."

Cassidy giggled into her coffee. "I'm glad."

"He promised to call me tonight so we can set up a date for this week!" Marissa beamed. Cassidy felt her heart swell. She was very happy for her friend.

"Do you know what restaurant you're going to pick?" Cassidy asked, taking a spoonful of cereal.

"No idea," Marissa laughed into her coffee. "Oh, my god! How was your night?"

Cassidy simply shook her head. "Um, interesting," she said, wincing.

"Please expand on that."

"Well, I went back to Pete's apartment, and things escalated pretty quickly." Cassidy paused to take another spoonful of cereal.

"And how was it?" Marissa prompted.

"Parts were definitely very good. Quick, though."

"Oh, dear." Marissa cringed.

"It's fine. We had a nice, awkward goodbye and I left – only to find out that he lives in Alex's building... when I ran into Alex in the lobby."

Marissa's eyes bugged. "Shut up!"

"Yeah, but it kind of worked out. Alex let me come up and have some food and then drove me home so I didn't have to pay for a cab."

"Yay, Alex!" Marissa cheered. She got up to make herself something to eat.

They were planning to head to the local park for a long walk in the June sun, then spend the rest of the afternoon lounging in front of the TV and ordering Chinese food for dinner. A perfect, lazy Sunday.

Cassidy tapped her pencil on her desk as she proofread the payroll form she was working on for one of her clients. It was the Thursday afternoon before a long weekend and Cassidy was ready to go home. Saturday was July 4th, but her office, and a majority of the city, were closing on Friday the 3rd to observe the holiday.

After confirming that the form was correct, Cassidy enclosed it in a manilla envelope and set it in her outbox to be collected by a mailroom clerk. She looked up at the clock on the wall. 4:45. Only fifteen minutes left until the long weekend. She let out a dejected sigh.

"Any plans this weekend, dear?" Gladys, the secretary, asked politely. Gladys was a small, thin woman in her early seventies. She'd been a secretary with the company since the late '50s and was beloved by all of the employees – beloved and feared in equal measure.

"Not much. My family is having a bar-b-que on Saturday, but that's it," Cassidy said with a small smile. "What about you?"

"We're driving down to Pittsburgh for the weekend to watch the fireworks and do some shopping in the city," Gladys said as she adjusted the leaves of the small, half-dead fern on the corner of Cassidy's desk. Cassidy quickly made note to water the poor thing before she left for the long weekend.

"Sounds wonderful!" Cassidy smiled at the sweet woman.

"Got to get my kicks while I still can!" Gladys winked before returning to her desk. Cassidy chuckled. She hoped she was that witty when she got that old. Although she also hoped she wouldn't still be working – at least not here.

Cassidy got up from her desk, patting her navy-blue skirt straight, before walking over to the large water cooler, filling a paper cup and returning to give her pathetic desk plant some nourishment. After tossing the paper cup in the trash, she started to clear off her desk and ready herself to leave. Filling the time, as best she could.

Once all her files, ledgers, and pencils were put away, she plopped her purse on her desk and pretended to search for something very important inside as the final minutes ticked down.

"Weekend time, Banker!" a male voice boomed as Cassidy stood up to leave for the day. She resisted an eye roll.

"Yep," she replied blandly as the tall, dark-haired man approached. Devon Parks. A sleezy coworker who spent most of his work day making rude jokes and boasting about his sexual conquests. He was probably harmless, but he still made Cassidy's skin crawl.

"I'm going to be spending my time out on the lake," Devon boasted.

"Mmmhmmm," Cassidy replied, scooting past. He deliberately stood in positions that forced her to brush against him.

"You're always welcome to join us. It's going to be great! Beer, bikinis, grilling, more beer – you'd love it." Devon started to walk with Cassidy towards the reception area.

"Quite an offer," Cassidy sighed dramatically. "However, I already have plans."

"Shame. You'd look hot on the lake," Devon said with a wink.

"Goodbye, Devon," Cassidy called as she waved her arm over her head and continued walking towards the door, leaving him behind. "Bleck," she grimaced as she exited the building onto the sunny sidewalk. The July heat smacked her right in the face.

Cassidy readjusted her bags on her shoulder as she strode towards the parking garage two buildings down. Despite being downtown, there weren't any really tall buildings to block out the sun. Normally she enjoyed the summer heat, but after spending the entire day in air conditioning, the sun felt brutal.

She made the walk to her car quickly and rolled the windows down as she started up the engine. Once out on the street, Cassidy cranked up the radio, drowning out the rush hour traffic with The Bangles.

After slowly weaving through the downtown traffic, Cassidy made it to the edge of the city and turned into her complex's parking lot, letting out a loud sigh. She was happy to be home.

Cassidy put her key into the door and let herself inside the apartment, dropping her bags on the floor. "Hi!" she called. Marissa generally got home later than she did, but she thought she'd spotted Marissa's Subaru in the lot. There was no reply, but Cassidy heard rustling.

She walked down the entrance hall and into the living room to find a set of men's feet hanging over the edge of the sofa. She quickly peered around to see Brandon and Marissa laying across the couch, limbs entangled in a full-on make-out session.

Cassidy cleared her throat, amused. Each one of the pair gasped and they scrambled to untangle themselves, the shock causing Brandon to thump onto the floor.

"Hello," Cassidy said with a cheeky smile.

"Hi, Cassidy!" Marissa said, blushing slightly. She and Brandon had been dating since that fateful night at the club the month before. Brandon was now spending one night a week at their apartment, and Marissa was at his once a week. They usually worked in a date night, as well. Cassidy was happy for her friend. Brandon was good to her and they seemed to be having a wonderful time together.

"How's it going?" Cassidy asked in a sing-song voice as she made her way to the kitchen for a snack.

"Well, it was great," Brandon quipped. Cassidy was leaning into the fridge, but she very clearly heard Marissa smack his chest. Cassidy chuckled to herself.

"Poor baby," she teased, emerging with a yogurt.

"Don't worry about him," Marissa said, heaving herself up from the couch and tousling Brandon's hair as she stood. He smiled up at her before moving to take a seat on the sofa.

"Didn't expect you to be home this early," Cassidy said, dipping her spoon in her yogurt.

"I took a half day," Marissa replied, coming over to rest her elbow on the counter next to Cassidy.

"Do you two have something special planned this evening?"

"No. Brandon's leaving tonight," Marissa said glumly. Brandon joined them in the kitchen, casually slinging his arm over Marissa's shoulder.

"Leaving?" Cassidy looked back and forth between the two.

"Driving back to Indiana for the long weekend and spending it with my family," Brandon explained.

"Hmm," Cassidy hummed.

"What?"

"Oh, nothing. For some reason, I thought you were from Ohio."

"No." Brandon shook his head. "I went to Ohio State, but I'm from Indiana. Just outside of Indy."

"Nice," Cassidy nodded.

"It's, like, a six-hour drive," Marissa chimed in, turning to wrap her arms around Brandon's middle, resting her head on the side of his shoulder.

"Just under six; it's not bad," Brandon assured her.

"When are you heading out?" Cassidy asked, downing the last spoonful of yogurt.

"Don't kick him out!" Marissa sassed.

"I'm not kicking him out, I'm just asking!" Cassidy rolled her eyes.

"It's fine," Brandon assured her. "Actually, I need to be heading out pretty soon. I promised parents I'd get in before midnight."

"Traffic is heavier going east. You should have a decent drive," Cassidy told him with a smile. Brandon nodded.

"You're leaving right now?" Marissa asked glumly. She tilted her head up to look at him.

"Yeah. I wanted to be on the road by 5:30 and that's in less than ten minutes. I need to head out." Brandon placed a light kiss on her lips.

Cassidy sighed. They were annoyingly adorable.

"I'll walk you out," Marissa sighed.

"See ya, Brandon," Cassidy said cheerily.

"Until next week," Brandon nodded. He took Marissa's hand and headed towards the door.

"Be back in a couple minutes," Marissa added to Cassidy as Brandon towed her along.

The door shut behind them with a click and Cassidy took a deep breath. She trudged her way to her bedroom and changed out of her work clothes, into a pair of running shorts and a light green tee shirt. After she tossed her hair up and quickly used the bathroom, she returned to the living room and flopped ungracefully down onto the couch. She had just reached for the remote when the apartment door opened and Marissa returned down the entrance hall.

"He left?" Cassidy asked, clicking the TV on.

"Yeah," Marissa said with a sigh. She took a seat on the armrest of the sofa by Cassidy's feet.

"Want to do anything tonight?" Cassidy asked, half-watching the MTV VJ babble on about some new album.

"Eh," Marissa shrugged.

"I want to hit the gym, but after that we can order pizza, if you want," Cassidy suggested.

"The pizza part sounds better than the gym part," Marissa replied, pulling both of her feet up underneath her so she was balancing on the arm of the sofa. Cassidy watched her for a long moment before lifting her foot up and gently tapping Marissa's thigh. Marissa teetered and lost her balance, flailing wildly before she caught herself and rebalanced on the arm, both feet now firmly planted on the cushion below. Cassidy chuckled to herself.

"You don't have to go to the gym," Cassidy assured her. "But we're not ordering pizza until after I'm back."

"Fine by me," Marissa said. "I've got a new book to read."

"Okay." Cassidy stood.

"Oh good, you're going now? Hurry up – I want pizza!" Marissa said, reaching over and smacking Cassidy on the butt.

"Ow," Cassidy whined, though it didn't really hurt.

"See ya," Marissa called as Cassidy exited the apartment. She quickly made her way down the stairs and into the small gym next to the main office and hopped on the treadmill by the window.

Chapter 6

Cassidy lazily chopped up a large head of broccoli as she waited for her Hot Pocket to finish warming in the microwave. It was just after noon on Saturday, but the long weekend made it feel like a Sunday. Marissa and Cassidy had spent their Friday off going for a long run in the park, shopping at the outlets, and going to the movies after dinner – finally seeing The Witches of Eastwick. They both loved it!

It was the first 'First Friday' in years that Cassidy hadn't spent at her parents' place, and there was an odd freedom to it. However, the freedom wouldn't last long. The only reason Friday dinner had been canceled was to allow for a family Fourth of July bar-b-que today. Cassidy was to be there no later than 3PM, and to bring a salad.

Cassidy brushed the chopped broccoli off the cutting board into the large bowl with her knife just as the microwave dinged. She quickly popped her lunch on a plate to let it cool as she grabbed a bell pepper to slice.

After adding the pepper to the salad, Cassidy took a bite of her lunch just as Marissa emerged from her bedroom, carrying the phone with her to return to its usual spot in the living room. She took a moment to untangle the long cord.

"How's Brandon?" Cassidy asked as she chewed.

"Good," Marissa replied as she set the phone down. "He got to his parents' at 11:45 and was asleep in his old room by 12:15."

"Sounds about right," Cassidy remarked absentmindedly. She was focused on her lunch.

"How's your salad coming along?" Marissa asked, coming to peer into the bowl.

"Not bad. I've got romaine, celery, carrots, broccoli, and bell peppers in there. I just want to add some pine nuts and radishes; then I should be all set," Cassidy said, taking another bite.

"Sounds good," Marissa said.

"Yes – too bad only my mom and I will eat it." Cassidy shrugged.

"The boys don't eat salad?"

"They do, but not if they have other options."

"Well, more for you, then," Marissa said.

"Good point!" Cassidy grinned.

Once Cassidy had finished her final bite of Hot Pocket, she put the finishing touches on her salad while Marissa returned to her room to get ready for the day. She was off to a family party that afternoon, as well.

By 2PM, both Cassidy and Marissa were dressed and ready to go to their separate holiday events; Marissa in a red sun dress and Cassidy in a knee length jean skirt and a white V-neck tee. Both girls sported ponytails as it was extremely hot out. They grabbed their bags, and left the apartment for the rest of the day.

Cassidy drove the forty-five minutes home to her parents' place. The Banker family home was in a small development, comprising a mere five streets in a grid formation, on the west side of town. The Banker's large, red brick house was set on the back corner of the one entrance street off the main road.

Cassidy loved this neighborhood. It had been a wonderful place to grow up. There were lots of other kids to play with and a safe place to ride bikes. There were even two girls Cassidy's age: one a year older and one a year younger. Her neighbor girlfriends definitely made growing up with four brothers easier – at least until they were teenagers and the neighbor girls started to find all of her brothers so cute! Ugh. Cassidy was actually fairly certain her twin had lost his virginity to one of them at sixteen.

Cassidy pulled into the wide driveway. Her parents, Art and Lynne, were both parked in the garage, but there were two other cars parked on the left side of the drive. She instantly recognized them as Ben's Chevy and Eric's Honda. Cassidy pulled up on the right side next to her youngest brother's car. With the large salad bowl tucked securely under her left arm, Cassidy walked to the entryway and let herself inside.

"Hi!" Cassidy called, closing the heavy front door behind her.

"Whatcha bring?" Ben called, bounding down the large, dark wood staircase. His chin-length blond hair bounced as he came.

"Nice to see you, too," Cassidy replied sarcastically as she made her way towards the kitchen.

"Oh, salad," Ben remarked with a grimace as he glanced over her shoulder.

"Wonderful!" Cassidy's mom, Lynne, chimed as they entered the spacious kitchen. Ben quickly pushed around his sister and made his way to the backdoor and outside.

"Hi Mom," Cassidy said, setting her salad bowl on the light blue counter.

"Hi, sweetheart," Lynne said, giving her daughter a quick peck on the cheek. She made her way over to the sink to rinse the potatoes. Lynne's blonde hair was cut short, just below her ears, and was just starting to show a few grey strands. Lynne and Cassidy stood almost the exact same height, but Lynne was slighter than Cassidy's muscular frame.

"What do you need, Mom?" Cassidy asked as she helped herself to one of the Wheat Thins sitting in a large plastic bowl next to the stove.

"Nothing right now," Lynne said. "I think we have everything under control, especially now that you're all old enough to bring stuff. Basically, I am on potatoes, your dad is grilling all the meat, and he picked up two cases of beer last night. We're all set."

"Glad we're all able to finally be helpful," Cassidy said with a smirk.

"Hey, I had five kids in seven years! I'm exhausted, I deserve a break," Lynne teased. Cassidy chuckled.

"So, who is bringing what?" Cassidy asked, popping another cracker in her mouth.

"Ben brought the crackers," Lynne said, nodding toward the bowl Cassidy was picking at.

"A box of crackers? Really?" Cassidy raised an eyebrow. Ben's contributions were always low effort.

"You're eating them," Lynne pointed out.

"Fair enough."

"Eric and Ellie brought dessert, Matty is bringing macaroni salad, and Alex and Laura are bringing fruit and chips."

"Fruit and chips?" Cassidy asked. "Shouldn't chips have been from Ben?"

"He picked up the damn crackers, Cassidy. Move on." Lynne was clearly not in the mood for her daughter's nit-picking.

"Sorry. I'm done." Cassidy sighed apologetically.

"Thank you."

"So, Ellie is here?" Cassidy asked.

"Yes; she and Eric are outside with your father."

Cassidy hesitated.

"Please be nice," Lynne said.

"Mom, I don't have anything against her," Cassidy said. She was only partially lying.

"Really?" Lynne asked. "Because you never seem happy about her."

"I don't really know her. We've only met what – two, maybe three times? No, today will be three," Cassidy counted on her fingers.

"Well, try to get to know her. She's going to be your sister-in-law. You've always wanted a sister!"

"I count Laura as a sister-in-law, even though she and Alex aren't married," Cassidy pointed out. She truly did adore Laura, and had ever since Alex first brought her home for a visit during spring break of their sophomore year at Mercyhurst.

"Laura is a sweetie, but I'm sure you'll enjoy Ellie just as much as the years go on."

Cassidy bit her tongue. "Where are Matty and Alex?" she asked, ready to change the subject.

"They should be here," Lynne said with a small eye roll. Alex was notoriously late. And Matty was a loose cannon – if he was late, he was most likely bringing something they didn't need, like more fireworks. "Why don't you take the big metal cooler from the garage out to the back deck so we can start filling it with ice and get the beers in there."

"Sure," Cassidy agreed. She headed through the side door to the connecting garage and collected the large metal tub. She rested it on her hip as she exited the back door and lugged it out into the yard.

She looked over to the large patio where her father, Art, was lighting the grill. Art was a tall, lanky man with a mat of wavy light grey hair on the top of his head. Both Matty and Ben were built just like him. Cassidy could only imagine that in thirty years, both of them, but especially Matty, would be dead ringers for their dad.

Further out in the grass, Ben and Ellie were playing a game of badminton. Ellie was thin and petite. Her long black hair and tan skin glistened in the bright afternoon sun. Ellie was absolutely gorgeous – gorgeous in that annoying, completely effortless way. Back on the patio, plopped on one of the lounge chairs with a beer can in hand, was Eric. His dark blond hair was greased back and he wore thick black sunglasses. Cassidy couldn't help but think he looked like one of The Outsiders. He glanced over as she made her way to the patio.

"Hi, Dad!" Cassidy called. Art turned from watching the large flames coming off the grill and smiled at his only daughter.

"Hey, Cassidy, glad you made it!" he said happily. Cassidy gave him a one-armed hug before setting the tub down a few feet away from the grill. No need for anyone to get singed when going for a refill.

"Mom said to fill this with the ice and beers. Are they all in the garage freezer?" Cassidy asked.

"Ice should be in the garage freezer, but I think the beers are still in the back of the Subaru," Art said.

"On it," Cassidy said with a smile. She turned to head back into the garage. Out of the corner of her eye she saw Eric leap up and follow her.

"Cassidy," he called as Cassidy reached the garage door.

"Hey," she replied.

"Hey," he repeated, pushing his sunglasses up onto his head. They stepped into the garage.

"What's up?" Cassidy asked, opening the freezer and retrieving two large bags of ice.

"I'm glad you're here early," Eric began.

"Really?" Cassidy asked, handing her twin one of the bags.

"Yeah, I, um – " Eric stuttered. "I wanted to give you a heads up."

"That sounds ominous," Cassidy said.

"I'm going to ask our brothers to be my groomsmen tonight," Eric said.

"Oh, cool."

"Really? I was afraid you'd be pissed."

"Dude, what? They're your brothers, and it's your wedding! I'd be more pissed and disappointed with you if you didn't have them up there with you," Cassidy said.

They stared at each other for a moment.

"I just didn't want you to be caught off guard, so I wanted

to tell you. But thank you for being cool," Eric said with a small smile.

"I'm always cool," Cassidy countered.

Eric scrunched up his face. "You're definitely not."

"Look in the mirror – your hair right now proves you don't know what cool is," Cassidy teased.

"Bullshit. This is in all the magazines," Eric said, pointing at his hair as he slowly walked backwards towards the door.

"What magazine? Boy Scouts of America?" Cassidy smirked.

Eric gave her the finger and Cassidy chuckled.

"Hey! Aren't you going to help me with the beer?" Cassidy called as Eric turned and dashed out of the garage.

"No!" Eric called back.

Cassidy sighed in annoyance, then walked over to her dad's car and opened up the back seat to find a large case of beer. She quickly tossed the bag of ice on top and heaved the case out of the car, kicked the door closed, and departed the garage.

By 4:00 everyone had arrived, the meat was on the grill, and all the other dishes were spread out on one of the large picnic tables. Cassidy was happily lounging on a towel on the grass next to Laura while her brothers and Ellie played poker on the other picnic table. Art carefully monitored the grill while Lynne hopped around, fussing over all the miniscule details and making sure that nothing was forgotten or mislaid.

"Alright, everyone! Burgers and dogs are ready," Art called.

"Now, now, everyone! Grab plates here, and then…" Lynne began, attempting to impose some sort of order on the meal, but she was quickly drowned out by the clamor of the crowd rushing over to the food in a chaotic, ravenous passion. Cassidy and Laura came around to the back of the herd.

"You tried, mom," Cassidy said sympathetically, patting her mother on the shoulder as she and Laura walked past. Lynne let out a defeated sigh. Cassidy didn't know why her mom had not yet learned that the Banker family was completely uncontrollable around food.

In less than five minutes, all seven Bankers, Ellie, and Laura had filled their plates and were all seated at the table, starting to dig in. Cassidy sat at the end of the long table with Alex on her right and Laura on her left. Her father was at the opposite end of the table. He playfully raised his beer can and nodded at her. Cassidy returned the gesture, adding a goofy wink. They chuckled at their own little joke before shifting their attentions to their food and those seated around them.

"So, what are we setting off tonight?" Matty asked. Cassidy rolled her eyes. Matty had a weakness for anything that went 'boom!'.

"Dad and I went 'cross the border to Ohio and got a few good ones – plus the sparklers from 7-11," Ben said excitedly.

"Sweet!" Matty cheered.

"You didn't tell me you bought illegal fireworks," Lynne scolded Art.

"Don't worry, they aren't commercial grade," Art said, his mouth full of macaroni salad.

"And they aren't illegal in Ohio, mom," Ben added.

"But we don't live in Ohio, we live in Pennsylvania!" Lynne said exasperatedly.

"How about tonight we set them off real quick, boom, boom, boom! By the time we're caught, the evidence will be gone!" Matty suggested, taking a bite of his burger.

"That is not a plan," Alex sighed.

"Evidence gone. Boom!" Matty replied dramatically.

"Just put me down for a sparkler," Ellie chimed in. There was a pause as everyone swiveled to stare at the newest person at the table, shocked that she was brave enough to contribute to a Banker squabble. Suddenly, Ben let out a loud guffaw. Everyone else followed suit.

"Well done, babe," said Eric, who was seated next to Laura. He kissed her on the cheek. Ellie looked quite proud of herself. Cassidy hated to admit it, but she was proud of her, too. It must be overwhelming to step into a Banker family function.

"Ellie," Art called from the head of the table once the laughter had died down.

"Yes?"

"What was it you studied, again?" Art asked.

Eric let out an annoyed groan. "Dad, I already told you, she teaches first grade," he whined.

"I knew that!" Matty chimed in obnoxiously. Art ignored him while Ben offered Matty a high five.

"I didn't ask her what she did, I asked her what she studied," Art retorted.

"Honey, she would have studied education," Lynne said.

"It's okay, Mr. Banker," Ellie interjected. "I did major in education, but I also minored in Native American studies."

"That's fascinating!" Art smiled at Ellie before turning to his second son. "I bet you didn't know that."

"I didn't know that," Matty agreed with a shrug.

"What made you want to minor in that?" Art asked.

"Both of my parents are Shawnee. Well, my mother is fully, her parents are, grandparents, and so on. My dad is only half.

68

His father, my grandfather's family is part of the tribe, but my grandma was just a girl from Dayton."

"Shawnee? Like the Indians?" Ben asked.

"Native Americans," Alex corrected. Ben winced.

"Oh, sorry Ellie," Ben apologized.

"It's okay," Ellie assured him.

Cassidy tilted her head to the side in thought. She had never considered the possibility that Ellie was a different nationality before. She knew she was always tan and her hair was a silky, raven black, but the reason for this had never dawned on her. But then, Cassidy never gave much thought to any person's nationality. All people were simply people to her. Come to think of it, though, it should have been obvious that Ellie was Native American, now that she looked at her.

Much to Ellie's relief, the conversation soon shifted from her to old family stories of past holidays. From there, it moved on to movies they loved and from there to former pets – mostly jokes about the Banker's former dog, Domino. He was a dalmatian they'd had when the kids were young, and he'd had the IQ of a meatball sandwich.

Finally, the stories had ended, the food was all eaten, and everyone was ready to get up from the table. After they quickly stacked their plates, Lynne shooed everyone away so she could clean up properly without any interference. Everyone else rushed out to the middle of the yard for a spirited game of volleyball. Cassidy was on a team with Alex, Laura, and Art, while Matty, Ben, Eric, and Ellie took the other side of the net.

Poor Ellie was given a quick crash course into the competitive nature of the Banker siblings. One hour, six skinned knees, a split lip, one bruised elbow, and lots of screaming, arguing, and obscenities later, they called the end of the game. Matty, Ben, Eric, and Ellie's team insisted they had won, though Cassidy verbosely disputed a few of their do-overs due to sun in their eyes or injury – Ben only bled a little bit, anyway.

Now that they had finished their game, they all tromped across the yard back to the patio where Lynne had reset the table for dessert.

"If you're all done killing each other, we can have some dessert," Lynne called.

"Who brought dessert?" Laura asked, resting her knee on the bench of the picnic table.

"We did," Ellie replied.

"What did you bring?" Matty asked.

"I'm starving!" Ben added.

"We just ate," Cassidy pointed out.

"I worked up an appetite," Ben shrugged.

"By cheating?" Cassidy asked, raising an eyebrow.

"Whatever you need to tell yourself – loser." Ben puckered his lips and gave the air two kisses.

Cassidy chuckled and patted his cheek. "Little boy," she cooed before walking past him to claim her spot at the picnic table. Ben rolled his eyes in annoyance.

"Shut up," he whined. Cassidy grinned.

"What did you bring?" Matty asked once more.

"Ellie made brownies and we brought ice cream, too," Eric said.

"Yes!" Matty cheered.

"Come on, everyone, dig in before the ice cream melts," Lynne instructed, and everyone ambled over to help themselves.

As everyone was finishing up their treats, or, in Ben's

case, his third helping of treats, Cassidy saw Ellie whisper something in Eric's ear. He quickly got up from the table and rushed over to the large metal tub, grabbed four beers, and returned to the table.

"Thirsty?" Alex asked.

"I'm sharing," Eric said, passing a can to each of his brothers.

"This is terrible sharing," Art commented, looking longingly at the beers that were not shared with him. "We raised you better."

Cassidy stifled a laugh.

"I'll get you one later, Dad," Eric said.

"What's going on?" Ben asked suspiciously.

"Do you just get us beers now? Because I'm fine with that," Matty smirked, cracking open his can.

"Definitely not. I got you guys these ones because I wanted to ask something," Eric said. He gave a big grin. Alex, Ben, and Matty, who were all sitting across from him, looked confused. Matty took a sip from his can.

"Go on," Ellie whispered, nudging Eric with her shoulder.

"I'd like to ask you three to be my groomsmen," Eric said proudly, raising his beer can in cheers.

"Oh, yeah!" Alex said, a big smile on his face.

"Hot!" Ben cheered.

"Fuck, yes!" Matty added, clinking his beer with Eric's.

"Matthew James!" Lynne scolded. Over the years she had learned to accept and ignore her children swearing. However, she drew the line on a few words, and that was one of them.

"I'm celebrating!" Matty protested.

Cassidy smiled as she watched her brothers toast each other. She was honestly happy for them. Lynne, Art, Laura, and Ellie all started to clap and Cassidy joined them.

"This is so sweet!" Laura smiled.

"Will you each have three people standing up with you?" Lynne asked, wiping a happy tear off her cheek.

"Five, actually," Ellie replied, positively beaming with excitement.

"Oh, wow!"

"It works out great for both of us. I get my brothers and also Derek and Jeremy," Eric explained, referencing his college and current roommate, as well as his best friend from childhood.

"Do you have a big family, Ellie?" Laura asked.

"No," Ellie shook her head. "I just have one sister, Kara. So it'll be her and my friends – I finally have them all picked." Cassidy's ears pricked. There was a weird feeling in her stomach.

"Oh," Laura paused. "No other family?"

"Nope, just Kara."

Cassidy felt like there was a rock in her throat as her stomach continued to churn, harder than before. She suddenly felt Laura's hand come to rest on her left knee under the table and give it a gentle, comforting squeeze. Cassidy glanced over and saw Laura biting her lip. Cassidy sighed. She was not invited to be a bridesmaid in her own brother's wedding. Hell, in her own twin's wedding. She wanted to vomit.

She was vaguely aware of everyone talking around her, but she couldn't absorb a single word. She was lost in a swirl of emotion.

Did she want to be part of the bridal party? No, not really. However, she had always expected that she would be, regardless. You're supposed to invite your future siblings-in-law into the bridal party, right? That's the tradition. Cassidy could not figure out why this hurt her so much. Generally, she hated Eric. Okay, maybe not hate, but they weren't friends. He'd probably told Ellie terrible stories about her to get her to skip her on the invite list. Did Ellie even know that he was a twin? Why did she even care?

Cassidy remained in her zoned-out trance until she felt Laura pulling her plate away from her. She quickly shook her head and brought herself back to reality. Everyone was done eating and starting to get up and gather the dirty dishes.

"Here, I'll take these," Cassidy said, taking the stack from Laura.

"Oh, hey, you okay?" Laura whispered.

"Never better," Cassidy replied sarcastically. She collected more dishes while both of her parents went into the house and her brothers and Ellie headed back to the yard with a soccer ball.

"Cassidy," Laura began, but Cassidy cut her off.

"Laura, please. I can't right now. I'm going to do dishes. Just, go and play soccer with the boys. Please," Cassidy begged. She was moments away from losing her cool, and she didn't want Laura to take the brunt of it. She didn't deserve it.

"Come sit with me later," Laura told her with a sigh.

"I will," Cassidy said with a forced smile before turning and heading towards the back door of the house, her arms full of plates.

After a small struggle with the door, Cassidy got herself inside and into the kitchen where she plopped the pile of dishes down onto the blue countertop. Lynne walked in from the other room and looked surprised to see her.

"Cassidy? What are you doing inside?"

"Thought I'd help with the dishes," Cassidy said. She turned on the faucet to let the water to heat up.

"Dishes over soccer? What's going on?" Lynne asked. Cassidy shrugged and stuck her fingers under the stream of water. Still only lukewarm.

"I'm just… frustrated," she admitted with a sigh.

"With what?"

"With the stupid wedding, obviously!" she grumbled.

"Eric and Ellie's?"

"Obviously," she repeated.

"Cassidy, this is Eric's wedding. He's allowed to talk about it and it's lovely how excited the boys are to be groomsmen," Lynne said with a smile.

Cassidy glared at her. "Of course he's allowed to be happy, and it's great that Alex, Matty, and Ben get to join in the big day, but did you not notice that your daughter is not involved?" Cassidy asked forcefully. She stuck her hand under the water once more. Finally hot. She began shoving plates into the sink.

"What are you talking about? Of course you can't be a groomsman, what are you thinking?" Lynne shook her head.

"I'm not a bridesmaid, either. And if they were each having one person stand up with them, I wouldn't care. But they're each having five people stand up, and I still don't make the cut." Cassidy angrily squirted an obscene amount of dish wash into the sink.

"Well, you don't really know Ellie," Lynne said. It sounded as if she was desperately trying to come up with an excuse.

"But I'm Eric's sister. His twin sister."

"A fact that you normally try very hard to downplay,"

Lynne argued.

Cassidy sighed inwardly. That one stung – especially because it was definitely true. "It's tradition, though," she whined. "Especially in larger wedding parties. You have your fiancé's siblings in the bridal party."

"Not all the time." Lynne shrugged as Cassidy shut off the water and started to scrub.

"If Ellie had four sisters, I wouldn't push, but she has one. She would still have room for three friends if I was there; Eric only gets two."

"Cassidy, this may shock you, but this is your brother's wedding. The day is not about you. Nor are the events leading up to it," Lynne said firmly.

Cassidy wanted to scream.

"I know it's not about me! Stop treating me like a petulant five year old!" Cassidy firmly stacked a plate into the dish rack to dry. She was surprised, though grateful, that she didn't break it with her less-than-gentle movements.

"Well, you're acting a little bit like one. Demanding to be involved."

"I'm not demanding. I'm upset that I'm suddenly not included in a family wedding that the rest of the family is included in," Cassidy argued, slamming another clean plate in the rack.

Lynne sighed, and came to rest her hand on Cassidy's back. "Why is this bothering you so much?" she asked.

"Why wouldn't it? I always assumed I would be involved in my brothers' weddings. If I get married, they'll be in mine."

"Well, now they don't have to be." Lynne shrugged.

"Mom, please stop being so blasé about this. I mean, I know for a fact at your wedding you had both your sister and dad's sister as bridesmaids," Cassidy pushed.

"Well, of course! I had to have Aunt Lucy as my maid of honor," Lynne said, referring to her older sister. "And I had Aunt Marie in because she and your father were close siblings."

"And you had friends. It was all fine," Cassidy pushed.

"But, in Ellie's defense, you and Eric aren't close."

"So you're saying that if Dad and Aunt Marie weren't as close, you wouldn't have invited her? Grandma would have had something to say on that one." Cassidy was proud of the logic of her argument. She put the final plate on the drying rack and unplugged the sink to drain.

"I don't know what I would have done if Dad and Marie weren't as close, but I will say, it wasn't an issue to have her because she was a sweetie," Lynne said.

Cassidy gasped. "What does that make me? Some miserable cow?" She dried her hands on the dishcloth before tossing it on the counter in a heap.

"That's not what I said! Do not put words in my mouth," Lynne said firmly, looking her daughter squarely in the eye.

"You know what, I'm just going to go," Cassidy sighed.

"No, you are not. You're staying here until after dark; I need you here to hold the second fire extinguisher," Lynne smirked.

"Mom, I am obviously not in a joking mood."

"Well, you'd better get in one, because I'm not having you sulk through a family event and ruin the night for everyone."

"I don't intend to ruin anything," Cassidy replied through gritted teeth.

"Okay, well, get your head back on straight, then come back outside," Lynne instructed. "The sun is starting to set and Matty is going to be champing at the bit to blow something up." She was out the back door before Cassidy had a chance to argue.

Cassidy stomped her foot in annoyance. She glowered for a long moment before huffing out of the room and into the hallway. She took a moment to use the downstairs bathroom and splash some water onto her face, hoping it would calm her. When she reemerged in the hallway, she heard a noise coming from her father's study off the foyer.

Cassidy wandered over and found her father sitting in one of his wingback chairs, sipping a glass of bourbon and listening to the radio. Only the table lamp had been turned on for light.

"Knock, knock," Cassidy called, coming to rest on the open doorframe.

"Ahh, someone found me."

"I promise not to reveal your location," Cassidy said with a wink.

"Much appreciated."

"What are you doing in here?" Cassidy asked as she stepped inside the small room and took a seat on the second wingback chair.

"Needed a moment. Love you kids, but I've gotten used to the empty house. This is a lot for me," Art explained.

"You sound like some grumpy old man," Cassidy teased with a smile.

"I'm getting there."

"No, you're not. I saw you play volleyball this afternoon – you've still got it," Cassidy assured him.

"Only in small doses," Art replied with a smirk. Cassidy laughed. "Besides, I wanted a drink," he added.

"There's a tub full of beers outside."

"No, I wanted a real drink, and I have no intentions of sharing the good liquor with your brothers. They'd clear me out." Cassidy grinned and nodded in agreement.

There was a long, comfortable silence between the two as Art sipped his drink and Bobby Darrin crooned from the stereo.

"What are you doing inside? You never miss an opportunity to trip one of your brothers, and on the soccer field you can make it look like an accident," Art said with a smile. Cassidy chuckled.

"Very true. I just needed a break."

"From wedding talk?" Art asked.

"See, even you caught it! Mom didn't!" Cassidy grumbled.

"Cassidy, do you even want to be a bridesmaid?" Art asked pointedly. The blunt question caught her off guard.

"Of course I do," she replied immediately.

"Really? You want to spend your weekends shopping with Ellie and her friends? Oooing and ahhing over every miniscule detail? Gushing with happiness and telling cutesie stories about your brother?" Art asked.

Cassidy grimaced slightly.

"Uhhh…" She hesitated. That did sound dreadful.

"Exactly. That's not you."

"You make me sound like the most miserable person in the world," Cassidy sighed.

"You're not miserable, but you would hate being involved in this wedding," Art said. Cassidy felt a rock in her stomach. "I am sorry you're not included. That has to hurt. But look at it as a blessing in disguise."

"Being left out doesn't feel like a blessing."

"I'm sure it doesn't. But if she had asked you to be a

bridesmaid tonight, you'd be miserable about all the bullshit you'd have to do for that," Art pointed out.

"And we're back to me being a miserable person."

"Pick your poison, Cassidy," Art said, taking a sip from his glass.

"You mean enjoy learn to enjoy being excluded from my brother's wedding?"

"Yep," Art said flatly.

Cassidy chewed her lip. "I'm still mad, but I'll be civil," she conceded.

"That's all we ask."

Cassidy sat with her father for a few more minutes while he finished his bourbon.

"Come on, the sun's setting. Let's go see what the boys want to shoot off," Art said, standing up and switching off the stereo.

"Oh, don't pretend like you aren't leading that charge," Cassidy teased.

Art simply shrugged. "Hurry up, then,"

Cassidy rolled her eyes as they made their way back outside. The soccer game was still going strong as the pinks and oranges of the late evening sky glowed above. Everyone except Lynne and Laura were racing along the grass after the ball. The boys and Ellie were running ragged while Lynne sat at the table chatting with Laura about preparing for the upcoming school year.

Cassidy took a seat next to Laura and listened to them talk, content to just observe the conversation.

As the sun set further, Art carried the large box of fireworks, firecrackers, and sparklers from the garage, which instantly lured Matty and Ben away from the game.

Art, Matty, and Ben spent the next thirty minutes setting up a large array of explosives while everyone else milled around the patio and drank beers. Cassidy sat with Laura the whole time, and actively ignored Eric and Ellie, who seemed to be lost in their own little world, curled up on one of the lounge chairs.

Cassidy remained on the patio with a lit sparkler in hand and watched her father and two brothers set everything off in the yard. They popped, sparked, and in a few cases, let out a loud bang that made everyone jump, as the colors swirled in the air. It was their most impressive display in years.

As soon as everything had been set off, they all cleaned up and collected their things to head home. Cassidy made her rounds of hugs and goodbyes to everyone until she got to Eric and Ellie.

"Hey, I'm heading out," Cassidy said flatly. Much to her surprise, Ellie rushed over and gave her a hug. Cassidy awkwardly hugged her back with one arm, her other clutching her salad bowl.

"Bye!" Ellie said.

"Yep, bye," Cassidy squeaked, pulling herself out of the hug.

"See ya, sometime!" Ellie said with a giddy smile. Cassidy didn't know why, but that really irritated her.

"Sure. Eric," Cassidy nodded at her twin. Eric took a step forward and leaned towards her ear.

"Please stop being shitty," he whispered. A sharp pang of annoyance shot through Cassidy's heart.

"You first," she whispered back firmly. The twins glowered at each other for a moment; then Cassidy felt a hand grip her upper arm and yank her the other direction.

"Come on, Cassidy! We're heading out too, and we parked you in," Alex said cheerily, as if he wasn't separating his siblings from killing each other. Cassidy tried to shake her eldest brother off of her arm, but he held his grip. She finally gave up and allowed herself to be led through the house and out the front door, Laura right on their tail.

Alex finally released his hold when they got to the driveway, and Cassidy instinctively rolled her shoulders a few times before opening the passenger door in her car to set the salad bowl on the seat.

"Don't let Eric get to you," Laura said, patting Cassidy on the back.

"I won't. I just need a moment," Cassidy grumbled.

"Cassie," Alex sighed. "Why don't you come home with us?"

"No, thank you. I just want to go home."

"Is Marissa in town?" Alex asked.

Cassidy nodded. "Yes, she was with family today, too. We should get home around the same time."

"Do you want us to come stay with you until she gets home?" Alex asked. Cassidy raised an eyebrow at him. Alex always tried to be overprotective of her. Cassidy had always loved him, but really needed him less than he liked. She was, however, always highly emotional, and Alex often took those opportunities to get to be her protector. I worked about half the time.

"Alex, I'm a fully functioning adult. I don't need a babysitter. I can stay home alone. It's okay."

"Normally, yes. But you're not in a good mindset right now. I really don't want you alone."

Cassidy felt a warmth around her heart. She appreciated

Alex being so protective and caring. Especially after another brother had left her out in the cold.

"Thank you very much, truly. But Marissa will be home very soon. I'll be okay." Cassidy smiled as she walked over to him.

"Call if you need anything, or just want to call people fucking assholes," Alex offered as he pulled her in for a hug. Cassidy laughed into his shoulder.

"I may take you up on that," she said, pulling back. Laura ran over and gave her a big hug as well.

"Sleep this all off," Laura told her. Cassidy nodded.

"Night, Cassie," Alex said before both he and Laura climbed into his car. Cassidy waved as they started the engine, and walked around to climb into the driver's side of her Toyota. She turned her key in the ignition and glanced at her rearview mirror. Alex and Laura were just turning out of the driveway and onto the street. She shifted into reverse as Matty exited the front door and waved at her.

Cassidy kept her foot on the break as she rolled down the window.

"Hey," she called. "Did you want to pull out first?" While Matty's car was on the other side of the driveway, he was the last car before the street.

"No," Matty replied, coming to lean against her open window. "Just sayin' goodnight."

"Goodnight," Cassidy chuckled. They had hugged goodbye less than five minutes prior.

"Sorry tonight was shitty for you," Matty added. Cassidy's head snapped up.

"You saw that?" she asked.

"You're terrible at hiding the emotions on your face," Matty chuckled. Cassidy groaned.

"I'll work on it," she replied sarcastically.

"I wouldn't. Let Eric and Ellie know you're pissed."

Cassidy thought about that for a moment.

"I'm sorry that you're being excluded. You would have been a lot of fun at the events. But that means we can just get extra shitfaced and dance our asses off at the reception," Matty said with a smirk. Cassidy smiled up at him.

"Thanks, Matty,"

"Alright, enough of this. Get the fuck out of here," Matty said, tapping the hood of her car twice.

"Goodnight," Cassidy laughed as she brought her foot off the break and reversed out of the driveway, onto the street, and sped out of the development.

Chapter 7

Cassidy made good time getting back to Erie and was thrilled to see Marissa's car in the complex lot when she pulled in.

"Hey," she called as she let herself in the apartment.

"Hey!" Marissa replied from the kitchen.

"How was your day?" Cassidy asked. She set her salad bowl on the counter and collapsed onto the couch.

"Pretty boring, honestly. But the food was good. We only ate and played with sparklers, so I got home early," Marissa explained, coming to sit on the chair next to the sofa, glass of Sprite in hand.

"Glad there was good food."

"Judging by your face, I'm nervous to ask how yours went."

"It was fine, except I found out that I'm not in Eric's wedding," Cassidy sighed.

"Oh, are they just doing a small wedding party? It would be hard for Eric to only pick one brother," Marissa said. Cassidy gave a low chuckle.

"Oh, no, they're having a large wedding party. All my brothers are groomsman, but I am not to be a bridesmaid," Cassidy glowered.

"What? Siblings are always in the bridal party!" Marissa said, looking confused.

"That's what I thought."

"That sucks, I'm sorry."

"My dad kept saying that I wouldn't like to be in the bridal party anyway, which honestly is true, but I'm still mad," Cassidy groaned.

"I think you have every right to be absolutely pissed," Marissa said firmly.

"I'm already there."

"What did everyone else say?" Marissa asked.

"Laura and Alex are upset. Alex has been extra sweet, which I appreciate. Even Matty took my side. But my mom didn't seem to care. She's just in wedding mode."

"Ugh," Marissa sympathized.

"At least I don't have to see Eric for another month," Cassidy said.

"Ellie doesn't come to the monthly dinners, does she?" Marissa asked.

Cassidy shook her head. "She came to one after they started dating, but that was it. Other than tonight, I only saw her once at our grandma's birthday back in February. I hope she doesn't start coming. I mean, Laura doesn't come, and she's my unofficial sister-in-law. She and Alex have been together forever."

"Do you think Eric told her it's just a sibling thing?" Marissa asked.

"I don't think he even told her that I'm his twin," Cassidy

said.

"Jesus," Marissa exhaled.

Cassidy didn't know why, but she suddenly started laughing. Perhaps it was frustration, or the exhaustion, or possibly the few beers she had, but Marissa's reaction cracked her up.

Both girls started laughing and Cassidy began to feel like she might just survive her brother's wedding.

It had been a week since the Fourth of July picnic and Cassidy had only spoken to her mother once since. While Cassidy felt she and her mother were back on good terms, there was still a low brewing frustration that seemed to haunt her thoughts.

Cassidy pulled into the small parking lot across the street from the Mexican restaurant downtown. She quickly shut off the engine, hopped out of the car, and jogged across the crosswalk before a pick-up truck zoomed past. Her light green sundress billowed as she went.

The bell on the heavy wooden door dinged as Cassidy pulled it open and stepped into the colorful interior of the restaurant.

"Hey!" Cassidy cried happily, spotting Laura sitting on one of the benches in the yellow lobby.

"Hi!" Laura said cheerily. She was in faded blue jeans with a black Beatles tee shirt that hung off her right shoulder perfectly. Damn, she was so cool.

"Were you waiting long?" Cassidy asked as they walked to the hostess stand.

"Nope! Less than three minutes."

"Just two?" the hostess asked in beautifully accented English.

"Yep," Cassidy nodded. They followed her through the maze of large wicker and glass tables, and were seated by the windows overlooking the parking lot and the large brick library situated on the other end of the block.

"So, how's it going?" Laura asked casually, sliding the ashtray on the edge of the table toward her and lighting up a cigarette.

"Pretty good. Work is kind of boring; it's our slow season now." Cassidy shrugged. "What are you up to, with school being out for the summer?"

"Well," Laura took a drag, "school is out, but we offer summer camps, so I'm working at a pottery camp for about six weeks."

"Oh, that's cool." Cassidy did not have a single artistic bone in her body, so she found anyone with the ability to create things incredibly talented.

"Yeah, the kids are fun, and they make pretty cool things!"

The server arrived at their table with a basket of chips and a large bowl of salsa. Cassidy waited about .05 seconds after they were set on the table before helping herself.

"Any more dates?" Laura asked after the server took their drink order and departed. She crunched a chip loudly.

"Dates?" Cassidy raised an eyebrow.

"Or, whatever the guy from our building was." Laura smiled widely.

"Pete," Cassidy sighed. She knew full well that her almost-sister-in-law was trying to wind her up. "He was a one-night stand, and just a bad decision. I'm not one of those girls."

"Was he really bad?" Laura asked curiously, popping

another salsa coated chip in her mouth.

"Well," Cassidy blushed, "some of it was quite nice. It just… ended poorly…" She trailed off with a sheepish smile before reaching for more chips.

"Oooof," Laura chuckled.

"Yeah."

"I think I know which guy he is in our building. I see him at the mailboxes," Laura said smugly.

Cassidy rolled her eyes. "Glad to hear it, Sherlock."

"You could have done much worse," Laura smirked.

The server came back with their drinks and the girls quickly ordered their favorites. They had both eaten there many times over the years.

"So, any others?" Laura asked once more.

"Nope."

"That's good. Don't rush anything. But I would suggest finding someone for Eric's wedding – otherwise you'll be miserable," Laura advised.

"You mean more miserable," Cassidy enunciated carefully.

"Exactly."

"I promise I'll find a date for the wedding. Or drag Marissa along."

"Perfect." Laura smiled.

"I have to ask, how on earth have you put up with my family for so long? I mean, we're a lot." Cassidy chuckled nervously. "Like, a lot, a lot. Your family must be a thousand times easier than us."

"Well," Laura laughed, "we have our own quirks."

"Please enlighten me. Because I'm imagining just cool, chill, people, maybe dancing in the rain on holidays?" Cassidy asked playfully.

"Okay, okay, we're hippies, but not that hippie," Laura joked.

"Fair enough."

"I mean, I know I'm an only child, but my family is still chaotic. My parents are high emotion, so they're either passionately in love with each other or passionately screaming at each other. My mom's parents absolutely hate my dad's parents, and vice versa, so we can never do joint family things. I have four cousins between the two sides, but my aunts and uncles all live out of state, so I don't get to see them often."

Cassidy listened carefully, completely captivated. Despite knowing Laura for many years, she was hearing most of this for the first time.

She'd known that Laura was an only child, and that she had artsy parents. Cassidy had met them at Alex's graduation. They were the polar opposite of Art and Lynn, and Cassidy found them fascinating. Laura's mother had actually gone to Woodstock! But somehow that was all she really knew about her almost-sister-in-law's background. Cassidy was starting to feel guilty for never making an effort to learn more about her.

"Are you close with your cousins? I mean, I know you don't see them much, but do you guys get along?" Cassidy asked.

Laura nodded. "Yep. I'm definitely closer with the three that live in Michigan. They're on my mom's side. We're all pretty close in age. The oldest is my mom's brother's son. He's a year older than me. Then her sister has a son and daughter. Beth is two years younger than me and Stephen is two years younger than her."

"Wow, I feel like dick for literally not knowing any of this," Cassidy admitted.

"No, no, you don't need to know my whole family history,"

Laura laughed, snuffing out the tiny nub of her cigarette.

"You've been with my family almost ten years, I should know more about you," Cassidy pointed out.

"You'll learn," Laura smiled.

Cassidy grinned. "I have a stupid question…"

"No such thing as a stupid question," Laura countered, eating another chip.

"You're a teacher to teenagers; you know damn well they have stupid questions," Cassidy pointed out.

Laura chucked and nodded. "Well, yeah."

"I was just wondering … does Alex know all this? Like, about your family? He knows to ask, right?" Cassidy had never given much thought to how her brothers acted in relationships. It was something she's rather not focus on, honestly. However, especially with someone she liked as much as Laura, she wanted to make sure she was treated well. She needed that confirmation.

Laura laughed.

"Yes, Alex knows. He knows my family, my childhood, my life, and I know his," Laura assured her.

"Good," Cassidy smiled.

"Did you honestly think I'd stay with him so long if he didn't take an interest in my family?" Laura asked, raising an eyebrow.

"I told you it was a stupid question," Cassidy sighed. "I just, you know, realized that I don't know as much about you as I should and wanted to make sure you're not putting up with the same shit from Alex. You deserve the best!"

"That's really sweet," Laura smiled. "But yes, Alex is a dream. Kind, thoughtful, always supportive, and so romantic and sexy. Like just last night, I was having a shower and –"

"No! Nope, stop right there," Cassidy insisted, her eyes wide in horror. "I'm thrilled he's good to you but I do not need to know about that."

"Oh, come on," Laura teased. "I'm happy to hear about your date nights! I love to, but I'm willing to share, too. I could give you tips!" Laura winked.

"Ugh! No, no, no, no, I do not want to hear about your 'alone time.' Even if you can teach me things. Especially if you can teach me things!" Cassidy countered, holding her hands up in defense. Laura nearly tipped over she was laughing so hard.

"Shut up," Cassidy jabbed as she started giggling herself.

Their laughter was interrupted by their server appearing at their table with a tray of delicious-looking food.

"Saved by my enchilada," Cassidy beamed as the warm plate was set in front of her.

The girls thanked their server and dug right into their meals: enchilada for Cassidy, fajitas for Laura. Not only did Cassidy love the food, but she loved spending time with Laura. She was so easy to talk to and laugh with. It was the perfect lunch and exactly the recharge Cassidy needed.

Chapter 8

It was Wednesday afternoon. There was only an hour left in the workday, and Cassidy was leaning against the wall in the conference room chatting with Gladys. The entire office staff was mingling in the conference room for Devon Park's birthday celebration, enjoying a large spread of nibbles, cake, and punch. While Cassidy appreciated the easy afternoon and the free snacks, Devon was her least favorite coworker and his usual obnoxiousness was only amplified with the attention his birthday brought him.

"I didn't think anyone could be that full of themselves," Gladys sighed, watching Devon animatedly retell a story to coworkers that hadn't been standing in front of him the first time around.

"Enter Devon," Cassidy remarked sarcastically, taking a large swig of her punch.

"I hope you're doing something fun after this terrible party," Gladys commented. Cassidy smiled.

"I'm going to head over to MU and watch some of their summer training game."

"What's that?" Gladys asked.

"The school's baseball team comes in over summer to do training and assess the players. They do a bunch of scrimmages. There's one today, so I'm going to go watch." Gladys scrunched up her nose.

"I could get behind going to see the Pirates, but a college scrimmage? No thanks," she said with a playful sigh.

Cassidy chuckled. "I would love to go to a Pirates game, but it's just too far for a weeknight." She shrugged.

"That's true."

"I'm just going to the campus field, grab a sandwich from the food truck, and enjoy a bit of a game."

"Oh, I love those food trucks!" Gladys's eyes smiled.

"My younger brother said they've got two on campus almost permanently. With the athletes back now for summer camps, I know at least one of them will be there," Cassidy said.

"Food trucks on a college campus - they must be doing a hell of a business!"

"Yeah, especially if they're open late nights, which I think they are."

"Well, hell, I'm in the wrong business," Gladys joked.

"Your next job," Cassidy suggested jokingly.

"Ha! Maybe next life. I'm retiring next year. I can't deal with the bullshit anymore."

"Devon is annoying," Cassidy winked. Gladys guffawed.

"You said it." Gladys lifted her cup and Cassidy clinked hers to it. She adored Gladys, and was heartbroken to hear that she would be leaving the office so soon.

Cassidy combed her wavy hair with her fingers and pulled it back into a messy ponytail before exiting her car. She was parked in one of the campus lots, only about a block away from the ball field. She brushed the front of her semi-casual knee-length dress. She loved this dress. It was black with tiny white daisies dotted over the fabric. Professional and dressy enough for a day in the office, but comfy and casual enough for the rest of the evening.

She slung her purse over her shoulder as she made her way to the sidewalk and the large, green food truck parked across the street.

"What'll it be?" a grouchy man with a backwards ball cap asked as he leaned on the white counter inside the truck window.

"Uh," Cassidy hummed as she glanced at the menu posted on the side. "Can I have a chicken wrap and a bottle of water, please?"

The grouchy man nodded. "$3.50." Cassidy placed the money on the counter and stepped aside to await her food.

"Why are you here? This can't be the only food truck in the city," a familiar voice rang out. Cassidy turned to see Ben walking toward her, with about six other boys trailing behind him. They were all in black workout shorts and green tee shirts with "Mercyhurst Soccer" written across the chest.

"Hey, kid!" Cassidy smiled at her youngest brother, honestly happy to see him.

"Shut up," Ben sighed.

Cassidy chuckled. "You boys on snack break?"

"No, we're walking to the fields for some drills, then I'm going to have everyone run again," Ben explained. A few groans came from the younger players standing behind him. Ben was starting his senior year in a couple of weeks, and Cassidy realized he was one of the captains leading the summer training. It felt weird to see him as the "oldest" or "in charge". She still saw Ben as her baby brother. She didn't like this feeling.

"Fun," Cassidy replied sarcastically.

"Anyway, we're supposed to be here. This is our school. What are you doing here?" Ben asked, looking down at his sister. He was clearly trying to regain his authority in front of the younger players.

"I'm going to watch the baseball scrimmage. Thought I'd pick up dinner, first."

"You're so weird," Ben sighed, shaking his head.

"I'm not weird, this is a lovely evening!" Cassidy shrugged.

"Chicken wrap!" The food truck man called out.

"That's me!" Cassidy beamed.

"Well, happy chickening," Ben said, nudging the boys to keep moving.

"And baseballing!" Cassidy added.

"Weirdo!" Ben called, moving off with his team. Cassidy rolled her eyes and decided to let him have that win. She'd get him back later.

Cassidy was one of about thirty people seated in the college ballpark that summer evening. Looking around, most of the other spectators seemed to be people involved in the MU baseball organization, a couple of the players' girlfriends giggling and gossiping, with a few overprotective parents sprinkled in.

She took a large sip from her bottle of water before setting it on the concrete and opening her wrap. Cassidy was seated about five rows up along the third base line. A perfect spot. There was something peaceful about sitting at the ballpark in the warm summer evening glow. The clang of the bats, the thump of the ball against the mitts. She was home.

The top of the first inning wrapped up just as Cassidy finished her dinner. She balled up the paper and tossed it to her feet to dispose of later. She heard a bit of a clamoring in the row behind her - someone rushing to get a seat. The place was pretty empty, though; she wasn't sure why anyone would be racing into a vacant row. She ignored the hustle as she watched the shortstop whack a line drive into left field.

"What inning is it?"

Cassidy turned to see a man in his late twenties sitting in the row behind her, about three seats to the left. He had thick, copper-colored hair that rested just above his ears and an oval face. His aviator sunglasses reflected Cassidy's image back at her.

"Um, bottom of the first," Cassidy replied.

"Oh, good! I'm not as late as I thought."

"It's a training camp scrimmage, I don't think this is super high stakes," Cassidy joked, turning back to watch the next player swing and miss.

"Strike one!" the assistant coach called.

"It may not be high stakes, but the guy keeping all the records should be in attendance," the guy joked.

"Records?" Cassidy raised an eyebrow.

"I'm a statistician. I work for the university. I teach Stats 305 and do the books for the MU baseball team," he explained. Cassidy was taken aback.

"Oh!" she said. "That's pretty cool!" The guy looked at her suspiciously.

"I don't think 'cool' has ever been used to describe my job," he chuckled.

"Well, most people don't get it. This is coming from a former competitive softball player and current certified public accountant." Cassidy smirked playfully.

"I think I just fell in love," he quipped.

Cassidy let out a loud laugh. "Happy to help cupid along."

"I'm Jake," he said, extending his right hand.

"Cassidy," she replied, giving a firm handshake. A loud clang from the bat sent a ball over the fence.

"Dammit, I need to pay attention," Jake winced, quickly pulling his notebook from his bag and fumbling for his pen.

"Good luck with the stats." Cassidy turned back around in her seat and faced the field. She couldn't shake the smile off her face. She quickly pulled her sunglasses from her purse and slipped them on, but they didn't hide the slight blush on her cheeks. She concentrated hard on the baseball scrimmage to distract herself.

But after two more innings of focusing on the scrimmage, she was dying to talk to Jake some more.

"How are they looking?" Cassidy asked, turning to look back at Jake, who was scribbling furiously in his notebook.

"Hmmm," Jake hummed. He finished his equation and looked up at Cassidy.

"How are they looking?" Cassidy repeated with a polite smile. Jake looked up and caught her eye. Cassidy felt a thump in her chest. What was happening?

"Oh, um, okay…" Jake said with an unconvincing sigh.

"That bad, huh?"

"Well, there are only two seniors and three juniors; it's a very heavy underclassman filled roster. There's a lot of learning going on," Jake explained, shrugging slightly.

"Ooof," Cassidy grimaced.

"Yeah, but in two years they'll be top of the league."

"Not this year, though?" Cassidy teased.

"No." Jake said firmly. "Not this year."

"So, did you go to school here?" Cassidy asked curiously.

"No, no, I went to Penn State."

"When did you graduate? My soon-to-be sister-in-law went there."

"Eighty-four."

"Her too! Did you know an Ellie Hammond?"

"It's a really big school," Jake replied with a slight smile.

"Yeah." Cassidy grimaced, feeling like a dumbass.

"What about you, did you go to Mercyhurst?"

"Edinboro."

"Pretty small school, right?" Jake asked.

Cassidy nodded. "Yep, but I loved it."

"I get that." Jake smiled. "So, what are you doing here watching MU summer baseball training?"

"I work half a mile away from here."

"Oh?" Jake looked intrigued.

"And my younger brother goes here," Cassidy added, hoping to not sound like some weirdo preying on college boys.

"Shoot, he's not one of the underclassmen I just said needs work, is he?" Jake asked nervously. Cassidy let out a laugh.

"No, no, he's a senior, and he plays soccer. Just saw him on a run with his teammates when I got here, actually."

"I feel much better, then," Jake said.

"You're all good," Cassidy smiled. A loud clink caught their attention just in time for them to turn and see a foul ball whiz mere feet from where they were sitting. They both reflexively flinched. The ball hit the metal bleachers, bounced to the floor, and rolled in the other direction.

Cassidy and Jake burst into laughter. They could hear the players on the field cracking up, as well.

"Guess that's my cue to pay better attention," Jake smirked.

"Okay," Cassidy hummed. She watched him for a moment as he clicked his pen a few times and turned to the next page of his black notebook before she turned around to face the field once more. She felt her heart flutter.

'Come on, Banker,' Cassidy mumbled to herself under her breath. She had had many crushes over the years, but never had one come on so quickly. This was more than finding Jake cute or charming; she couldn't figure out what she was feeling.

The next few innings went by without a hitch, and without any more talking to Jake. Cassidy tried very hard to concentrate on the game, but as the top of the ninth came to a close, she had no idea what the score was. Her mind had been lost in a world of daydreaming.

The first three batters were quickly and consecutively struck out, ending the game. Cassidy let out a contented sigh.

"So," Jake's voice floated behind her. Cassidy turned around to find him stuffing his notebooks and pens back into his bag. He gave her a small smile. Cassidy couldn't help but grin back.

"So, what?" she asked playfully.

"How'd you like the scrimmage?" Jake asked.

Cassidy shrugged. "It was alright. It's just nice to be in a ballpark in summertime."

"Yeah," Jake chuckled, looking amused. Cassidy realized

she must have sounded like an idiot. Her brain was not working properly. She knew the sport inside and out, and she wanted to impress him with astute observations and play analyses. But the honest truth was that she'd spent most of the game in a foggy daydream. Shit.

"What did you think about the game?" Cassidy asked lamely.

"Eh, definitely a rebuilding year." Jake shrugged.

"Yeah, that's right, you had said…" Cassidy trailed off. She was sure her face was bright red. She was off her game and felt like an idiot.

"I gotta get these numbers to the coaches," Jake said. "Maybe I'll see ya at another game - hopefully a better one." He smiled.

"Oh, yeah, yeah," Cassidy stumbled as she watched Jake stand up. "It was nice to meet you."

"You too, Cassidy." Jake nodded as he tucked his notebooks under his arm. He gave her a final flicker of a smile before gracefully shuffling across the bleacher and down the metal steps, making a beeline for the dugout.

Cassidy sighed shakily, annoyed that she was feeling so rattled.

Chapter 9

"Hi," Cassidy called down the hallway as she shut the heavy red apartment door behind her with a thunk.

"Hey," Marissa called back in a garbled voice. Cassidy could tell she had a mouthful of food. She walked into the living room and found Marissa seated cross-legged on the floor with a Styrofoam container of Chinese food on the coffee table in front of her. The local news was playing on the TV.

"Ooo, what's that? Looks good," Cassidy commented as she flopped onto the sofa.

"Orange chicken and lo mein," Marissa replied, placing another forkful in her mouth.

"Nice."

"I thought you were picking up food, so I didn't order you anything," Marissa said, covering her mouth as she chewed.

"I hit a food truck downtown," Cassidy said, rolling onto her back to look at the ceiling.

"How was the game?" Marissa asked, popping another piece of chicken in her mouth.

"Nothing special. It was nice to be out in the ballpark, though," Cassidy replied, her eyes still on the ceiling. She could feel Marissa's eyes on her. The reporter on the TV droned on about a robbery.

"What's going on? You're off," Marissa commented. Cassidy slowly turned her head to face her friend's big brown eyes and lightly freckled face.

"I was sitting by myself on the bleachers, and this guy sat right behind me…" Cassidy began.

"Hmmm?" Marissa raised an eyebrow, clearly intrigued.

"We chatted a bit; he works for MU. He does the team stats. He's…. he's pretty cute."

"Mmmmm," Marissa grinned. "So, when are you going out?"

"We're not." Cassidy rolled her eyes.

"Why not?" Marissa asked, slurping a lo mein noodle.

Cassidy shrugged, feeling oddly irritated. "I don't know."

"Hmmm."

"What does that mean?" Cassidy pursed her lips.

"I'm just surprised. You're not exactly shy, and if you felt so much as a spark, which clearly you did, you wouldn't have ignored it."

Cassidy sometimes found it irritating how well Marissa knew her. "I'm not shy! It's just, I don't know… It was a stupid, fluke thing. I don't know why we're even talking about it," she said defensively. She wasn't quite sure why her defenses were even up at the moment.

"You brought him up," Marissa shrugged.

"Well, it doesn't matter."

"So," Marissa chewed. "What's his name?"

"Jake." Cassidy smiled to herself.

"Mmmhmmm," Marissa hummed. "And what does Jake like to do?" she enunciated carefully.

"Dunno. We mostly talked about the game."

"Ah, that's right! Baseball and math nerd," Marissa noted.

"Hey!" Cassidy protested.

"Sorry, connoisseur," Marissa quipped. Cassidy couldn't help but chuckle.

"I mean, it's stupid that I even care. We chatted for a moment. Why is he in my head?" Cassidy groaned.

"Crushes are weird like that."

"I feel like a stupid teenager," she sighed.

"Just enjoy it! It's a fun high. Return to adulthood tomorrow," Marissa smiled. Cassidy rolled her eyes.

There was a comfortable silence. Marissa returned her attention to her dinner while Cassidy stared at the ceiling, half listening to the weatherman talk about the humidity. Her mind was in a constant loop of the events of her evening at the ballpark, and it was irritating her.

"When was your last crush?" Cassidy asked, breaking the quiet.

Marissa let out a snort. "Well, I am dating Brandon right now."

"I know, but he doesn't really count," Cassidy countered.

"Why not?"

"You never wished or waited for him. You two met, hit it off, and got together right away. It's different."

"Ahh, so you mean someone I've pined for." Marissa playfully waggled her eyebrows.

"I wouldn't use that term, but yes."

Marissa thought about it.

"Was it Mike from the soccer team?" Cassidy asked,

thinking back to Marissa's last long-term boyfriend in their junior year. Marissa had liked him since freshman year and was thrilled when they started to date two years later. The relationship only lasted six months, but - especially in the early months - Marissa had been obsessed.

"Ugh," Marissa groaned at the memory. Their breakup had been unpleasant. "Mike was probably the last one that came true - unfortunately. But I did like the guy in my psych class, senior year. Colby."

"I forgot about him. Did you two ever go for a drink?"

"No," Marissa snorted. "As far as Colby was concerned, I didn't even exist. I don't think he ever knew my name."

Cassidy sighed.

"Doesn't matter, though. I'm with Brandon and all is glorious!" Marissa said smugly.

"Very true."

"So, what are you going to do about Jakey-boy?" Marissa asked, taking a deliberate bite off her fork.

"I can't do anything. I mean, I met him once; I'm being an idiot. Jake's probably like Colby, doesn't even remember my name."

"I'm sure he does."

"Whatever." Cassidy sat herself up on the couch. "I'm going to have a drink and not even think about it anymore."

"Good luck," Marissa replied in a sing-song voice. Cassidy reached down and gave her shoulder a playful smack as she passed by.

"Ow," Marissa laughed.

"You deserved it," Cassidy smirked as she pulled an empty glass out of the cupboard.

Chapter 10

The engine of Cassidy's blue Toyota rumbled to a halt on the left side of Art and Lynne Banker's driveway. It was the first Friday in August and Cassidy was dutifully returning home with the rest of her siblings for their family dinner. The only car she didn't see parked was Alex's, though he was often the last to arrive.

She straightened her light pink sundress as she got out of the car before walking up to the house and letting herself inside.

"Hi," she called loudly as she closed the front door behind her.

"Oh, hi, darling," Lynne called from the kitchen.

"Hi, darling," Matty parroted in a mocking, nasal tone. Cassidy entered the kitchen to see her mother stirring something on the stove while Matty casually leaned against the island with a beer in hand, smirking.

"Hi, mom," Cassidy said happily, walking over and giving Lynne a side hug. Lynne smiled and gave her a kiss on her temple as she continued to stir.

"Hello," Lynne smiled. She enjoyed having her children

home.

"Hey, babe," Cassidy said in a playful, nasal tone as she walked to Matty and gave him a gentle pat on his chin. They grinned at one another. Cassidy and Matty had never been super close, but he was always the most playful of her brothers and they had spent so much time over the years playing pranks on one another, talking in silly voices, telling dumb jokes, quoting movies, and laughing until they could barely breathe. Matty was fun. He taught tenth grade biology at the high school two towns over. He had only taught there for the last four years, but he was consistently the student body's most favorite teacher.

"Does thou lady wanteth some bubbly?" Matty asked. He had now switched to a botched English accent that caused both Cassidy and Lynne to cringe.

"I'll just get my own beer," Cassidy said in her normal voice. She opened the fridge and helped herself to a can.

"How was your week?" Lynne asked her daughter.

"Pretty boring," Cassidy said as she cracked the can open and took a sip.

"Well, isn't that special?" Matty interjected in a surprisingly good impression of the SNL Church Lady. Cassidy chuckled.

"Oh, there are my middle two," Art said as he entered the kitchen.

"Hi, Dad," Matty and Cassidy chorused.

"What are you looking for?" Lynne asked suspiciously as Art opened the refrigerator.

"Nothing. Just looking," Art replied in a bored voice.

"Dinner is going to be ready soon; get out of there!" Lynne scolded. Art gave a defeated sigh, grabbed a can of beer, and shut the refrigerator door. Cassidy and Matty exchanged knowing looks.

"Who are we waiting on?" Art asked, taking a sip.

"Alex," Cassidy replied.

"As per usual," Matty added.

"Well, dinner's not ready yet anyway, so he still has plenty of time," Lynne said in defense of her eldest.

"We're still two down," Art commented, nodding towards Cassidy and Matty.

"I think they're downstairs," Lynne said offhandedly as she reached for the colander sitting in the sink. The Banker house had a half-finished basement where the kids had often been sent to watch TV or play games when their parents needed a break. It became the prime hangout spot when they were teenagers.

"Yeah, Ben's obsessed with his new Nintendo game and is thrilled that Eric will play it with him," Matty noted.

"Well, get them up here. As soon as Alex gets here, I want to eat," Art instructed. Cassidy couldn't help but smile. Her father was usually pretty passive at meal times, unless he was very hungry - which he clearly was today.

"Art," Lynne grumbled. "That's not how dinner works. Even if Alex appeared this instant, the food isn't cooked yet. We have at least fifteen minutes left on the oven timer. Here, eat some bread and go sit in your study." Lynne handed him a roll from the bread basket on the island and gave him a gentle push towards the hallway.

"He's just hungry, mom," Cassidy said in defense of her father as he ambled towards his office, munching on the roll as he went.

"He's driving me batty, is what is happening," Lynne commented before returning her attention to her vegetables.

"Okay…" Cassidy let out a low breath as she and Matty exchanged a glance. Their parents loved each other dearly, but after thirty-one years of marriage, sometimes their little quirks got under each other's skin.

"I need one of you to set the table and one of you to fill up the water pitcher," Lynne instructed.

"Pitcher!" Cassidy and Matty called in unison. They instantly locked eyes and stared at each other for a few seconds before Matty raised his fist in the air. Cassidy followed suit. With a silent nod, they both began to shake their fists. One. Two. Three. Cassidy threw scissors, Matty threw rock. Cassidy scrunched her nose in defeat as Matty tapped her fingers with his fist.

"Set that table real nice," Matty said slyly as he grinned and collected the large blue glass water pitcher from the cupboard. Cassidy sighed, but carried the dishes out to the dining room to start prepping for dinner.

Thirty minutes later, the table had been set, Alex had arrived, Ben and Eric had been lured away from their video game, the lasagna was out of the oven, and the seven Bankers were taking their seats at the dining room table. Everyone always took the spots they'd sat in since childhood, out of habit. Art and Lynne at the head and foot of the table, Matty and Eric on one side, Alex, Cassidy, and Ben on the other.

"Get those cigarettes off the table," Art warned his eldest son firmly as he picked up the serving spoon.

"Sorry." Alex quickly picked up the cardboard box from next to his fork and dropped it on the floor beneath his chair.

"Don't throw them on the floor," Lynne groaned as she helped herself to some salad.

"I don't have any pockets," Alex huffed, motioning to the

maroon gym shorts he was wearing.

"You're such a disappointment," Matty commented sarcastically.

"Shut up," Alex sighed, glaring his closest brother who was seated diagonally from him at the dining room table.

"Pass the bread around, Matty," Art ordered, handing him the breadbasket. Matty smiled proudly as he took the basket from his dad.

"Eric, any wedding updates?" Lynne asked curiously.

"Um," Eric hummed as he passed the Lasagna dish. "We're actually thinking about early next year in between our birthdays, since mine is in January and hers is in February."

"I thought she didn't want to have a snowy wedding," Cassidy said.

"Yeah, weren't you thinking summer '88?" Lynne asked.

"We were, but that just feels so far away." Eric shrugged.

"Oh, my god, is she pregnant?" Ben asked excitedly. The sound of Lynne's fork being dropped onto her plate reverberated through the room.

"No!" Eric groaned.

"He'd have to have sex to get her pregnant," Matty teased.

"You'll get there someday, bud," Alex added as Ben cackled. Eric rolled his eyes at his brothers' taunting, and Cassidy couldn't help but chuckle at her twin's annoyance.

"Boys, stop it," Lynne sighed as she took a sip of wine.

"Cassidy, you still working at the nerd capital?" Eric asked over the laughter, clearly desperate to get the attention off of him.

Cassidy scrunched up her nose and glowered at him. "I didn't say a word; don't throw me under the bus," she grumbled before shoving a forkful of lasagna in her mouth.

"Cassidy, be nice," Art said blandly. His focus was on his dinner.

"What?" Cassidy squeaked in annoyance. She caught Ben's eye, as he was sitting between her and her father, and he was grinning, thoroughly enjoying how quickly dinner had turned to chaos.

"Just asking," Eric backtracked.

"I didn't call you a virgin! But I don't think Ellie is pregnant. If she was, waiting until second trimester to waddle down the aisle would be just stupid," Cassidy reasoned.

"Thanks, I guess," Eric sighed.

"Anyway!" Lynne said loudly. "Eric, what other wedding decisions have you made?"

"I know Ellie and her sister have been looking at flowers, and invites, but I don't think much else. I guess if we are moving it up, decisions will have to be made more quickly." Eric took a bite of his dinner.

"What's the color theme?" Lynne asked curiously.

"Oh, yes, please, tell us the color theme!" Matty said mockingly. Cassidy couldn't help but chuckle. Eric shot her an annoyed look.

"I don't know, mom, I'll let you know at soon as I do." Eric turned his focus back to his meal.

"I'm just asking." Lynne shrugged.

"Ben, did you get your apartment yet? I want you moved in before classes start," Art asked pointedly. Cassidy was thrilled for the change in topic. The last thing she wanted to hear about was Eric's wedding.

"Yeah, yeah, I think Steve and I are signing the paperwork sometime this week after practice. But we definitely got in with the lottery for the upper-classmen apartments. So we'll still get to be on campus," Ben replied.

"I'm glad you've been able to stay on campus for all four years," Lynne said with a smile. "I don't want you to have to deal with driving in the city during rush hour to get to and from school."

"Mmm-hmmm," Ben agreed with his mouth full of lasagna.

"Yeah, now he can just stumble to the bar, stumble to practice, stumble to his apartment, then repeat. No driving required!" Matty said sarcastically.

"The damn classroom better be part of that stumble," Art advised.

"Excuse me, but I've been on the Dean's List every semester!" Ben pointed out.

"As through Ds get degrees," Alex said in a sing-song voice, causing all five Banker kids to chuckle.

"That's terrible advice for your younger brother," Lynne sighed. Alex shrugged, clearly unbothered.

Quickly Art changed the subject to the construction on Main Street and the closing of the local hardware store, and the rest of the meal was uneventful. Dinner and cleaning up was followed by a round and a half of Pictionary before arguments broke out, causing Art to huff off to his private study and Ben to stomp upstairs to his bedroom. Alex, Matty, Cassidy, and Eric quickly finished their beers, kissed their mom goodbye and headed back to their separate homes. They all had reached their fill of family time for the evening.

Chapter 11

Cassidy slammed her car door as she flopped into the driver's seat of her Toyota. It had been the Tuesday from hell at work and she was beyond ready to get back to her apartment. As soon as she got out of the parking garage, she cranked up the radio as she merged onto the city street.

She had made it a mere four blocks from her office, Madonna blasting from her speakers, when she heard a loud pop and her car suddenly jerked to the right.

"Shit," Cassidy screamed, frantically weaving to the side of the road. Cars honked as she pulled off the busy street and onto the safety of the shoulder. She quickly turned down the music before switching off the engine.

"Shit," Cassidy whined, her head tilting back on the headrest. She didn't need to get out of the car to know what happened. She had popped a tire. This was absolutely the last thing she needed today.

After a long minute of feeling sorry for herself, she carefully got out of her car during a break in traffic, and scooted to the passenger side where she could safely inspect the damage to her front passenger-side tire.

It was completely flat. There was no way it could be patched and salvaged. Cassidy bit her bottom lip as she tried to process her situation. She opened the trunk of the car and saw there was a donut as well as the car jack, still in its box, that her father had bought her when she was sixteen and insisted she keep in her trunk. Cassidy sighed. She guessed it was a good thing she'd never thrown it out.

The only problem was – she had no idea what to do next.

She knew the basic principles of changing a tire, but she had never done it herself before. When Cassidy and Eric were sixteen, a week prior to their driving tests, Art had dragged them both outside to give a tire changing demonstration. Eric watched and took notes. Cassidy sat in the grass next to her twin and peeled the neon green nail polish off of her fingernails, occasionally repeating Eric's answers when Art checked to make sure they were paying attention.

As a matter of fact, she had only had one flat tire in her life. It was Easter break during her senior year of high school. Both Alex and Matty were home from college for the week and all five Banker siblings were outside and playing one of their longstanding, made-up games with ridiculous rules and many chances for injuries. This one in particular was a combination of baseball, rugby, and lawn darts. Surprisingly, none of the siblings got injured; however, during one of Ben's lawn dart throws, he had stepped out of bounds, which, according to the rules, meant he could be tackled. Unfortunately, Eric tackled him when he was in mid-throw and the lawn dart careened off course and landed squarely in the tire of the little, beat up Dodge that Cassidy drove all through high school and college. It let out a pathetic squeal and deflated unceremoniously in the driveway.

Matty, who loved cars, had stepped right in and quickly changed the tire for her before either of their parents caught them, knowing they would all be in serious trouble.

Unfortunately, at this exact moment, she did not have any of her brothers or her dad around her to rescue her. Cassidy debated taking her purse, walking into one of the nearby stores and using a payphone to call for a cab. However, she knew she'd regret having to rescue her car later. Not to mention the earful she'd receive from her father if he heard about it.

Cassidy reluctantly pulled the jack out of the trunk and opened the box, trying to ignore all the cars passing by on their way home. She tossed the cardboard box into trunk as she pulled the crisp metal device out. As she walked back around to the front of the car with the jack in hand, determined to try to figure out how to actually use it, a tan pick-up truck pulled up behind her and shut off its engine.

Cassidy sighed. The last thing she wanted was an audience to her humiliation.

"Do you need any help?" a male voice called as the truck door opened.

"Um," Cassidy hummed. She was not in the mood to interact with a stranger; however, she was not exactly in a position to turn down help if she wanted to get home anytime soon.

"Oh, hey, it's you!" the male voice called. Cassidy's head snapped up. It was the statistician from the MU scrimmage last week!

"Hi," Cassidy said, with a surprised smile. She hadn't thought she'd ever see him again. However, she had mixed feelings about him witnessing her terrible mechanical skills so early in their acquaintance.

"Cassidy, right?" he asked. Cassidy felt herself blush slightly. She was thrilled that he remembered her.

"Yeah," Cassidy smiled. "Jake?"

"Yep," Jake smiled as he walked around the car to stand next to her.

Cassidy bit her lip.

"Tire issue?" Jake asked, looking down at the flat.

"Yep," Cassidy said, trying not to sound as defeated as she felt.

"Jeez, that's a nasty one," Jake remarked. Not the uplifting words Cassidy was hoping for.

"That's what I was afraid of," Cassidy sighed.

"Well, lucky for you, I can change tires in my sleep," Jake smirked. Cassidy felt her heart give a hard thud and a tingle shoot through her body.

"Yeah?" she mumbled, like a dope.

"You have a spare, right?" Jake asked.

"Umm, I think so." She fumbled for her keys and walked around Jake to the back of her car and unlocked the trunk. She rummaged past her gym bag and the laundry basket of old towels that she'd had every intention of taking to the Salvation Army four months ago. After some shifting, she was able to locate the donut spare wheel.

"Perfect," Jake said, looking over her shoulder. Cassidy reached in to grab it at the same moment that Jake did, causing their shoulders to bump.

"Oh, sorry," they said in unison. Cassidy fought the urge to shiver. She could smell his aftershave. It was alluring.

"I got it," Jake said, reaching past her as she paused, completely lost in the moment.

Jake plopped the tire on the sidewalk and got to work.

"Do you know what you hit?" Jake asked casually as he started to unscrew the lug nuts from the hubcap.

"No, not a clue," Cassidy said as she crouched down next to him to watch him work. She was a sudden mix of fascinated, insanely grateful, and incredibly turned on. In short, she was completely enamored; her heart pounded as she watched him work, sliding the jack underneath the car and starting to lift it.

"Are you sure you're not a mechanic?" Cassidy asked playfully. Jake chuckled.

"No, just learned as a kid. I always thought it would make me seem cool… I was wrong," he signed. Cassidy couldn't help but laugh as he placed the old tire on the ground next to her.

"I think it's very cool," she said.

"Oh, shit, I should have been telling you what I was doing so you could learn," Jake said, looking over at her. Cassidy blushed.

"No, no, this is better," she said, causing Jake to let out a short laugh. "I was taught as a teenager. My dad insisted I learn, but the truth is, I didn't pay attention and let my brother do all of the work."

"Ahh," Jake hummed. His focus was now on getting the donut wheel screwed on. Cassidy watched him in silence for a couple of minutes.

"I am really glad you stopped for me," Cassidy said as he started to lower the jack.

"I can't stand the idea of anyone stranded," Jake replied. Cassidy felt her stomach twitch. The comment was sweet, but it also reminded her that he hadn't stopped for her specifically, he just stopped to be a good Samaritan.

Cassidy's Toyota returned to ground level and Jake pulled the jack out.

"Oh my god," Cassidy sighed happily at the sight of a functioning wheel.

"Don't drive far on it. It'll be enough to get you home and then to the mechanic's soon to get a real tire," Jake said. He gathered up the jack and the split tire and headed back to the open trunk of Cassidy's car and deposited them inside.

"Okay."

"You should be all good now," Jake said, closing her trunk with a thump.

"Thank you! Seriously! So much! How, how can I ever thank you?" Cassidy asked frantically.

"Dinner?" Jake asked nonchalantly.

"Yes, absolutely!" Cassidy gushed. She would love to spend more time with this man.

"Oh!" Jake looked surprised at her quick reply. "Really?"

"Of course!" Cassidy insisted.

"Um, yeah, okay, dinner would be great," Jake said nervously. It seemed Car Hero Jake had much more confidence than Regular Jake. She found it kind of cute and endearing. Cassidy waited a moment, but he didn't say anything else.

"I'm free Sunday," Cassidy smiled.

"Oh! Oh, yeah, um, Sunday would be good for me," Jake said.

"Great!" Cassidy grinned up at him.

"Oh, um, how about the Chinese food place on Fourth? Do you like Chinese food?" Jake asked.

Cassidy nodded. "Love it. That sounds great."

"Great, great." Jake smiled nervously. Cassidy was completely charmed by his polite nerves.

117

"So, I'll see you there? 7-o'clock?"

"Yeah, yeah," Jake grinned. Cassidy grinned back.

"I'll meet you out front," Cassidy said as she started to slowly walk towards her car door.

"I'll be there," Jake said. "Drive safe!"

"Thanks again," Cassidy said as she climbed in the driver's seat and Jake shut the door behind her. She heard Jake give the roof of the car two pats and she grinned as she turned the key in the ignition.

Glancing back in her rear view mirror, she saw Jake getting back into his truck before signaling and merging back onto the road.

"Holy shit," Cassidy sighed as her car rumbled down the road. "I have a date with a stranger!" She chuckled at the sudden realization that this was her first proper date since college. Cassidy swore under her breath and gave another hearty laugh as she processed what her weekend held.

Chapter 12

Cassidy swirled the straw in her Pepsi glass with her left hand as she smoothed her dress over her knees with her right hand under the dark wooden table at the Chinese restaurant. Jake sat across from her, his wavy copper hair shimmering in the ornate red and gold light above them.

Their date had started only fifteen minutes ago and Cassidy was already having a great time. They'd met at the front door of the restaurant. She wore a knee-length purple sundress and he was in jeans, a white button up, and brown sports coat pushed up to his elbows. He looked very handsome.

They had already gotten their drinks and put in their order, and were finally able to enjoy a moment for conversation.

"Are you from Erie?" Cassidy asked, absentmindedly stirring her Pepsi.

"Oh, no, from Johnsonburg," Jake replied.

"I've heard of that," Cassidy smiled.

Jake chuckled. "Pretty small town, but it was nice. What about you? Local?"

Cassidy shrugged. "From Meadville, so not too far. I've been living in Erie since I graduated, though."

"Where did you go to school?"

"Edinboro."

"Ooo, that's a small school," Jake commented.

Cassidy giggled. "It is. Far cry from Penn State, I know," she said.

Jake looked startled. "Shit, you knew I went to Penn State? Have we already had this conversation?" he asked.

"We had a very brief conversation at the scrimmage, so it doesn't really count," Cassidy said, not wanting him to feel guilty.

"Still," Jake shrugged, taking a sip from his glass of iced tea. "What about your family, are they still local?"

"Yep. My parents are still in Meadville - same house I grew up in, actually," Cassidy smiled. "Are your parents still in Johnsonburg?"

Jake nodded. "Yeah, well, it's just my mom,"

"Oh! Has it always been just you and her?" Cassidy asked, curious.

"No, I had both parents growing up - a younger brother, too. But my dad passed away about four years ago."

"Oh, I'm so sorry," Cassidy said. She felt her heart thump. She could not imagine the unavoidable moment of losing either of her parents. It was something she truly dreaded, and hoped it would be a long way off. A very long way off.

"No, no, it's okay," Jake said with a nervous smile.

"How is it okay?" Cassidy asked.

"I mean, it's okay, I'm not sad anymore. And, well, I, um… I wasn't super close to my dad, anyway," Jake explained, looking down at his drink.

"Oh." Cassidy didn't know what to say. She often took for granted how close she was with her family, and was always surprised that other families weren't as close.

"Please, don't be sad," Jake said with a smile, clearly desperate to move the conversation to a happier topic.

"You're right. You're okay, I'm okay," Cassidy smiled back.

"Do you have any siblings?" Jake asked. Cassidy grinned. She knew the exact reaction she was going to get – it was the same every time. Ever since preschool. Four brothers is a lot to process, apparently.

"Yes, I'm one of five."

"Five, wow," Jake said. Cassidy noticed a cautious look creep onto his face.

"I have four brothers," she added. Jake's eyes bugged for a second before he quickly composed himself. Cassidy couldn't help but giggle. She loved peoples' reactions.

"Are they older or younger?"

"Two older, one younger, and one my age," she explained.

"Oh," Jake nodded, processing for a moment. "Same age? Does that mean you're a twin?"

"Yep. And I'm older by twelve minutes," Cassidy said proudly.

Jake smiled widely at her. "I always thought that would be kind of cool," he mused. "Is it?"

"Umm," Cassidy chuckled, "it's okay. I mean, I love my brother, but we're not super close."

"Ah."

"What about you? You said you have a younger brother, right?"

"Yeah, Will is one year younger than me," Jake said.

"That's nice. Are you guys close?

"Nah, not really. I mean, we get along great, but we're really different. He's in law school outside of Harrisburg, so he's about five hours away," he said.

"That's cool… I mean about the law school, well, and that you get along," Cassidy said, processing as she spoke.

"Yeah."

Before they could say anything else, a waitress arrived at their table with two heaping plates of delicious-looking food. Jake had sweet and sour shrimp while Cassidy ordered sesame chicken. They quickly thanked her before digging in and enjoying their food for a minute.

"What was it like growing up in a big family?" Jake asked as he finished his egg roll.

"It was fun! I mean, I guess I never paid much attention to it. I actually always thought our family was small since we only have a couple of cousins and they all live out of state," Cassidy said, popping a slice of carrot in her mouth.

"Five kids is a small family?" Jake playfully mocked.

Cassidy laughed, now hearing how silly it sounded. "I was used to friends at school seeing so much extended family at every holidays, or on weekends. We just didn't have that," she explained.

"Hmmm," Jake thought as he took another bite.

"What about you? Did you always feel like a small family? Or did you have a lot of extended family?"

"Yeah, my family always felt really small. My dad traveled for work a lot, so he was gone often. My brother was in sports, so my mom just drove around for that. I was either with my friends or at his games, doing the stats," Jake shrugged.

"Ooo, so the statistics love started early," Cassidy smirked.

Jake blushed a bit.

"Yeah, I was always a bit of a math nerd and frankly, it gave me something to do at Will's games," he shrugged. Cassidy watched him for a moment. There was something beautiful and raw about his words, but she couldn't quite put her finger on it. It was at that moment that she knew this was not going to be their only date.

"I love that," she said. He smiled back at her.

They spent the rest of the meal talking about work. Jake loved both teaching and working with the baseball team. Cassidy couldn't help but feel her office accountant job was quite boring in comparison. However, they both enjoyed being numbers geeks. And there wasn't a moment of silence; they both had so much to say to each other. Cassidy's cheeks hurt from smiling so much.

They finished their meal, and Jake insisted on paying. As they slowly headed outside the restaurant to the noisy street, Cassidy realized she wasn't ready for the date to end.

"Do you want to go for a walk?" Jake asked.

Cassidy perked up happily. "Would love to."

They walked the two blocks to the lake front and commented on all the odd people they came across on their way: the drunk college kids, the angry business men, the random older people out on a late walk.

"Do you want to walk down the pier?" Jake asked. Cassidy nodded.

"I haven't been out here in years," she said as they walked. The summer breeze and the sound of the lake lapping against the shore was intoxicating.

"I made the walk out here only once, and it was the day I moved out here for work. I thought it was so cool," Jake said.

"It's fun in the summer, but an absolute nightmare in the winter. My friends and I would always be daring each other to go out in the snow. How we didn't die back in college, I have no idea," Cassidy laughed. She could feel Jake watching her, smiling.

"Other than working with numbers and risking your life on a pier in the snow, what do you like to do?" Jake asked. Cassidy gave a little snort.

Cassidy turned to rest against the metal railing along the edge of the pier. "I like going to the gym, spending time with my best friend, Marissa - we have an apartment together - and, I don't know, movies, being outside, I guess. I'm pretty boring,"

"I definitely would not call you boring," Jake said, leaning on the railing next to her.

"What about you?" Cassidy asked playfully.

"I like movies, board games, beer…"

"I like beer, too," Cassidy winked.

"No - I mean, yes, but I like trying new beers," he said.

"New beers?" Cassidy asked. Her dad had been drinking the same brand of beer her entire life. She knew there were others - she'd had cheaper brands in college - but honestly, she'd never paid much attention to any of it.

"Yeah, like beer tastings, stuff like that."

"I know nothing about any of this, but I officially need to know more," Cassidy said, looking at him intently. This was the first time she had even heard of this hobby. She'd dated plenty of guys who did things she had no interest in, but she knew nothing of the world of beer tastings.

"Well, there's a festival here in a couple of weeks. We could, uh, go, if you'd like?" Jake said nervously.

"Here in Erie?"

"Yeah, it's like the fifth annual one or something," Jake shrugged.

"Shit, I'm really out of it," she said to no one in particular.

Jake grinned at her. "I'm happy to teach you... Well, if you'd like."

"I would like that a lot," Cassidy said.

"Good."

"Okay, let's get back to something I do know: games!"

"Yes?"

"I should remind you, I have four brothers. I'm competitive as hell. You have been warned," Cassidy smirked.

"Duly noted," Jake nodded.

"Which are your favorites?"

"Oh, anything. From good old Scrabble to Pictionary. I like Risk, Monopoly, Trivial Pursuit, Taboo, even Battleship, Clue, Sorry - honestly, whatever. Enjoy learning new ones, as well," Jake explained.

Cassidy smiled. "Nice! Monopoly and Trivial Pursuit generally end in fist fights, in my family," she added.

"Fist fights?"

"Four brothers," she reminded him.

"But no fighting for you?" Jake asked playfully.

"Oh, hell yeah," Cassidy said firmly. Jake laughed. "But I'm never the one to start the fights."

"Clearly a difference," Jake teased.

Cassidy and Jake spent the next hour telling game-playing stories from their childhoods, although Cassidy's stories revolved more around the arguments that broke out during game play than the actual games. However, Jake hung on every word she said. Cassidy was elated at how fascinated he seemed to be with all of her stories. She loved his honest interest and passion for his hobbies; it was a trait she honestly wasn't used to seeing much of. Most of the people she hung out with were so nonchalant about everything. She loved Jake's enthusiasm.

As the breeze off the lake started to pick up, they slowly made their way back down the pier and into downtown, towards the Chinese restaurant where their evening had started.

"Where are you parked?" Jake asked.

"Just over here." Cassidy pointed to a street parking spot where her blue Toyota sat. They made their way over and Cassidy rested her left hip on the driver's side door.

"So, um," Jake stuttered nervously.

"I had a good time tonight," Cassidy interjected with a smile. A grateful smile spread across Jake's face.

"I had a good time tonight, too," he said.

"Yeah," Cassidy nodded, dying for him to make the next move. She was used to guys being more forward, but she was charmed by Jake's shyness.

"I'd love to hang out again… go out again," Jake corrected himself.

"Me too," Cassidy smiled.

"So, um, can I call you and set something up?" Jake asked. Cassidy felt her heart swell. She couldn't remember the last time a guy had been so nervous around her.

"Yes, let me give you my number," she said, quickly reaching in her purse. She always carried a pen with her, a trait she'd picked up from her mother when she was a little girl. Even in the little girl purses she wore for playing dress up, there'd always been a pen in her bag.

After only a couple seconds of searching, Cassidy produced

a blue gel pen and hastily pulled off the lid.

"Here, give me your arm," she instructed. Jake extended his left arm. His sports jacket sleeve was still pushed up to his elbow and Cassidy took hold of his forearm and quickly scribbled out her seven digits. "There!"

"Thanks." Jake smiled, looking down at his new marking.

"I really did have a good night," Cassidy smiled, taking half a step closer to him.

"Me too," Jake grinned. There was a pause. The air felt heavy. Cassidy gazed up into his hazel eyes as he looked down at her. Without any hesitation, Cassidy pushed herself up slightly and connected her lips to his. Instantly, she knew she had taken him by surprise. He didn't push her back, he just froze.

After a long moment, Cassidy slowly pulled back from the kiss. Her eyes fluttered open to find Jake looking pleasantly surprised.

"I," Cassidy started to explain herself, but Jake interrupted her by leaning forward and again pressing his lips to hers. Cassidy smiled into the kiss. It was nice to be kissed back. His lips were soft and warm, and she felt a tingle of electricity at their touch.

Too soon, Jake pulled back. They grinned at each other for a long moment. Cassidy's heart was racing. She hadn't felt like this on a date in a long time. Actually, she couldn't even remember the last time she'd been on a proper date like this. She loved it.

"Well, goodnight," Cassidy said, attempting to hide the giddiness in her voice.

"Well, good night," Jake repeated, reaching past her to open up her car door. Cassidy got in and waved as she started up the engine. Jake smiled and retreated towards his car.

"Oh my god!" Cassidy whispered to herself in elation before shifting her car into gear and heading home, anxious to tell Marissa everything.

Chapter 13

Cassidy towel dried her hair after changing into her pajamas. She had immediately taken a shower after returning to her apartment, needing a moment to process her thoughts and, frankly, cool herself down a bit. Not to mention, Marissa was out, and she didn't have anyone to talk to.

She tossed her towel onto the hook on the back of her bedroom door before emerging to hear the TV on and the sound of the Cheers theme song ringing through the living room. NBC always played reruns in the late night.

"Hey!" Marissa called from the sofa.

"Hi," Cassidy smiled as she made her way into the room and plopped down on the opposite side of the couch. She pulled her feet up underneath her. "When did you get home?"

"About ten minutes ago," Marissa replied. She was still in her floral dress from her date with Brandon that evening.

"Good time?" Cassidy asked. Marissa looked at her aghast.

"Yes, but who cares? What happened?" Marissa enunciated

loudly.

Cassidy grinned. "It was good. Really good."

"Yeah?" Marissa pressed, leaning forward slightly.

"He was just so easy to talk to! I, I really like him," Cassidy admitted with a blush.

"Ahhh," Marissa gushed.

"He's a good kisser, too," Cassidy smirked.

Marissa looked at her wide eyed for a moment before leaning forward and smacking her knee. "Why didn't you open with that?!" she asked.

Cassidy guffawed. "I mean we just kissed twice, but both were really nice. Well, the second was much better," she said dreamily.

Marissa tilted her head. "I'm guessing you're seeing him again?" she asked.

"Yeah, I think so. I mean, we both wanted to, and I gave him my number, so… here's hoping he calls soon," Cassidy sighed.

"He will!" Marissa assured her. Cassidy smiled. Marissa didn't know Jake from a stranger, yet she was already defending his good intentions just because Cassidy liked him. Everyone deserved a friend like Marissa.

"I just got home like half an hour ago, so he definitely won't call tonight," Cassidy said.

"It's almost midnight. It would be creepy if he called now," Marissa said. Cassidy snorted.

"True. But I think he'll call tomorrow."

"Definitely. I'll make sure the answering machine tape is clear in case he calls while we're at work," Marissa said.

The girls stayed up and talked for another fifteen minutes, gushing about their dates and discussing the food they had eaten, one of their favorite topics, before heading to bed. They both had work the next morning.

It took Jake less than twenty-four hours to call Cassidy after their first date. They spoke on the phone Monday after work for over thirty minutes. Cassidy relished how natural conversation continued to feel with Jake. It was just easy.

Jake surprised her by inviting her to go bowling with him on Thursday and Cassidy happily accepted. She had never bowled on a date before, but Jake seemed to be ready to take on her competitive spirit, and she figured it was better to scare him off now rather than after they got attached.

Cassidy was even more thrilled when he asked if he could pick her up this time. It felt like a good sign - like he wasn't planning on bailing. Plus, she always loved riding in guys' cars.

The days seemed to drag until Thursday finally came around. Marissa even made sure she got home before Jake arrived to pick her up at six-thirty to get a chance to catch a glimpse of the famous Jake. The grin she gave Cassidy as she was leaving leaving made it clear that she fully approved.

They were now on their ninth frame and second plate of cheese fries in the large bowling alley about ten minutes west of the city. Cassidy was ahead by seven points and enjoying her lead. She had to admit, Jake held his own - not only in the game, but in the competitive spirit and playful trash talk. She could just relax and be herself.

"Wooo! Spare!" Cassidy cheered loudly as she spun around after her turn and skipped back to their bench.

"I can still catch up," Jake smirked as he stood up for his roll.

"I highly doubt that," Cassidy giggled as she sat down where he had just been and popped a cheesy fry into her mouth. Jake bowled the dark red ball down the lane and managed to topple only three pins. Cassidy laughed.

"That doesn't bode well for your score," she teased.

"I've got one more roll and one more frame," Jake grinned. Unfortunately for him, his next roll got only him an additional two pins. Cassidy tried to hide her glee.

"My turn! If I get at least five, I win - you can't catch up!" Cassidy gloated as she playfully bumped into his shoulder on her way to pick up her green ball from the return.

"You could always get a gutter ball," Jake teased.

"Oh, very unlikely!" Cassidy laughed, before rolling her ball down the lane. The ball gave a satisfying thunk as it hit the pins and knocked down seven.

"Shit," Jake laughed, as Cassidy screamed in joy. She skipped back over to him and reached up, grabbed his face with both her hands, and placed a hard kiss on his lips. Jake jolted slightly, taken by surprise. Cassidy pulled back and grinned at him.

"I won," she said in a sing-song voice.

"You did," Jake conceded with a smile. Cassidy beamed – not only at the win, but because they had had so much fun. He wasn't intimidated by her competitive spirit! He was, however, intimidated by her natural reaction to kiss him. Cassidy knew she could get him used to that.

"This was so much fun!" Cassidy said.

"What, winning?" Jake teased. Cassidy snorted.

"That was part of the fun, but I enjoyed playing with

someone else who likes to play."

"I told you, I like games," Jake said.

"You did."

Cassidy and Jake gathered their things and returned their shoes, before heading out of the bowling alley into the warm summer night air.

"What do you want to do now?" Jake asked.

"Want to go for a drive?" Cassidy suggested. What she really wanted to do was kiss him again, but she knew he was a little jumpy and she didn't want to push too hard. Not to mention, he was her ride, and she had absolutely no idea where they were.

"Sure," Jake said, leading her to the car and opening the passenger door for her.

"Thank you," Cassidy said, and smiled.

Jake started up his truck and the engine rumbled as they made their way out of the parking lot and onto the road. They drove for about fifteen minutes, happily chatting about some of the more interesting patrons they'd seen at the alley that evening.

"Where do you want to go?" Jake asked.

Cassidy chuckled. "I thought you knew where you were going,"

"Nope, just driving. Seeing where we end up," Jake admitted with a chuckle of his own.

"Well, where did we end up?" Cassidy looked around. It looked like Erie suburbs - nothing special.

"Hey, there's a diner. Up for a malt?" Jake asked.

Cassidy agreed, seeing the red neon sign glowing a top a nondescript small white brick building.

They pulled into the lot and got a seat in a corner booth

along the window and ordered two chocolate malts.

"I feel like I'm in Grease," Cassidy teased.

"Is that a bad thing?" Jake asked.

"Definitely not." She'd been to see that movie four times in theaters when it came out in her sophomore year of high school.

"Tell me something I don't know about you," Jake posed.

Cassidy raised an eyebrow. "This is our second date. There's a fair number of things you don't know about me yet," she giggled.

"Then enlighten me with something," Jake said. Their waitress walked over and placed two frosty malt glasses in front of them. They thanked her and each took a large sip. It was very sweet and chocolatey. It reminded Cassidy of her childhood.

"Something about me…" Cassidy hummed in thought.

"Could be anything! Just something I don't know yet."

"Okay, um… I actually hate accounting. Well, no, hate is a strong word. I don't care about accounting. It's just that math was always really easy for me, and I wanted a job that could be easy so I didn't have to be consumed by it and would be able to just enjoy my life." Cassidy chewed on the tip of the straw anxiously. She had never admitted that fact out loud before.

"Wow!" Jake gave her a surprised smile. "Playing the system, then, huh?"

"Never thought of it like that," Cassidy chuckled. "Alright, your turn. Tell me something new."

"Alright, well… I guess that my younger brother and I are polar opposites." He shrugged.

Cassidy scrunched up her face a bit. "That's not a secret."

"You didn't say it had to be a secret, you said something

134

you didn't know yet. You didn't know that, did you?"

"Well, no." Cassidy giggled again before taking a long sip.

"See, I played your game," Jake smirked.

"You started the game; it's your game!" Cassidy pointed out playfully.

They spent another thirty minutes at the diner enjoying their malts. The conversation flowed easily, and they ended up discussing baseball until they left.

Jake weaved through the city as they made their way back to Cassidy's apartment complex. She smiled over at him as they drove in silence, Bon Jovi crooning through the radio speaker. It felt comfortable and safe.

After about ten minutes, Jake pulled into one of the empty spaces in the complex lot and shifted the truck into park.

"I had a really good time tonight," he said, smiling over at her. Cassidy felt her heart flutter.

"So did I," Cassidy said. She leaned forward and pressed her lips to his. A spark shot through her body at the touch of his lips. It was wonderful. Jake kissed her back firmly for a few seconds before pulling back. Cassidy let out a small sigh at the loss of his lips.

"I'll call you tomorrow, but I'd really like to see you again," Jake said, reaching over and taking her hand in his. His hands were large and secure. They weren't soft, but they were not calloused, either.

"The date doesn't have to be over." Cassidy gave a playful shrug as she smiled up at him. She was more than happy to have Jake follow her upstairs.

"It doesn't?" His eyes were on Cassidy's hand entwined with his.

"You're welcome to come on up," Cassidy said, leaning

over and placing a soft kiss on his cheek. Stubble brushed against her lips. She loved it.

"No, no, not tonight," Jake said, shaking his head. Cassidy watched him for a long moment. She wasn't used to a guy not pushing for sex at the end of the second date. She wasn't sure if she found it flattering or annoying.

"Oh, um, okay," she said, trying not to sound too disappointed. Jake looked over and their eyes locked.

"I'll call you tomorrow after work," he assured her, leaning over to place a soft kiss on her cheek. Cassidy smiled.

She opened the passenger door and stepped out of the truck into the warm air.

"Good night. I had a good time," Cassidy assured him once more.

"Me too. Night."

She shut the door and made her way to the entrance of her apartment complex, stepping into the lobby without looking back – grinning widely as she went.

Chapter 14

Cassidy paced in front of the phone in the living room, her right forefinger absentmindedly twirling in the coil cord as she listened to the ringing and waited for a pickup. She'd found Ellie's phone number in the phone book and decided to reach out. She was good at winning people over. Perhaps, the thought, she could befriend Ellie and get her on her side.

After the sixth ring, someone picked up.

"Hello?" Cassidy did not recognize the female voice.

"Hi, is Ellie there?" Cassidy asked politely.

"Yes, she is; who's calling?"

"Cassidy Banker."

"Okay, hang on."

Cassidy waited patiently. She heard the receiver being set down and a muffled conversation in the background.

"Hi, um, Cassidy?" Ellie's familiar, gentle voice sounded in Cassidy's ear. She sounded confused.

"Hi, Ellie! How are you?" Cassidy asked perkily. She knew she'd have to really sell it. There was a long pause.

"I'm great. You?"

"Great!"

There was an uncomfortable pause.

"Cassidy, why are you calling?" Ellie asked.

"Look, I know we didn't get off on the right foot, or any foot, for that matter, but you are marrying into my family, so I was wondering if you wanted to get together and talk about the wedding, maybe? You can tell me all your exciting plans," Cassidy offered.

"Oh, uh, wow," Ellie stuttered. Cassidy winced; she knew she was coming on too strong.

"Maybe next week?" Cassidy pushed gently.

"Well, I don't have a lot of things together yet. My sister and I have been looking at tons of magazines; it's getting a little chaotic. More so since we moved up the wedding," Ellie chuckled.

"I'm happy to let you bounce ideas off of me," Cassidy suggested.

"Yeah, yeah, I mean, I know you're not super into wedding stuff, but I appreciate the offer," Ellie said. Cassidy scrunched up her face, really glad they weren't having this conversation in person.

"Happy to talk through ideas," Cassidy said simply.

"Well, that's great! Um, yeah, let me talk to my sister and see what day she has free next week and I'll let you know," Ellie said. Her tone had turned from confusion to excitement.

"Let me give you my number," Cassidy offered before reciting the seven digits. The girls bid their goodbyes and hung up. Cassidy let out a sigh as she slumped into the large blue chair next to the TV.

"What was all that?" Marissa asked, emerging from her room. Cassidy shrugged.

"Just thought I could reach out to Ellie, maybe get in her good graces," Cassidy said.

"Are you honestly trying to worm your way into being a bridesmaid?" Marissa asked pointedly.

"What?" Cassidy asked. She couldn't even feign confusion, though; Marissa knew her too well.

"Cassidy!" Marissa scolded.

Cassidy shrugged.

"You don't want to do this. You're going to hate being a part of that wedding, and you're going to make Eric really mad at you!" Marissa pointed out.

"Why would he be mad at me? I'm trying to be nice to his future wife. He should be happy," Cassidy argued.

Marissa sighed in defeat.

It was mid-week and Cassidy was just returning from her lunch break in the small kitchen in the back corner of the office.

"Banker," her boss, Mr. Jelif, called out curtly before she made it all the way back to her desk.

"Yes?" Cassidy asked. Mr. Jelif was a naturally grumpy man; she had learned to tune out his curtness when he spoke.

"My office," Mr. Jelif ordered. Cassidy shrugged and placed her empty lunchbox on her desk before turning to head toward his large office with the double doors.

"Private meeting, huh?" Devon crooned suggestively as

she walked past his desk.

"Luckily it's not with you," Cassidy mocked sarcastically. Devon rolled his chair back and started to stand up.

"That could be arran—"

"Not in a million years, Devon," Cassidy interrupted firmly. The thought of Devon even touching her arm was enough to make Cassidy shudder. Devon swore under his breath and rolled back to his desk as Cassidy approached the large office doors, knocked ceremonially, and let herself inside.

"Banker," Mr. Jelif nodded. He was an older man, early sixties, at least. Tall, with white hair and a beard. He almost never cracked a smile.

"Sir," Cassidy nodded in return. She liked working for Mr. Jelif. He'd taken a chance on hiring her right out of college, and held her to high standards. As long as she met every benchmark and deadline, which she always did, he never micromanaged her. Cassidy appreciated his management style and was grateful she had him as her boss.

"Close the door," Mr. Jelif ordered. Cassidy did as he asked before coming to sit in one of the brown wooden chairs in front of his large desk.

"What can I help you with?"

"I need you to look over some accounts for me," Mr. Jelif instructed.

"Me?" Cassidy asked, surprised he was reaching out to the youngest member of the accounting team.

"Yes. You are the most detail-oriented person here, and I need an eagle eye to find out if there's anything left to save," Mr. Jelif explained, handing her a large portfolio. Cassidy took it from him and opened it, giving it a cursory look to see if she had any questions before she left.

"Looks pretty typical of a company about to go under," Cassidy commented as she glanced over the columns of red numbers.

"No saving it?" Mr. Jelif asked. Cassidy shrugged.

"Never say never, but there would have to be a lot of changes and cutbacks. It would take a lot to get them out of the red. There's too much overhead and way too many personnel," Cassidy said, scanning the pages as she flipped through.

"I'll need you to put together a revival plan once you go through the numbers. Make this your top priority and give it your full attention," Mr. Jelif said. Cassidy looked up at him. She felt honored, but very confused.

"Mr. Jelif, what is this?" Cassidy asked.

He took a deep breath. "Our company," he admitted. Cassidy's eyes bugged.

"What?" Her heart was in her stomach and she felt like she could not breathe.

"We're going under, Banker. We have been for over a year, but I was hoping it would even out, or a miracle would happen in the market. But nothing came."

"I, I, I don't understand how we could be doing this poorly," Cassidy stuttered. She was in shock.

"This is business, Banker. Something you don't understand yet," Mr. Jelif said firmly.

"I don't know how to run a business. What do you expect me to do about this?"

"What you do is, you comb through every single line and digit with an eagle eye. I want a full report of how to turn this around - no matter what it costs," Mr. Jelif instructed.

Cassidy felt her heart thump. She willed herself to not tear up. This was not an easy assignment. "But," she started.

"No 'buts.' I need you to do this. And don't you even think about telling a single soul in this office. If you do, you'll be fired immediately," Mr. Jelif warned. Cassidy didn't know how to react.

"When do you need this by?" she asked timidly. She was extremely shaken.

"As soon as you possibly can. Take it home and work on it. Ideally by Friday," Mr. Jelif said.

"Friday?" Cassidy repeated. That only gave her two days.

"As you said yourself, Banker, this company is going under."

Cassidy wanted to scream; she wanted to argue. She was at a loss and her mind could not make sense of what was happening.

"Um," Cassidy mumbled.

"That is all. You are excused - but remember: not a word," Mr. Jelif reiterated firmly. Cassidy nodded. She stood up, closed the portfolio and exited the office, trying very hard to make her face look neutral.

"What was all of that about?" Devon asked, wiggling his eyes suggestively as she walked by. Cassidy hated that she had to pass him to get back to the safety of her desk.

"Nothing," Cassidy lied. Oh, how very much she would like to tell him it was about him getting fired. However, given that everyone here was about to be out of a job, it was a morbid thought.

"Oh really?" Devon asked. He started to follow her.

"Devon, I'm very busy and I have a lot of clients to tend to," Cassidy said. She took a seat at her desk and popped the portfolio in the top drawer.

"And what's that?" Devon asked, referring to the recently

hidden portfolio.

"Private client documents. Please leave and let me do my job," Cassidy said, avoiding his eyes. He drove her nuts. Thankfully, growing up with four brothers had given her a high tolerance for male bullshit.

"Oh, I bet you do a good job," Devon winked.

"You're disgusting. Go away," Cassidy grumbled.

"Just let me dream," Devon said playfully before turning and sauntering off to his desk. Cassidy rolled her eyes as she watched him go, letting out a sigh the moment he was out of her space.

Cassidy opened her desk and glanced at the portfolio. She didn't want this responsibility. Even if it could mean saving her job, she knew she would be destroying others. The weight of the situation felt like a noose around her neck.

Cassidy slammed the drawer shut and quickly opened one of her regular client folders, desperate to be distracted by monotonous work for a few minutes before taking on this monumental task.

The white wine in Marissa's glass sparkled against the side lamp in their apartment living room. Cassidy looked at it longingly. She was sprawled out on the living room floor looking through the thick company portfolio as Marissa lounged on the sofa reading a book and sipping wine. Cassidy had abstained from any alcohol that evening as she knew she had to work - and work a lot harder than usual. She'd always been quick, requiring little effort to succeed at her studies or work. But she wanted this to be exceptional. It had to be exceptional.

"Ugh," she groaned loudly. Looking at her company's books was making her mind spin. How could they be doing this poorly?

"How's it going?" Marissa asked, not looking up from her book.

"Not great."

"Can you explain something to me?" Marissa asked, lowering the paperback to her lap.

"Hmm?"

"How exactly did saving the company fall to you?" Marissa asked.

"I'm not doing this to save the company. I need to come up with a breakdown report so others that are much higher up can make informed decisions on what to do," Cassidy explained as she flipped to the next page.

Marissa raised her eyebrows.

"What?" Cassidy asked.

"I just don't understand why you specifically were chosen to do this."

"Who knows! Maybe since I've only been there two and a half years, I have the least to lose? I really have no clue," Cassidy replied, feeling even more frazzled. Why had she been chosen for this?

"Okay," Marissa said skeptically.

"You have more to say, don't you?" Cassidy knew Marissa too well to imagine she'd just roll over and accept a situation.

"Well, kind of. But also, if your company really is collapsing, I don't feel it's right for me to find more holes in the already-porous game plan," Marissa said. Cassidy let out a frustrated breath, mostly annoyed that Marissa was right. Her world was collapsing and she had no idea what was going to happen. Cassidy hadn't expected to have to search for a new job any time soon. She was comfortable, and she liked being comfortable.

Chapter 15

Cassidy tapped her toes on the concrete steps excitedly. It was Friday night and she was standing in front of Jake's house, a half house he was renting on the east side of the city. Jake had called her a few times this past week, which had been a good distraction for Cassidy since work had been hell. Yesterday he'd invited her out for their third date at his house to play board games. Cassidy was thrilled.

"Hi," Jake said with a smile as he opened the door. He was in jeans and a blue Penn State t-shirt.

"Hey!" Cassidy smiled. Jake had told her to dress casually since they would be hanging out at his house, so she was in her comfortable yellow sundress. She appreciated the lack of formality; it made it easier to relax.

"Come on in." Jake stepped aside to let her in. Cassidy stepped into the living room, giving Jake a light peck on the lips as she walked past. Despite the fact that he had lived here for the last two years, the room was fairly stark: nothing on the walls and a few mismatched pieces of furniture. It was clean, but definitely not homey.

"Nice," Cassidy commented as she looked around. She was only half lying. There was a lot of space and everything was nice, it was just the lack of personality holding her back from loving it.

"Do you want a tour?"

"Definitely!" Cassidy beamed.

The ground floor consisted of the living room, dining room, and kitchen, all with bare walls and minimal furniture. The stairs off the dining room took them to a paneled hallway leading to three small bedrooms and a white and beige bathroom at the end of the hall.

After the tour, Jake brought her back to the kitchen to get a snack.

"I have some pizza rolls in the oven right now; they should be done in a few minutes," Jake said.

"Great," she chuckled. Total bachelor food. Not that she was mad about it.

"I've pulled a few games out in the living room. As soon as the rolls are done, we can head in," Jake said. Cassidy could tell he was nervous. She wanted him to know how happy she was to be there, so she closed the gap between them.

"We can pass the time," she whispered before pushing herself up slightly and pressing her lips to his. Jake let out a surprised chuckle, but cupped her face with his left hand and kissed her back.

Their lips moved slowly together and Cassidy's heart started to race. She loved the feeling of his lips on hers and the smell of his aftershave. She snaked her arms around his shoulders as they kissed.

The kisses were soft but firm, never deepening, but their

mouths moved with vigor and passion, both enjoying being on the cusp of something more.

They were interrupted by the beeping of the timer Jake had set on the microwave. They pulled apart with a jolt of surprise and both chuckled.

"Dinner," Jake teased. Cassidy smiled as she watched him shut off the timer before tending to the oven. She was reveling in the warmth that filled her belly. It was only going to get better as the night went on.

She wanted this night. She needed this night.

Five minutes later, they were seated on the brown shag carpet in the living room. A large plate piled high with half-exploded pizza rolls sat on the coffee table between them and Jake was setting up a game as they ate.

"I cannot remember the last time I played Parcheesi," Cassidy said, popping a hot pizza roll into her mouth.

"I love it," Jake said, focused on the set up.

"Enough to lose miserably to me?" Cassidy teased.

Jake looked up at her a smirked. "In your dreams, Banker."

Cassidy laughed. She was always pleasantly surprised at how well Jake handled her competitive nature. She liked having someone that she could be herself around. She liked having someone that wouldn't be scared away by her family. This was only the third date, but it was the start of something. Cassidy could feel it.

"How was your day?" Cassidy asked. She knew that once game play started, there was a low chance they would be having deep conversations.

"Good. I gave a test to my stats class, so there wasn't a lot for me to do," Jake said. "But I had to go over some of the books with the baseball coach after lunch to figure out some

148

of the starters."

"Oh, cool." Cassidy was intrigued.

"Well, we'll see how it plays out on the field. What works in the books doesn't always work in real life."

"That is true."

"What about you? Did you get that report in?" Jake asked. Now that he had finished setting up the game he popped two pizza rolls into his mouth at once. Cassidy tied to hide her smile as he winced from the heat.

"Ugh," Cassidy groaned. "Yes, I did. But I have no idea what's going to happen. I was shooed out of the room as soon as I turned it in. Didn't talk to Mr. Jelif the rest of the day… or even really see him."

"What was your suggestion in the report?" Jake asked.

Cassidy shook her head frantically. "Oh, no! I didn't give any suggestions. I mean, I don't have any right to. I just had to give the facts and figures. We're spending more money than we're bringing in. I mean, like, we're hemorrhaging money."

"But you're smart, you have to have some ideas. It can't just be the end of the line," Jake said. "If it was one of your clients, you wouldn't tell them to just throw in the towel!"

"If it was one of my clients, I absolutely would. You have to cut your losses at some point if you want any hope of moving on," Cassidy groaned.

"I understand, but you have to find a next step, too, right?"

Cassidy bit her lip. "Ideally, yes. But it feels weird that I was even given this data. I'm most likely out of a job within the next year," Cassidy said glumly. She'd never put much thought into her working life. She'd always just assumed there would be a job waiting for her. She hated the realization that there might not be.

"Do you want to talk about it?" Jake offered, popping another pizza roll in his mouth. Cassidy felt her heart thud. She looked over at his sweet, sincere face. He truly cared. He was actually offering to just sit and talk. But Cassidy was tired of thinking about work. She had been looking forward to the distraction of the night and wasn't going to let anything to get in her way. Good intentions or not.

"No," Cassidy shook her head gently. "I just don't want to think about it for a bit."

"Oh, okay." He gave her a small smile, which Cassidy reciprocated.

"Hand me the dice," Cassidy said, happily changing the subject and holding out her hand.

"You know what you're doing?" Jake asked playfully.

"Definitely," she winked, and rolled the dice. Their game night was on!

Cassidy loved to play games and enjoyed being with someone who could not only keep up, but could dish out the banter like she was used to. Jake won the first game. Then Cassidy picked Guess Who for their second game, and she was able to pull out a win. Not only was Jake good at banter, he was a good competitor. He played to win, but the results didn't affect his temperament. Cassidy was similar. She liked to win, but hated playing with people who threw the board when they lost.

This was a good sign.

By the time they were packing up the game box, the pizza roll pile had been completely devoured and they were both on their third beer.

"Do you want to do something else?" Cassidy asked slyly. She had enjoyed the games, but she was ready for the real event of the evening. She was ready to sleep with Jake. She wasn't used to waiting this long, but with Jake the pace felt natural, and she wanted the moment to be perfect. Given how much fun they had been having that evening, this could definitely be it.

"Another game?" Jake asked, his attention focused on the game box.

"No. I was thinking you could come sit by me," Cassidy suggested, biting her lip in anticipation.

"Huh?" Jake asked before looking up. The instant he saw the look on her face, he knew what she wanted. "Oh! Oh, yeah," he agreed in a stutter, setting the box aside and scooting his way to the other side of the coffee table where Cassidy was leaning up against the base of the couch.

"I'm really having a good time with you," Cassidy whispered, looking over at him. Jake scooted a bit closer and slid his right arm around her shoulders. Cassidy felt a flutter in her belly.

"I'm having a good time with you," Jake replied as he leaned down and lightly pressed his lips to hers. Cassidy smiled against his lips and kissed him back.

Their kisses started slowly: playful pecks. But after a minute, they become longer, more deliberate. Cassidy felt a tingle shoot through her body. His lips tasted so good, she felt intoxicated. Suddenly Jake pressed his lips harder on hers, pushing them open. Cassidy responded enthusiastically and deepened the kiss immediately. The feeling of his warm breath and his tongue on hers was fantastic. Sparks shot up her spine. Cassidy flung her arms around his shoulder and pulled him closer. Jake moved his hands to her waist. The quick shifts caused them to teeter slightly and fall back on the carpet, Jake landing on top of her. Cassidy gave a gasp of elation at the feeling of his weight on her and kissed him with even more fervor.

Jake propped himself up on the brown carpet while leaning over Cassidy, his right hand slowly running up and down her side, their kiss never once breaking.

They kissed for many minutes. Cassidy plunged her right hand in his copper, wavy hair and held on to his upper back with her left, practically clawing at him. She wanted to be closer, she needed to be closer. The sensations shooting through her were incredible.

Jake eventually pulled back from their kiss and slid his lips down her jaw line. The touch was so light, it almost tickled, but mostly, it drove Cassidy crazy. After tantalizingly trailing his lips all along her jaw, he settled on the side of her neck, where he kissed and licked the sensitive skin.

Cassidy gasped and twitched under him. She was buzzing from his touch. She never wanted this to end. How on earth could he be affecting her so much already?

"Jake," Cassidy panted in a low voice. Jake took the hint and moved his mouth from her neck back to her lips and their passionate kissing resumed immediately.

She reached down and caught Jake's right hand, and led it down to the hem of her dress. Unfortunately, Jake didn't seize the opportunity to rip off her dress, but rather let his fingers play with the fabric along the top of her thigh. Cassidy couldn't deny this felt amazing, but it wasn't really what she was hoping for at the moment. She decided he needed another hint. She slid her hand down from his shoulder and trailed it over his chest and stomach, which felt delightfully firm even through the fabric of his tee shirt. She trailed her hand down further, to the waistband of his jeans, where she worked quickly to pop open his top button. Jake chuckled against her lips before pulling back.

"What are you doing?" he asked, amused.

"What do you think?" Cassidy smirked.

Jake shook his head with a small smile. "Not tonight, babe," he said, leaning forward and giving her a gentle peck on the lips.

Cassidy giggled. "Oh really?" she teased, moving both hands to the front of his jeans. Jake intercepted her hands in his and moved back.

Cassidy raised an eyebrow. She no longer understood this game.

"Look, I like you, and this, this, is great. But it's as far as we're going tonight," he explained.

"Sure about that?" Cassidy asked again, eyeing the front of his pants. She had been positive she'd felt a bulge. Jake sighed.

"Yeah."

"I don't understand."

"Cassidy," Jake groaned. He sat himself up and re-buttoned his pants and adjusted them.

"Jake," Cassidy mimicked, sitting herself up as well so they were facing each other.

"I just, it's too soon," Jake admitted with a shrug.

"But it's the third date," Cassidy countered.

"What does that have to do with anything?"

"I mean, generally, the third date is where things move into the bedroom... or the floor," Cassidy said with a shrug. She was actually used to this stage coming much earlier in the courtship. The waiting had been fun, but she was ready to

153

move forward.

"That's not a law!"

"Maybe it should be," Cassidy joked, desperate for this awkward moment to end. She was in uncharted waters, and she hated it.

Jake simply stared at her for a long moment. He looked hurt. Cassidy was confused.

"Is that what relationships are all about to you? Sex?" Jake asked seriously.

"It's not the only thing, but it is an important part. I mean, don't you think so?"

"Of course I do, which is why I don't want to sleep with you tonight."

"This makes no sense to me!" Cassidy threw her hands in the air emphatically.

"Cassidy, I've been hurt before. Really hurt. I'm not ready to jump into a physical relationship immediately," Jake admitted.

Cassidy wanted to make a joke, break the tension, but the look on his face hit her. He was… sad. Vulnerable. She had never seen him look like this before. She wasn't used to seeing any guy look like this.

"Oh," she said quietly.

"What does that mean?" Jake asked.

"It means, I, I never really thought about that," Cassidy admitted.

"What are you talking about?"

"About you being hurt."

"You think no one ever gets hurt?" Jake asked. Cassidy again felt her heart thud – but this time with a twinge of shame. He looked annoyed. She felt like an asshole.

"No, I know people do. But like, not guys… I don't know." Cassidy shrugged.

"Is that what you want? A guy that doesn't feel anything and just wants to sleep with you all the time?" Jake asked.

Cassidy had honestly never thought about it. All of her past relationships had been fairly surface level. They never talked about feelings. She'd dated Kevin for almost two years, and while she knew almost everything about him, she'd never thought of him getting hurt. He never let her see that side of him.

"No, no, I'm just… not used to it."

"Used to what?"

"Used to hearing what a guy is feeling. I guess my relationships were never super deep," Cassidy trailed off. She was starting to feel bad for herself. Had she spent her entire life in a shallow bubble and not even realized it?

"Do you just want something light and casual?"

"No," Cassidy said immediately. She wanted a deep relationship, and it scared the hell out of her because she knew, in that moment, that Jake would hold her to it.

"I don't want something light, either," Jake said with a small, slightly embarrassed smile. Cassidy grinned.

"But does that really mean we won't… you know … tonight?" Cassidy asked playfully. She hoped he might change his mind. She was desperate to be physical with him again.

"For me, it does," Jake told her. Cassidy swallowed her disappointment.

"Okay. I can wait," Cassidy replied, telling herself as much as she was telling Jake.

"Don't look so disappointed," Jake chuckled.

"It should be a compliment to you!" Cassidy covered her

face in embarrassment.

"It is," Jake smiled, pulling her hands off of her face. Cassidy looked deep into his eyes. She knew there was no turning back, that this could be the start of something real and deep and permanent.

"Can we still kiss, or do we just start knitting now?" Cassidy teased. Jake leaned forward to press his lips gently to hers.

Chapter 16

Cassidy turned onto her childhood street for the second time in the month of August. It was a Sunday evening and she and her siblings were all returning to their parents' house to celebrate Ben's 22nd birthday. Ben's birthday had actually been that Friday, the 15th, however, he had partied with his friends the nights before so the family was getting together on Sunday. Cassidy assumed Ben would be hungover as hell this evening, and looked forward to watching everyone annoy him by being as loud as possible, which she knew her brothers would gladly do.

She turned into the long driveway to the familiar brick house and was surprised to find most of the cars there already.

She quickly parked and grabbed Ben's present – a new Nintendo game – and headed to the house. As she approached the front porch, the door opened and Alex emerged.

"Hey," Cassidy said happily.

"Hey." Alex pulled a green lighter out of his pocket and quickly lit his cigarette.

"Does mom know you're out here?" Cassidy smirked. Their parents hated that Alex smoked so much. Cassidy didn't love it either, but she was used to it.

"No." Alex took a drag. "And don't give me away!" He nodded to the far end of the porch, out of view of the large bay window in front. Cassidy followed him to the secluded corner. They all knew about the invisible corner. Cassidy herself had used it many times in high school when returning home from dates.

"How is it in there?" Cassidy asked, leaning against the rough exterior of the house. Alex settled on the porch railing across from her.

"Eh, not bad."

"Is Ben hungover?"

"Yeah. He already took a swing at Matty for popping a balloon by his head while he was lying down on the couch."

"I'm sober and I'd take a swing if someone popped a balloon at my head," Cassidy chuckled.

"Fair point."

"Everyone's here early," Cassidy commented.

"Just waiting on you and Eric," Alex said, flicking some ash off the railing.

"Is Eric bringing Ellie?"

Alex tilted his head and shot her a knowing look.

"What?" she asked.

"I was going to talk to you about that," Alex said.

"Ellie is coming?"

"No," Alex replied, "but you need to stay away from her."

"What? Why?" Cassidy scrunched up her face.

"Cassidy, I don't know what you're playing at, but leave her alone," Alex said firmly before taking another drag.

158

"I don't know what you're talking about," Cassidy countered, although she was fairly certain she did.

"You called Ellie the other day."

"It was last week, actually, and I'm still waiting for a call back," Cassidy said sassily. Alex just watched her for a moment. He didn't look amused.

Cassidy felt a weird pang in her chest, like she was a little kid in trouble.

"Why did you call her?"

"Sounds like you already know," she said defensively.

"Do you actually want to be her friend, or are you trying to weasel your way in?"

"Weasel?" Cassidy looked taken aback. "That's low."

"It may be, but I know damn well you're pissed about the wedding and are taking things into your own hands."

"First I'm supposed to be nice to Ellie, so I reach out, and now it's a problem?" Cassidy waved her arms dramatically.

"Cassie," Alex said in a low, warning tone.

"Why is this any of your business, anyway? I can be friends with whomever I want."

"Because we know you're not reaching out to Ellie out of the goodness of your heart."

"We?"

"Ellie told Eric you called. Did you honestly think she wouldn't?"

Cassidy paused. Honestly, she hadn't thought that far. Shit. "What does that have to do with anything?

"Eric is pissed."

"Why?"

"Ugh," Alex groaned. "Because you need to just let them have their day."

"But why are you the one cornering me if Eric is so pissed?" Cassidy asked.

"Because he doesn't want to deal with you."

"Deal with me?"

"You know what I mean," Alex sighed.

"No, I don't, and I don't appreciate you taking his side," Cassidy whined, aware that she was sounding very much like a child. She hated this feeling.

"I'm not taking anyone's side," Alex assured her, stepping forward to rest his hands on her shoulders as he looked down at her.

"It feels like you are," Cassidy said in a low voice.

"Why do you say that?"

"Well, I don't know. You already talked to Eric, so clearly you got his story first," Cassidy shrugged. Alex gave her a quizzical look.

"Eric, Matty, Ben, and I meet for drinks now and then. We happened to get together earlier this week, and Eric walked in pissed. He said that Ellie just told him you called to butt in."

"He's being dramatic," Cassidy grumbled.

"Since when has Eric been the dramatic one?" Alex raised an eyebrow. Cassidy let out an annoyed huff.

There was a long pause. Alex gave her shoulders a squeeze and then stepped back to his place at the railing.

"Why did you call her?" Alex asked quietly.

"I don't know. I just offered to get together," Cassidy replied sulkily.

"And do what?"

"Look at wedding stuff. I don't even know their theme or colors!"

"Really?" Alex asked in disbelief.

"Yes, really!" Cassidy was on the defensive. "And she sounded open to it! She was going to talk to her sister to find a date. It just sounds like Eric threw a fit about it and fucked it up."

"Of course, you're blaming Eric." Alex rolled his eyes. He stubbed out his cigarette butt on the brick post and flung it into the wisteria.

"What does that mean?"

"Cassidy, he is not the sum of all of your problems."

"I never said all of them," she shrugged. Alex let out an audible sigh.

"Can you just please be nice and let Eric and Ellie have their day?" Alex asked.

"I just want to be involved in their day," Cassidy countered firmly. She could feel a lump forming in her throat.

"Ugh, come here," Alex said. He looked sad for her. Cassidy set the gift bag down and let him wrap her up in a hug. She rested her head on his chest and inhaled the familiar scent mix of smoke, Old Spice, and Doritos that had been his signature smell since he was about sixteen.

"Look, I know this sucks, and you're pissed, but if this was your wedding, would you invite Ellie to do anything?" Alex asked. Cassidy paused for a moment. It was annoying that Alex was winning this argument with logic.

"That's completely different."

"No, it's not. Ellie is celebrating her day with her sister and her friends. There is nothing wrong with that," he said. Cassidy pushed herself off of him so she could look Alex in the eye.

"But–"

"No! You know you wouldn't invite Ellie to anything.

She and Eric have been dating for years and you've hardly acknowledged her," Alex pointed out.

"Fine. Ellie didn't invite me, but neither did Eric. This worked out perfectly for him. I'm not a brother – easy option to exclude me."

"And I'm sorry about that," Alex sighed.

"So, what am I supposed to do?"

"Ignore all the politics, show up to the wedding, clap, dance, and drink. It'll be great," Alex assured her.

"It won't," Cassidy huffed.

"If it sucks, you don't have to deal with any of it."

Cassidy was silent, considering his words. They heard a car engine in the driveway and the sound of a car door slam. Eric had arrived.

"Great."

"Be nice." Alex said firmly.

"Always am."

"Bullshit," Alex smirked. Cassidy smirked back. They walked around to the front of the porch as Eric approached.

"Hey," Eric said, looking slightly suspicious at the two of them walking towards him.

"Hey," Alex said pleasantly. Cassidy simply nodded.

"What's up?" Eric asked.

"Cigarette," Alex answered.

"Oh."

"Heard you guys met for drinks this week," Cassidy mentioned airily.

"You did? That's great," Eric replied blandly. He continued towards the front door.

"Guys," Alex said in a warning tone.

"What?" Cassidy and Eric snapped simultaneously. Alex

looked mildly surprised at their joint reaction.

"Do you have anything to say to each other?" Alex asked.

"Nope."

"No."

"Really?" Alex groaned.

Suddenly the front door swung open to reveal Matty looking shocked to see the three of them standing on the doorstep.

"Whoa!"

"Hi Matty," Cassidy said with a smile, happy for the distraction.

"What the hell is going on out here?" Matty asked.

"Apparently Alex was just having a cigarette," Eric said skeptically.

Alex let out a low breath. "Okay, we all know – Cassidy called Ellie, Eric is mad, Cassidy is mad, and everyone is just being stubborn."

"Stubborn?" Cassidy and Eric asked in unison before turning to glower at each other. They so rarely spoke in unison anymore, it was weird and unnerving when it happened – especially now that they were in their twenties.

"Echo!" Matty teased, knowing exactly how irritated they were. He fed off the chaos.

"Guys!" Alex said, reaching for them both. "Let's call a truce."

Cassidy raised her eyebrow in suspicion.

"Just reset to last week. Cassidy didn't call Ellie, Eric didn't get annoyed, we're all good!" Alex suggested.

Cassidy ground her teeth in irritation. Yes, she had started all of this, but she hated that everything was her fault.

"Reset? Okay, Mr. Sci-fi," Matty mocked. Cassidy and Eric looked at each other, brows furrowed, for a long moment.

163

"Fine," Eric said with a defeated sigh. Cassidy simply grunted.

"Great!" Alex gave a forced grin.

"You're not pulling any more shit, though," Eric grumbled at Cassidy.

"Why would I do anything? I don't even exist to you," Cassidy said in a low voice.

"Heaven forbid the world doesn't revolve around you all the time," Eric said before turning to push past Matty and go inside.

"It doesn't!" Cassidy screamed after him. Suddenly, their mother, Lynne was at the front door.

"What in the world are you all doing on the porch? Get inside!"

"I'm trying!" Cassidy said defiantly.

"Try harder. I'm serious, get inside all of you. The food is almost ready and Ben is falling asleep on the couch," Lynne said in an exasperated tone.

"What a hoppin' party," Matty joked.

"Shut up, and get Ben up and moving," Lynne instructed. Matty gave their mother a nod before turning inside.

"That's not going to end well," Alex said gently.

"I know," Lynne sighed, waving her remaining children inside.

Alex and Cassidy followed her into the foyer just as Ben let out a loud scream. Cassidy bit her lip as she heard Matty's footsteps making a run for it, Ben's tread in hot pursuit.

"Boys!" Lynne screamed, marching towards the family room at the back of the house.

"You're going to be okay," Alex said, giving Cassidy a nudge.

"Yeah," Cassidy sighed, disheartened.

"Come on. It's Ben's birthday, he's hungover as hell, mom's pissed – this'll be great!" Alex grinned. Cassidy couldn't help but laugh.

"Best party ever." Cassidy smiled up at her eldest brother before the two made their way into the family room to join the commotion.

Chapter 17

Cassidy was furiously punching numbers into her adding machine as she looked over third quarter reports for one of her clients when a shadow appeared over her desk. Her boss, Mr. Jelif, was standing in front of her.

"Banker," he said, as soon as she looked up. "My office, two minutes."

"Sure thing, Mr. Jelif," Cassidy said. He turned and strode away as she swore under her breath.

Cassidy quickly finished calculating the line she was on, marked her spot, and got up from her desk. She felt the eyes of her coworkers on her as she walked through to Mr. Jelif's large office at the far end of their floor. She quickly brushed her hands over her tan skirt before knocking on the door.

"Enter," Mr. Jelif called from inside, and Cassidy let herself in.

"How can I help you?" she asked.

"Take a seat." Mr. Jelif motioned to the chair in front of his large desk. Cassidy quickly sat down.

"What's up?" she asked as calmly as she possibly could.

"We've gone over the proposal you made up the other week," Mr. Jelif began.

"We?"

"The board and I."

"Ah." Cassidy felt her heart give a loud thud. She felt like there was a rock in her stomach.

"We clearly need to make some cuts."

"Oh," Cassidy gulped loudly. "Wait, am I getting fired? Did I write a proposal to fire myself?"

"Well…"

"Shit!" Cassidy swore before remembering herself. She gasped loudly as her eyes bugged in surprise. "I'm sorry!"

"You're okay," Mr. Jelif said with amusement.

"Um, thanks," Cassidy stuttered. "But, am, am I getting fired?"

"Not right now."

"Not right now," Cassidy repeated.

"Banker, I need you to let me finish a sentence or we'll be here all day," Mr. Jelif said.

Cassidy nodded frantically and brought her fingers to her lips to locked them. She realized after the fact that the gesture was childish, and probably not helpful to her hopes of staying employed.

"Go ahead, sir."

"We need to make some cuts. This is going to be the first step in trying to get us back in the black."

"What cuts?" Cassidy asked nervously.

"We need to consolidate. Drop our lowest preforming accountants, and drop all of our smallest clients. Split up the medium-to-large clients between the remaining accountants.

You'll all just have to adjust and work overtime," Mr. Jelif explained. Cassidy's mind was swimming.

"But if we can pay overtime, we can pay the accountants to stay," Cassidy nervously countered. The thought of her coworkers suddenly losing their jobs while she stayed on made her very uncomfortable.

"We're not paying overtime. We don't have the funds."

"But then why would people work overtime?"

"Because they want a job," Mr. Jelif said flatly.

"I don't see how this is the best option."

"Banker, come on! You saw our books. You know the situation we're in - you know we don't have any wiggle room," Mr. Jelif said firmly.

"I thought cuts would be made to the coffee station or the snacks," Cassidy said, refraining from adding "or larger salaries."

"We need to think bigger, and more long term." There was a long, awkward pause. Cassidy willed herself not to cry.

"Mr. Jelif, can I ask a question?"

"You've never held back before," he chuckled.

"Why am I looking at all these books with you? Like, how, how am I in this position?" Cassidy asked nervously. Almost everyone else in the office had more experience than her.

"Because you're smart as hell and I can't waste time worrying about seniority. I knew you were smart enough to read these books and give us a quick rundown, and you did," Mr. Jelif said plainly. Cassidy felt both honored and overwhelmed.

"Um, thank you."

"I'm going to make some phone calls, but I need you to keep pulling reports of our finances."

"How much could have changed in a few days?" Cassidy asked. She knew the money market was fickle, but she didn't want to have this responsibility.

"A hell of a lot," Mr. Jelif replied, shuffling the papers on his desk into a stack. Cassidy paused for a moment, finding the courage she needed to ask her one remaining burning question.

"Do - do I still have a job, since I'm helping?"

"For now," Mr. Jelif replied plainly. "We're going to try our best to keep this damn place afloat, but you need to work hard for me. I know you coast on your brains and natural smarts, but you'll have to put your nose to the grindstone if you want to pull through."

Cassidy gulped. She couldn't tell if Mr. Jelif meant that as a pep talk or not, but it sounded more like damnation to Cassidy. Her palms were sweating.

"Okay," she replied softly, knowing she had to at least say something.

"Go pull those reports before you leave tonight and you can do a write up tomorrow."

"And don't say a word to anyone?" Cassidy questioned.

"Not a word, or you're out on your ass, brains or not," Mr. Jelif said, motioning to the door. Cassidy nodded. Her stomach was in knots as she trekked back to her desk. She could feel eyes on her. Her coworkers must have known something was up; it was too obvious with all of the private meetings suddenly happening. She hated this feeling of secrecy so much. Generally, Cassidy enjoyed her work and office, even with creeps like Devon around. But she was coming to dread her time here. What was she going to do?

Jake listened intently as Cassidy regaled him with the latest developments in her work saga. They were seated in his pick-up truck at the local A&W car hop for dinner. They had placed their order about ten minutes ago and were waiting for the overly perky high school girl on roller skates to bring the tray of food to their window.

"I don't know what to do," Cassidy whined, tilting her head back on the headrest of the car seat. She hated feeling so rattled.

"Is it worth starting to put feelers out for a new job?" Jake asked.

"I don't want to look for another job," Cassidy sighed.

"Well, it sounds inevitable." Jake pointed out.

Cassidy gave a low groan. "I mean, what if I can find a way to fix things?"

"Cassidy, come on. It sounds like it's already too late anyway. I don't think there's anything you can do - I think they pulled you in to help them tread water just a little bit longer," Jake said.

"I still don't want to give up yet," Cassidy told him honestly.

"Okay, that's your choice."

"You sound like you disagree with me."

"I don't know what to tell you," Jake said. "I'm not in that situation."

"Well, what would you do?"

"I'd look for a different job - but again, I'm not quite as invested as you are."

"You don't like your job? I thought you did."

"Oh, I do," Jake said. "I like my work, but I don't think Mercyhurst is my forever job," Jake said with a shrug.

"Hmmm." Cassidy wasn't sure what to think. As she

pondered, the enthusiastic sixteen-year-old skated to the truck with a tray full of food. They thanked her and took their sandwiches: a chicken sandwich for Cassidy and a burger for Jake. They shared an order of fries.

"I can't believe you came to a drive-in and didn't get a burger," Jake said playfully as he took a bite. Cassidy smirked.

"Forgive me for wanting functioning arteries," she teased, popping a French fry into her mouth.

"Yeah, that's just like eating a bowl of spinach," Jake teased nodding at her large, condiment-filled chicken sandwich. Cassidy let out a snort, knowing he was right. She enjoyed having someone to verbally spar with.

The two talked and ate happily until they had had their fill. The young car hop skated back over, took their tray and trash, Jake paid, and the truck rumbled back to life as they departed the busy parking lot.

"So, what do you want to do now?" Cassidy asked innocently. Both of them fully knew what she wanted.

"Want to go for a walk?" Jake asked as he cruised through the next intersection.

"It's 8 pm. Where would we go, other than the lake?"

"Okay, what do you suggest?"

"You can come back to my place," Cassidy offered.

Jake gave a knowing smile. "Mm hmmm."

"My roommate is home; you can properly meet her. Marissa is my best friend, you'll love her!" Cassidy offered. Marissa had been begging to meet Jake for weeks; now Cassidy could satisfy her curiosity and get a chance for some much-needed feedback from her best friend.

"Um, sure," Jake replied with a shrug.

"No, come on - it'll be fun! You'll like her," Cassidy said.

Jake gave her a quick glance and grinned.

"I'm sure I will," he said.

In less than ten minutes, Cassidy and Jake were back at her complex. He parked the truck and they headed inside. Cassidy bounded her way up the stairs with Jake right in tow before letting herself inside the red door that groaned as it opened.

"Hi!" Cassidy called loudly.

"What the hell are you doing back already?" Marissa called from the direction of the living room.

"I brought you a friend," Cassidy replied, taking Jake's hand and leading him down the entrance hall into the open living room.

"A friend?" Marissa asked excitedly. Cassidy smiled at Marissa who sprawled across the length of the sofa, leaning back on Brandon who was stretched out beneath her, resting his back on the arm rest. Marissa was resting her head on his chest. The two hardly ever let themselves not be touching when together. They were practically magnetic.

"Hey Marissa, Brandon," Cassidy greeted. "This is Jake Sullivan."

Marissa quickly clambered up and around the sofa to greet Jake.

"Jake! It's great to finally meet you!" Marissa gushed excitedly, surprising him with a big hug. Jake was clearly caught off guard, but recovered quickly and reciprocated.

"Babe, he just got here," Brandon chuckled. Marissa pulled back from Jake, but continued to beam up at him.

"Come on, sit down and tell us everything," Marissa said, gently pulling him into the seating area. Jake took a seat on the plush blue chair by the window, and Cassidy balanced herself on the wide arm of the chair. Marissa tapped Brandon's leg to sit up as she sat down next to him, pulling her legs up and crossing them.

"Want a beer?" Brandon offered. Jake nodded. Brandon got up and headed to the fridge.

"So, what do I need to know about you, Jake Sullivan?" Marissa asked playfully. She straightened her back as if she were conducting a proper interview.

"Wow, that's a question," Jake chuckled, taking the beer can Brandon offered him.

"He works at Mercyhurst - he's a professor!" Cassidy said. She had already told Marissa all of this after their very first chance meeting, but she was proud of him.

"I teach one class," Jake chimed in. Cassidy looked over at him taking a sip of beer. She didn't understand why he didn't want to brag about himself. She wanted to brag about him.

"He's really smart," Cassidy added with a big smile.

"Did you go to Mercyhurst?" Brandon asked. Jake shook his head.

"No, Penn State."

"Ooof." Brandon scrunched his nose. "OSU," he clarified.

"Ah, the enemy," Jake said with a smile. Cassidy watched the boys interact attentively. Please get along, she thought.

"What did you guys do tonight?" Marissa asked, sensing the need for a new topic.

"We had dinner at the A&W," Cassidy said.

"Oh, I love that place," Marissa said dreamily.

"Me, too," Brandon added.

"Let's go!" Marissa cheered. Brandon smiled, then leaned over and kissed her forehead. Cassidy felt her heart swell. She loved that her best friend had such a loving man in her life. How she hoped Jake would be that for her.

"Is that a concert tee?" Jake asked, nodding at Brandon's black and white shirt.

"Oh yeah!" Brandon grinned, pulling the fabric on his stomach forward slightly to look at it. "Van Halen!"

"Were you there?" Jake asked.

"Yeah, saw him in Indianapolis back in '78. Great show! I was a senior in high school and my friends and I drove into the city for it." Brandon gushed.

"That's awesome! I went to his show in Pittsburgh in '84 – my senior year of college," Jake grinned.

"I actually thought about going to that one," Brandon smiled.

"Civic arena?"

"Yep."

As the boys continued to talk about concerts, Cassidy looked over at Marissa and caught her eye. They exchanged quick, excited grins, thrilled that their boyfriends were getting along so easily.

"What was your first concert?" Brandon asked.

"Oddly enough, Sinatra," Jake chuckled.

"What?" Marissa gasped.

"Oh my god!" Cassidy said in shock, smacking his shoulder

"Seriously?" Brandon looked stunned. Jake just nodded.

"Yeah, um, he came to Pittsburgh and my parents were big fans. My brother and I grew up listening to the records, so they took us into the city for the day then we went to the show that night," Jake said.

"I can't believe this!" Cassidy said in awe.

"It was a good show. Like, I was a weird kid who grew up on oldies, so I enjoyed it, but I don't think I appreciated it as much as I should have, you know?"

"How old were you?" Brandon asked.

"Like, fourteen? It was in the fall of my freshman year of high school. Will and I were definitely the youngest people there," Jake snickered.

"Damn." Brandon sighed in awe.

Jake nodded with a smile.

"Cassidy, what was your first concert?" Marissa asked, deep in thought.

"Journey, I think," Cassidy mused. "It was the end of the last week of school, my junior year of high school. Like, I think I had finals earlier that day," she laughed.

"Drove all the way to Pittsburgh?" Brandon asked.

Cassidy shook her head. "No, no, they came to Erie - the Field House. My friends and I went. My mom was so pissed when I stumbled home at 1AM." Cassidy sighed deeply at the memory. She had been in a lot of trouble, especially since she had conveniently forgotten to mention to her parents that she was going to the city for a concert and not studying at a friend's house. She'd spent the first two weeks of summer holidays grounded for that one. The punishment had initially started at a single week of grounding, but as soon as Cassidy found out it was Ben who ratted her out, she punched him and split his lip. An additional week was tacked on.

"You guys?" Cassidy asked, nodding at Brandon and Marissa.

"Eagles," Marissa said. "My older cousins took me. I was in high school."

"Nice," Brandon said. "I think my first one was Aerosmith… Yeah that was the first one. Early high school I ended up going to three in one summer. I was hooked, loved it."

"Live music is the best," Cassidy said with a smile.

"The best," Marissa sighed dreamily.

"So, what have you been up to this evening?" Cassidy asked.

"Nothing, just hanging out," Marissa lightly, looking up at Brandon. Cassidy instantly knew she and Jake had interrupted a make-out session.

"Yeah, we watched some TV," Brandon said, looking at Marissa with a smile.

"Cassidy, do you want to give Jake the rest of the tour of the apartment?" Marissa asked slyly.

"Rest of the tour?" Jake asked, looking confused.

"Oh, um, sure," Cassidy chuckled. She knew Marissa not only wanted to regain her private time with Brandon, but also was being an excellent wing woman.

Jake raised an eyebrow. Cassidy stood up and took his hand.

"Follow me,"

"Have a good night," Marissa called as Cassidy led Jake back down the hallway toward her bedroom.

Chapter 18

"Oh," Jake said as they stepped into the room. He looked around happily. Cassidy shut the door behind them.

"So, this is my room," Cassidy said in a low voice.

"I like it," Jake said, with a small smile.

Cassidy watched him take in the room. She slowly walked over and stood beside him, gently brushing her arm against his. Jake looked down at her and smiled at her touch.

"Hey," Cassidy whispered.

"Hey."

They slowly turned to face each other and Cassidy trailed her hands up his front to wrap her arms around the back of his neck. Jake's firm hands reached for her hips and pulled her close. Cassidy loved the feeling of his grip.

After a long moment of staring into each other's eyes, Jake lowered his head and Cassidy leaned up and pressed her lips onto his. The kiss was soft and sweet. They pulled back after a few seconds and just rested their foreheads together, tightening their hold on one another. There was electricity in the small space between them. Cassidy's heart rate accelerated.

Slowly Jake leaned down and kissed her again, over and over, sweet, slow pecks. Cassidy's body was tingling in anticipation. The kisses began to build in intensity, no longer soft and sweet, but full of passion. Before they knew it, their mouths were moving in sync. Cassidy loved the feeling of his lips on hers.

Without warning, Jake slid his tongue along her bottom lip. Cassidy gasped and Jake quickly slid his tongue into her mouth. Cassidy felt a spark shoot up her spine.

Cassidy held onto his shoulders tightly with one hand and plunged her other into his thick, copper hair. Jake kept one hand at her hip while the other slid down and cupped her ass, making Cassidy squeal inside his mouth.

After several minutes, Cassidy tightened her grip on Jake and began to walk backwards toward her bed, pulling him along with her. In a few steps, Cassidy felt her mattress hit the back of her thighs.

Jake slid both his hands under her backside and gripped firmly before lifting her off the ground. Cassidy was caught off guard; she gasped and wrapped her legs around his trim waist. They remained in that position for a few seconds, then Jake pushed forward and they crashed onto the bed. Jake landed on top of Cassidy, her legs still around his middle.

They both grunted as they hit the mattress. However, the impact only distracted them for a moment before their lips connected once more, the kiss deepening immediately. Cassidy reveled in the feeling of Jake's weight on her, especially as he ran his hands up and down her thighs. Even through her jeans, she loved the feeling of his fingers on her body. She could feel a warmth growing in her belly.

Cassidy slid her hands down Jake's back and found the fabric of his shirt, tugging it upward. She had only pulled the shirt up a few inches when Jake pulled away, leaving Cassidy bereft. However, disappointment was quickly replaced with excitement; Jake pulled the shirt off over his head and tossed it on the floor. Cassidy smiled widely at him and he grinned back. His chest was quite toned for his slim build, and Cassidy ached to touch it.

But Jake didn't give Cassidy long to eye up his body, leaning back down to kiss her once more. Cassidy reached down to the hem of her own shirt and started to tug the fabric up. Jake pulled his lips away again to help her slide her top over her head. Together, they tossed it to the side. Cassidy felt her heart give a thud. She loved the moment when clothes start to come off.

She bit her lip with anticipation as she watched Jake's eyes rove over her body before he caught her eye and grinned. Their kisses resumed with fervor. Cassidy relished the feeling of his bare stomach against hers. Sparks shot from her core to her extremities.

Jake used his left forearm on the mattress to balance his weight while his right hand began to slowly explore her body making Cassidy shiver with delight. The feeling of his fingertips deliberately sliding over her skin was intoxicating.

Cassidy wasted no time returning the favor. Her left hand ran over his strong chest and stomach, while her right hand was practically clawing his bare back with excitement. She nipped at his bottom lip with her teeth while her fingertips happily twirled through his chest hair.

They kissed deeply as their hands explored for many more minutes. Time was no longer a concept Cassidy understood;

179

she was living touch to touch. Jake's mouth and hands were addictive and exhilarating. Her body felt like it was on fire.

Cassidy brought both of her hands to Jake's shoulders, got a firm grip, and pushed him to the side, rolling them over on the mattress so she was on top. She sat up proudly on his lower abdomen, resting her hands on his chest, while Jake looked up at her in surprise and pleasure, his hands holding onto her thighs. She noticed his eyes had settled on her chest. The black bra she was wearing was lacy, floral and quite sheer. Cassidy smiled, happily allowing his eyes to linger.

Jake's gaze returned to her eyes after a long moment. They shared a smirk before Cassidy leaned down to press her lips to his. Jake immediately deepened the kiss and his hands tightened their grip on her thighs. Cassidy was soaring. She wanted more – she needed more.

Slowly, she trailed her fingers down Jake's chest and stomach, and landed on his waist. Her fingers fumbled for the button on his pants.

Without warning, Jake suddenly flipped them back over so he was on top once more. He grabbed both of Cassidy's wrists and pinned them to the mattress on either side of her head. Cassidy let out a loud gasp, practically trembling with anticipation.

"Nope," Jake whispered barely an inch above her lips. Cassidy let out a shaky breath as she fluttered her eyes open.

"Yes," she replied in a low voice. Jake continued to hold her wrists, but he propped himself up a bit so they could see each other's faces clearly.

"We've got to hit pause," he said, taking a slow breath. Cassidy gave a small smile.

"You sure?" she asked.

"Yeah."

"Well, I'm pretty sure that you're the one pinning me down," Cassidy smirked. Jake gave her a light peck on the lips before releasing his grip on her wrists. Cassidy brought her arms down and rolled onto her side, facing him.

"Hey," Jake began.

"Hey."

"We have to stop now, otherwise I won't be able to," Jake explained, reaching over and brushing her cheek lightly with his thumb. Cassidy's heart gave a thud and a shiver ran through her. His touch was electric.

"We don't have to stop ever," Cassidy insisted.

"Well, I do." Jake let out a small, embarrassed chuckle.

"Talk to me."

"I, I - I think I'm… falling for you," Jake stuttered. Cassidy gulped. She wanted to scream with excitement, but all she could seem to do was grin at him like an idiot.

"Really?"

"Yeah."

"But, then, why are we stopping?" Cassidy asked. Jake hesitated. He looked like he was trying to muster up some courage.

"Because I don't want this to end."

"I don't either," Cassidy said.

"Look, my last relationship moved quickly. Well, the physical stuff, anyway. And I fell hard, but, but, she didn't. And when she left, it … it hurt. Hurt like hell. It took me over six months to even go on another date. And that went poorly. I, just… I can't do that again," Jake admitted.

Cassidy bit her tongue inside her mouth. She hadn't known how badly he had been hurt. She hated to think of Jake ever being broken-hearted. Cassidy was suddenly aware of the silence in the room. She had to say something, to let him know that he hadn't just bared his soul to thin air.

"I don't want that to happen to you again, either."

"Oh," Jake hummed. It was a raw moment. Cassidy did not want to fuck it up.

"I mean, I won't let that happen with me. I want us to have a deep relationship because… well, I think I am falling for you, too," Cassidy admitted with a small smile.

Jake looked as if she had lifted an enormous weight off of his shoulders. Cassidy giggled as she watched him absolutely beam. She leaned forward and placed a slow, gentle peck on his lips.

"I've had so much fun these past weeks, I don't want to lose it," Jake said. Cassidy watched him for a long moment before speaking.

"Do you want to spend the night, but just… talk?"

"Yeah, I do," Jake said, leaning forward and placing a soft kiss on her lips.

"Okay." Cassidy rolled away from Jake and stood up off the bed.

"Where are you going?" Jake asked.

"I'm getting comfy for the night," Cassidy said. She walked over to her dresser and pulling her sleep shirt out of the top drawer. Cassidy turned her back to Jake in the bed and quickly unbuttoned her jeans, slid them down her legs and stepped out of them before tossing them in the hamper. She didn't turn around to look, but she could feel Jake's eyes on her. She wanted them on her. She loved the feeling.

She reached back to unhook her bra and hung it from her closet door, and was left standing in nothing more than her light pink panties with the knowledge that Jake was watching her. She pulled the grey sleep shirt over her head. The hem rested just an inch above her knees. Now dressed in her pajamas, Cassidy turned around with a smile. As expected, Jake was lying on the bed watching her keenly.

"Now I'm comfy." Cassidy smiled as she walked back over to the edge of the mattress, resting her right knee on it.

"You always know what you're doing, don't you?" Jake asked with a smirk.

"Only some of the time," Cassidy smiled back. "Give me a minute?"

Cassidy turned and made for the bathroom. She took a quick peek in the living room, but Brandon and Marissa had abandoned the sofa. She could only assume they had also moved their evening into the bedroom. Good. Cassidy didn't need any distractions at the moment. She quickly used the toilet, brushed her teeth, and splashed some water on her face before returning to her room and offering Jake the same opportunity. She had left the large bottle of Scope on the counter.

While she was waiting for Jake to return, Cassidy got herself settled under the covers on the right side of the bed, closer to the window. She let out a low, deep breath. Her mind was swirling. It had been quite a long time since she had just slept with a man. As much as she wanted to be with Jake physically, Cassidy did really want this relationship to grow. She willed herself not to toss her nightshirt on the floor before he returned.

Jake was back in her room, closing the door behind him in a matter of minutes. Cassidy bit her lip as she looked over at him. His wavy copper hair was slightly mussed and he was wearing just his dark red and black plaid boxers. He looked like a dream.

"Hey," Jake said softly.

"Hey." Cassidy smiled as he walked over and climbed into bed next to her.

She could smell him; his aftershave still lingered along with the crisp laundry scent that always seemed to be there. Cassidy loved it. As soon as he was settled in, Cassidy rolled to her side and scooted toward him. She placed a soft kiss on his lips and they smiled at each other.

"Ask me a question," Cassidy posed.

"Hmm?"

"You want us to really connect, so ask me a question. Anything you want."

Jake looked pleased. "Um, what was your favorite summer vacation as a kid?" he asked. Cassidy scrunched up her face. She'd been hoping for something more intimate.

"Well, we always went down to Kennywood in the summer, but when I was ten, we went to Cedar Point in Ohio and it was so much fun. All those roller coasters and rides! Oh, and the little beach there. We had a blast. Yeah, that was definitely the best vacation when I was a kid." Cassidy smiled at the memory.

"I've been to Kennywood a lot, too, but we never did Cedar Point."

"What about you? What was your best childhood vacation?"

"Definitely the beach. We went out to the Jersey shore for a week every summer. I loved it. We'd rent a place in Atlantic City. My parents could gamble and go to shows, and my brother Will and I played on the beach. It was the best."

"Your parents didn't like the beach?"

184

"They did, but they couldn't stay out on the sand or in the water all day like Will and I could. We'd all go down in the morning, but by lunch time, my mom was too hot and my dad was pissed about something, so they would go in. Will and I just had to be back and cleaned up by dinner. Easy to do." Cassidy smiled as she thought about that. The freedom Jake must have felt just enjoying the beach. Cassidy and her brothers had always been so chaotic, their parents had kept them all on tight leashes - which Cassidy had to admit, they had needed.

"Okay, next question. Something deeper," Cassidy smirked. Jake looked like he was thinking hard.

"Have you been in love before?" Jake asked. Cassidy gulped.

"I thought I was. I mean, for real thought I was. I used the word a lot when dating in high school, but I had no idea what I was talking about. But my last year in college I fell in love with my boyfriend. We dated for two years and then he left. It hurt like hell." Cassidy looked down, her eyes on the mattress. She rarely even thought about Kevin these days, and she definitely no longer had an iota of a romantic feeling for him, but the memory still stung.

"What happened?" Jake asked gently, reaching over to brush her cheek with his thumb. Cassidy tried not to focus on how good his touch felt.

"Honestly, I don't know. Maybe the writing was on the wall and I was just delusional and didn't see, but it felt very sudden to me. I was planning my future with him, and then all of that was gone."

"I'm sorry," Jake said sincerely. Cassidy slowly looked up and met his eyes. They shared a small smile.

185

"Well, what about you? Were you in love?" Cassidy asked, shifting herself slightly on the mattress.

"I thought I was."

"When?" Cassidy asked gently.

"College." Jake took a deep breath. Cassidy could see this was hard for him. "She was a girl from my dorm. It felt like it was happening so naturally. We started hanging out, then we started making out, and it progressed from there. We spent all of our time together for months - and then, suddenly, it was over."

"Why?" Cassidy asked.

"I honestly don't know. One day Dina told me that she was scared of how intense things got and - that night, she was gone."

"Fuck," Cassidy whispered. She instantly hated this Dina girl.

"I had never been serious with a girl before. At least, I thought it was serious with her," Jake said quietly. He looked so sad, like the wound was still raw, though she knew it had to have been at least three years.

"I'm sorry she hurt you."

"I mean, it's kind of the reason I don't…"

"Don't want to jump into bed immediately," Cassidy finished his thought. Jake nodded, looking slightly ashamed. Cassidy leaned forward and placed a light peck on his lips.

"Yeah," he mumbled.

"I get it, and I like that you want to be sure. That's… that's better than me," Cassidy admitted.

"Not better than you; you're brave and you put yourself out there," Jake countered.

"You're making me sound really good, and cool," Cassidy

chuckled.

"You are good, and very cool. You're a little intimidating,"

"Intimidating?"

"I cannot be the first person to ever tell you that," Jake chuckled. Cassidy giggled.

"Well, no, but I haven't heard it since, like, high school."

"I figured you were one of those girls."

"One of those girls?" Cassidy gasped in amused shock, smacking Jake on the shoulder. He looked proud of himself.

"You know what I mean."

"No! Explain it to me," Cassidy challenged.

"Right there! What you're doing right now – you're looking at me just right so that I back down. You do always know what you're doing!" Jake smirked.

Cassidy let out a loud laugh. "I try to make it look like I know what I'm doing, maybe," she admitted.

"You're succeeding."

"You know, I really wasn't one of those mean, bitchy, popular girls in school. I was popular, but that was because I was really good at softball."

"There was at least one other reason." Jake gave her a knowing look.

"Are you saying I was a slut?" Cassidy gave another shocked looked.

"I definitely did not say those words," Jake pointed out.

"You insinuated them."

"No, I did not! I was referencing your looks."

"My looks?"

"Oh my god, Cassidy, you know that you're fucking gorgeous. And I'm sure you were gorgeous back then, too. Come on, don't play dumb." Cassidy blushed. While she had been complimented for her appearance since childhood, it always caught her off guard.

"Gorgeous may be a stretch. That's a compliment for someone like Brooke Shields or Demi Moore," Cassidy said. "I'm pretty."

"Gorgeous," Jake insisted.

"Well, you're handsome," Cassidy smiled, kissing him lightly. Jake shook his head.

"You're in a league of your own."

"I still don't know what that means."

"It means you wouldn't have given me a second glance in school," Jake said. Cassidy rolled her eyes.

"I definitely would have, but do you know what?"

"Hmm?"

"We're out of school, and we don't even have to think about those stupid things anymore," Cassidy grinned.

"You're telling me you didn't like school?"

"Oh, I loved it! I had a blast. But it's over now. I've had to make peace with that and move on; I want to make sure that I have a good life after school," Cassidy said. This was the part of growing up she was struggling with. She didn't want to become one of those people who can only talk about the old days, because it's all they have. But she hadn't found her place yet as an adult.

"What's the best part about being out of school?" Jake asked. Cassidy bit her lip.

"You go first."

"Oh, well, that's easy. I don't live at home anymore. I get to keep my own schedule, for the most part, and I really love teaching, especially in college, because the students want to be there. I'm teaching a specialized course, and my students like this shit as much as I do," Jake smiled. Cassidy smiled back, soaking up his pride and happiness.

"That's what I want."

"To teach?"

"Oh, well, I was thinking more of how content you are in life and how happily you look forward to the future."

"You don't like looking forward?" Jake asked.

"I mean, I did, especially with Kevin, but then that ended, and well… I just didn't know what my future would be. Shit, this is becoming a heavy conversation." Cassidy rolled her face in the pillow for a moment before looking back up at Jake.

"You don't want to have heavy conversations with me?" Jake asked.

"Oh, I do. You're so easy to talk to, I just find myself opening up to you. But that doesn't mean this isn't hard," Cassidy told him.

"That's fair."

"But I want to look forward with excitement, like you do," Cassidy said firmly.

"What would make you do that more often?"

"Well… um… you," Cassidy admitted, biting her lip. The moment froze. It had been a very long time since she'd been so honest with a guy. Jake just brought it out of her, in the best way possible.

"Me?" Jake looked surprised, yet quite touched.

"Yes, you."

"How did I get that honor?" Jake asked playfully, still smiling.

"You're positive and happy, and you're just… you. Unapologetically you."

"That's good?"

"That's wonderful. I've never met anyone like you, and that is amazing," Cassidy gushed. Jake smiled, looking slightly overwhelmed.

"Um, thanks, I guess," Jake chuckled nervously.

"Look, my words aren't right, but the feeling is. You're a good person and you make me want to be a better person. Heck, I feel like a better person when I'm around you," Cassidy explained.

"Wow, that's… wow." Jake was unable to meet her eyes, and Cassidy could have sworn he was blushing. Cassidy leaned forward and placed a soft kiss on his lips, which Jake happily reciprocated. The two shared a slow, light kiss for a long minute before pulling back and smiling at each other.

"You know, I love just getting to lie here next to you in bed. It's comfortable," Cassidy said.

"I love getting to lie next to you," Jake said softly. Cassidy snuggled into place at his side and rested her head on his shoulder.

"This is perfect," Cassidy hummed.

"Want me to shut off the light?" Jake asked.

"Sure." Jake reached over and switched off the bedside lamp. The room was engulfed in just darkness. Cassidy and Jake both let out contented sighs as they settled into place and slowly fell asleep.

Chapter 19

The small galley kitchen of Cassidy and Marissa's apartment was busier than usual the next morning, with not only Cassidy and Marissa attempting to make coffee and scrounge something to eat before dashing out the door, but also both Brandon and Jake taking up room as they joined the busy morning shuffle.

While it was a little touch and go at times, with one bathroom and one coffee maker, all four of them managed to make it out the door on time. Cassidy was resting her left hip on the driver's side door of her car as Jake leaned over to say goodbye for the day.

"I'm glad I stayed last night," Jake grinned.

"I'm glad you did, too."

"So," Jake began.

"So," Cassidy mimicked.

"It was a little crowded this morning."

"Mmmhmmm,"

"I was thinking… would you like to come to my place

tonight?"

"Your place?" Cassidy smirked, attempting to play it cool.

"You could stay over and, well, we could have a good night, and space to ourselves and, and, maybe do a little less … sleeping," Jake said with a playful shrug. Cassidy bit her lip. She wanted to burst. To stop herself from screaming like a school girl, she leaned forward and pressed her lips firmly against Jake's.

"Is that a yes?" Jake chuckled as she pulled back.

"Definitely a yes," Cassidy gushed. "I would love to come over this evening."

"7:00? I'll order us a pizza."

"I'll bring a bottle of wine," Cassidy offered.

"Two Polacks pretending to be Italians," Jake teased. Cassidy snorted with laughter.

"It's a date, amore," Cassidy grinned.

"Have a good day," Jake said, leaning down to kiss her once more.

"You, too," Cassidy said before turning to get into her car. She buckled her seatbelt, leaned her head back on the headrest and let out a happy sigh. A part of her life was actually perfect. Completely perfect!

Cassidy had barely pulled open the large, glass door to her office when Gladys hopped up from her desk in the front lobby and hustled toward her.

"Cassidy!" Gladys said in a low, intense voice.

"What's going on?" Cassidy asked worriedly.

"Something's going down. Williams is packing up his

desk. Started a few minutes after he arrived. I think he got canned!" Gladys told her frantically. Cassidy felt her heart sink. Downsizing. How could this be happening so quickly?

"Oh no," was all Cassidy could say. She couldn't tell Gladys that she'd known this was coming, she couldn't say that she'd been spending nights looking over the books and desperately trying to find ways to save jobs. She couldn't say that she'd known this was inevitable. She really hadn't known, however, who the first target would be.

"Can you find anything out? Mr. Jelif likes you," Gladys said. Cassidy glanced down at the older woman, wanting to tell her everything. Wanting to tell her to get out while she could, wanting this burden of knowing to be taken away from her.

"I'll do my best," Cassidy lied. They nodded at each other, and then Cassidy continued through the lobby and into the bullpen filled with desks and cubicles. She had to pass Williams' desk on the way to her own. She bit down hard on her tongue as she walked by, trying to give him the dignity of respectful eye contact and a nod without staring curiously or making a horrid pity face.

Cassidy plopped down at her desk. If her stomach hadn't already been feeling unsettled, it went into a complete knot when she saw the note laying on her desk: "See me," written in thick red ink. Must have been a Sharpie. It wasn't signed, but there was no mistaking that it came from Mr. Jelif himself. Cassidy sighed deeply before standing and heading to the boss's office, summons note in hand. As she walked through the office, a hush fell. The air was thick; everyone was tense but no one dared to ask what was going on.

Cassidy was aware that there were eyes on her as she

marched, however she refused to look at anyone. She couldn't. When she finally reached Mr. Jelif's office, the door was open. He was sitting there working as if nothing was amiss. Cassidy knocked on the door frame. He looked up at her.

"You wanted to see me?" Cassidy asked, holding up the note.

"Yes, Banker, come in," he instructed. "Close the door behind you." Cassidy did as he asked and took a seat in one of the chairs in front of his desk. Behind her, the door made an ominous thud.

"What's going on?" Cassidy asked.

"I've let Williams go."

"Yeah, I see that. The whole office sees that," Cassidy replied, aware she was being far too sassy toward the guy that signed her paycheck. She bit her tongue.

"It is not something I'm enjoying. However, your cost analysis showed that he is the lowest producing employee. He has the least number of clients, and they're all small fish. I had to make the decision," Mr. Jelif explained solemnly. Cassidy appreciated that he was taking the matter seriously. She had heard too many stories on the news of companies firing whole departments without any remorse. It seemed like this was bothering Mr. Jelif, too.

"So, with Williams gone, and some cost cutting around the building, we'll just need to bring in more clients and we can, at least, finish up the fiscal year," Cassidy said, bouncing her knee anxiously. She knew this would not be the end of it, but maybe if she convinced Mr. Jelif it was possible, she could buy some time to consider other alternatives.

"Banker…"

"I think we could do it! Just give me more time," Cassidy

rambled. Mr. Jelif watched her quietly for a long moment.

"Cassidy," Mr. Jelif began. Cassidy felt her head snap up. She couldn't remember the last time he'd used her first name. "Go back to your desk. Pull yourself together and focus on your regular work today. Tomorrow we'll reconvene and look at the numbers again."

"Um," Cassidy began.

"Focus on your work," he reiterated. Cassidy nodded.

"Okay. Thank you, sir," she said, standing up and letting herself out of his office.

None of her coworkers were even attempting to hide the fact that they were watching her reemerge into the bullpen. The eyes followed her as she walked back towards her desk.

"Hey, Banker, what did he say?" Devon asked as she passed his desk. Cassidy looked over at him. For once, he wasn't leering or smirking at her, but looked genuinely concerned.

"He said to focus on my work," Cassidy replied honestly before continuing her walk. She heard Devon swear under his breath.

Cassidy once again flopped down at her desk and let out a sigh. It took almost ten minutes before she could bring herself to dive into the stack of papers in her inbox. The day was long and silent. Williams and his cardboard box of possessions departed the office by 10AM. His absence left an odd void.

Chapter 20

Jake took Cassidy's empty plate from her and headed to the kitchen. She smiled as she watched him. They had just finished their pizza dinner – Jake had even gotten green peppers and onions on half for her, keeping the pepperoni for himself on his side. Cassidy had offered to help him clean up, but Jake insisted that she just relax at the table. Cassidy couldn't remember the last time she hadn't had to clean up after a meal, aside from going to restaurants. It was an odd feeling, but nice.

There was a sudden, loud noise that sounded like something falling in the dishwasher. "Sure you don't need help?" Cassidy called.

"No," Jake replied in a strained voice. Cassidy giggled.

Within five minutes, Jake returned to the small dining room carrying two bottles of Coors Light.

"Sorry, I'm out of wine," Jake said, handing Cassidy a bottle as he took his seat. She took the chilled bottle from him happily.

"No worries; I'm more of a beer person, anyway," Cassidy replied. They clinked their bottles and took a sip.

"I'm glad you came over. I know it was rough day in the office today," Jake said.

"Thinking about tonight is what got me through," Cassidy smirked.

"I'm honored," he chuckled. Cassidy took a long drink, feeling calmer and happier than she had all day.

"It's just nice to relax," she said.

"I want to take care of you tonight," Jake said. He bit his lip slightly as if he were a tad nervous, but recovered quickly.

"Oh yeah?" Cassidy felt her stomach flutter slightly.

"You deserve a break. Tonight, you don't have to lift a finger - or even think," Jake said as he took a sip.

"Where has thinking ever gotten us anyways?" Cassidy asked sarcastically.

"Absolutely nowhere," Jake winked. Cassidy couldn't help but laugh.

"So, what's on the table for this evening of no thinking?" she asked.

"Well, really, anything," Jake shrugged. "We can get ice cream, we can watch a movie, but, at some point, I would love to show you the new comforter I got," he trailed off as he brought the bottle to his lips and turned his gaze from her. Was he blushing? Cassidy's heart gave a hard thud.

"I would like to see the comforter now."

"Now?" Jake asked, raising an eyebrow.

"Yes, please," Cassidy grinned. Jake smiled at her for a long moment before taking a long drink of his beer and standing up from his seat. He extended his left hand toward Cassidy. She also took a large gulp before setting her half-empty bottle next to his and placing her hand in his.

Jake gave her hand a squeeze and led her out of the dining room and up the stairs.

"Oh," Cassidy said suddenly, "after this, I actually do want ice cream. But you know, after." Jake looked back at her and grinned.

"You got it."

As they hit the landing on the second floor, Jake turned to the right and into the large bedroom that took up that end of the hallway. Cassidy looked around. While it was dark in the room, the last hints of sunset shone through the large windows across from a king-sized bed that sat along the wall next to the door. The room had old-house charm, with high ceilings, long, antique windows, white walls, and dark hardwood floors.

"Nice comforter," Cassidy whispered. She could feel Jake watching her. She didn't mind in the least. After a long moment, she felt Jake's fingertips come to rest lightly on either side of her hips. She bit her lip at his touch and slowly turned to face him. Without hesitation, Cassidy leaned up and pressed her lips to his. Jake kissed her back, hard.

Cassidy wrapped her arms around the back of his neck as his grip tightened on her hips. There was a difference in his kisses tonight. No politeness, no hesitation, Jake knew what he wanted and Cassidy was happy to give it to him.

She felt his tongue slide across her bottom lip and parted her lips to let him in, his warm breath engulfing her as his tongue slid along hers.

Jake suddenly lifted Cassidy off of the ground and practically tackled her onto the mattress. He caught himself on the mattress with his left hand so only some of his weight was on Cassidy – she didn't mind, she loved the feeling of him so close, not to mention the adrenaline of his sudden movements. She brought her right foot up to the bed frame and used it to push herself back on the mattress, so they were now in the middle of the large bed.

Under her hands, Jake's hair felt thick and silky as their passionate kisses picked up their pace. Cassidy felt like she was on fire already. Jake's right hand slid from her hip, up her side, to cup her breast. They kissed with little variation for a while, Cassidy's body continued to warm at his touch and the feeling of his mouth moving with hers. She could feel sparks shooting through her body. She never wanted it to stop.

Jake moved his hand from her chest and came to the hem of her white and pink stripped t-shirt and slipped his fingers underneath. Cassidy barely had a chance to feel her heart give a loud, excited thump, when Jake rolled them to the side and quickly pulled her shirt upward. She moved her arms from around his shoulders to help him remove her top and toss it to the side. Jake sat himself up and ripped his navy blue PSU shirt over his head and thew it on the floor. Cassidy grinned up at him as Jake leaned back down and attached his lips to hers once more. She relished in the feeling of his mouth moving in sync with hers.

Cassidy slid her right hand down his chest. She could feel his muscles tense under her fingertips; she loved that she could have this kind of effect on him. Her hand trailed to the waistband of his jeans and fumbled with the buckle. Jake slid his hands from her hips and rolled to the side so he could unzip. Cassidy took the moment to unbutton her own jean shorts and shimmy them down. Jake ripped off his jeans and tossed them on the floor, pulling his socks off in the same movement. Cassidy's shorts were just past her knees when

Jake, in just his dark red boxers, pushed her hands aside and took over slipping her shorts off her feet. She bit her lip as they joined the growing pile of garments on the floor.

And then Jake was kissing her once more. Cassidy immediately deepened the kiss, pulling his body down on top of hers. Their kissed continued as their hands explored each other's bodies. She loved the feeling of their limbs intertwined in a feverish passion.

Slowly, Jake moved his right hand from her side to the center of her back. Cassidy knew he was going for her bra, and grinned against his lips.

"What?" Jake whispered playfully, pecking her still-grinning lips.

"You're going for the bra," Cassidy hummed.

"I am," Jake smiled as he moved to kiss her jawline.

"It won't work, though," Cassidy breathed, distracted by Jake's lips teasing her sensitive skin.

"Why's that?" Jake asked, his fingers still fumbling at her back.

"Because the clasp is in the front," Cassidy said with a smile. Jake's fingers stopped moving and he pulled his mouth off of her neck.

"Front," he repeated fuzzily. Cassidy apparently wasn't the only one distracted by kissing. She grinned wider. Jake untangled himself from Cassidy and propped himself up on his knees. Cassidy let out a shaky, excited breath as his hands came to her chest. She watched with bated breath as he eyed up her light pink bra before reaching out and slowly tracing the fabric with his fingers. From the straps, down the top of the cups, and to the center clasp, he left a trail of goosebumps in the wake of his painfully light touch. Cassidy let out a shaky breath as his fingers finally worked on the small hooks between her breasts. In a few seconds, she felt the release. Jake looked up and their eyes locked for a moment before his gaze returned to her chest. He opened up her bra and exposed her.

Cassidy smiled, watching him. He looked mesmerized. He collected himself after a few long seconds and looked back up at Cassidy's face.

"Better?" Cassidy smirked.

"Much better," Jake said, pressing his lips to hers. Cassidy sat up slightly and slid her bra off her shoulders. Jake helped her free herself from the lacy fabric, then gave it a toss before pushing her firmly back on the mattress and climbing on top of her.

Cassidy loved the feeling of her bare breasts against his chest. His chest hair almost tickled as it rubbed against her. Their kisses turned heated. Jake's hands roamed her body, and she bucked up against him whenever his fingers slid over her nipples. Cassidy's left hand gripped his hair tightly while her right hand ran along his muscular back. She was about to burst into flames. Her heart was racing and her extremities were tingling with anticipation. This was perfection.

They continued kissing for a few, long minutes, before Jake moved his lips from hers and started to work his way down. He kissed her jaw, her neck, trailed down her chest onto her left breast. Cassidy gasped as his tongue ran across her nipple. She tightened her grip on him. She was pretty sure she was hurting him, but Jake didn't seem to mind - his focus was on her body.

Jake kissed and licked the entirety of her breast before kissing his way over to her right one and repeating the process. Cassidy was soaring at his touch. She was in no way inexperienced, but this was the first time any man had paid this much attention to her breasts. She was elated, and she found she was almost panting. Once her right breast had been fully explored, Jake's mouth moved to the center of her chest, then began to slowly trail kisses down her stomach. Goosebumps broke out over her body.

Jake paused at the waistband of her grey panties. The air was heavy with anticipation.

"Hey," Jake whispered, looking up at her.

"Yeah?" Cassidy smiled as she tilted her head to look down at him.

"I want to try something."

"Hmm?"

"I want to kiss you."

"You've already done that. You already get an A for that," Cassidy teased.

"No," Jake chuckled as his fingers looped into the sides of her panties. "I want to kiss you here," he said, quickly sliding the grey fabric down her legs and tossing her final covering onto the floor with the rest of their clothes. Cassidy trembled in anticipation.

"Okay," Cassidy said in a low voice. She felt her heart give another excited thud. It had been years since a guy had gone down on her. Kevin was the last, and that was just when they first started dating. She was dying to experience it again.

Jake smiled at her as he pushed himself up and stood at the foot of the bed. Cassidy noticed the large, protruding bulge in the front of his boxers. She felt the junction of her legs start to quiver. However, she couldn't focus on it for long - Jake's hand suddenly wrapped around her left ankle and pulled.

Cassidy felt herself slide across the sheets, stopping just shy of the edge of the mattress. Before she could take a breath, Jake parted her legs, propped her heels on the low, wooden base of the mattress, and lowered himself to his knees.

Cassidy brought her hands to her sides and gripped fistfuls of the sheets beneath her as her heart pounded. There was a spark in the air as Cassidy waited. It was a pause of just a few seconds, but it felt like an eternity. Then suddenly, a touch! Cassidy inhaled sharply as she felt Jake's finger tips slowly trail the perimeter of her labia. He made three circles – his light touch driving her wild - before his fingers slid inward and rubbed across her clit. Cassidy bucked slightly into his touch. His fingers were quickly replaced by his lips. Cassidy let out an involuntary moan as Jake's mouth took over, kissing and licking her most sensitive skin. His tongue trailed across her vulva and Cassidy gasped. She tightened her grip on the sheets as he continued, needing to hold on to something. Her head tipped back as her breathing became labored and loud. Her body was heating up and a bubbly, tingly sensation was shooting the whole way down to her toes. Cassidy lost track of time, unable to process much besides the soaring feeling that was overtaking her. As his lips lingered on her clit once more, Cassidy suddenly wanted nothing more than Jake inside of her. She let go of the death grip she had on the sheets and grabbed for his hair. Jake looked up at her in surprise.

"Up," Cassidy panted. Jake grinned and quickly scrambled back onto the bed, and climbed on top of her once more. He pressed his lips against hers, sharing the new taste with her. It didn't deter Cassidy in the least. She parted her lips and Jake took advantage of the opening, deepening the kiss. He slid his left hand underneath her and cupped her backside firmly.

Cassidy gripped tightly onto his back while Jake used his knee and forearm as leverage and scooted them further up the bed until Cassidy's head hit a pillow. They kissed deeply, then Cassidy slid her hand down his chest and onto the waistband of his boxers.

"Hey," Cassidy breathed, pulling her mouth off of Jake's.

"What?"

"Why the hell are you still wearing these?" Cassidy teased, snapping the elastic waistband against his skin. Jake chucked.

"No idea," he replied, rolling off of Cassidy to slip them off. Cassidy smiled at the sight of him. He was ready to go.

"Much better!" Cassidy grinned. She brought herself up on her knees and pushed Jake onto his back, then climbed on top of him. She straddled his torso, her knees resting at his sides. Jake looked as elated and excited as she felt. He suddenly reached to his left, fumbling for the drawer on his bedside table for a moment before retrieving a small, silver packet. Cassidy took it from him, ripped it open, and scooted back onto his thighs so she could slide the condom onto him. Jake bit his bottom lip as she worked. Cassidy loved seeing him so excited. Once the condom was in place, she lifted herself onto her knees, hovering over him. Jake nodded and gripped her hips while she rested her hands on his stomach.

Jake's hold on her tightened as he lowered her onto his shaft. Both he and Cassidy gasped as he entered her. She raised herself up slightly and dropped back down, pushing Jake deeper inside. Cassidy was flushed from her face to her chest. Her breaths consisted of little gasps.

They very quickly got into a rhythm, Jake supporting and guiding the movement of her hips. They moved faster; Cassidy could feel Jake's eyes glued to her chest as she bounced.

She felt so free - full and fiery with Jake inside her. Elation overtook her every emotion. Cassidy's gasps turned into cries of pleasure; she was ready to burst. She could tell Jake was feeling the same thing. Their eyes locked in a powerful moment, and Jake began to tremble beneath her. Cassidy lowered herself down onto him one final time, and they both cried out. The sparks that had been building in her since they met finally caught, flaring into a towering inferno.

She collapsed on his chest. Jake gently helped guide her off of him as he pulled out. He turned away briefly to deal with the condom, and then his hands returned to her lower back, resting on her bare skin. Cassidy snuggled back into him, trying to soak up all the contact she could with all his skin on all of hers. It took a moment to get their breathing back to normal. But even then, they stayed in place, simply enjoying the peace and satisfaction of the moment. No talking, no distraction - just comfort. Cassidy rested her head on his upper chest, and his chest hair lightly tickled her ear. She loved it.

They lay in precious silence for about ten minutes when Jake lifted his head and placed a gentle kiss on her forehead.

"You're not getting up yet," Cassidy said in a playfully firm voice. Jake chuckled. He returned his head to the pillow and they rested peacefully for another long minute.

"That was great, by the way," Jake murmured, breaking the quiet.

"Yes. Yes it was," Cassidy agreed with a smile.

"Thank you for letting me try something new."

"That definitely was not something new for you," Cassidy giggled.

"It was! I've never done that before. It was awesome."

"Lies! You knew exactly what you were doing!"

"I figured it out as I went," Jake countered.

"Bull. Shit." They both chuckled. Jake placed another soft kiss on her forehead.

"We should get up," Jake said with a sigh.

"Why?"

"Because I promised you ice cream and I can't follow through if all the shops are closed by the time we get there," Jake explained.

Cassidy perked up. "Oh, yes!"

"Glad we can agree," Jake smiled.

"Kiss me first," Cassidy demanded. Jake leaned his head up and pressed his lips to hers.

Chapter 21

Cassidy licked the black raspberry ice cream from her cone as she and Jake walked hand in hand down the sidewalk, lazily meandering through the downtown. Their conversation was easy and fun. Cassidy pointed out spots she and her friends had been to when they were in college, including the infamous storm drain that Marissa once tripped over, falling into a puddle and turning her green party dress a nasty brown. Marissa, trooper that she was, didn't let it faze her and walked into the neighboring bar, demanded a drink for her troubles and danced for another hour with dirty leaves stuck to her. Jake laughed, and Cassidy was sure to add that these days, Marissa would have gone straight home, changed into sweats, and had a drink on the sofa instead.

After thirty minutes of wandering and storytelling, ice cream now long gone, Jake gave Cassidy's arm a firm tug and pulled her from the sidewalk into a grassy patch under a tree. He kissed her. Cassidy, caught off guard by his spontaneity, took a moment to react, but then happily kissed him back.

"Cassidy?" a loud, familiar voice called, causing them to startle and pull apart. "Hey!" the voice yelled excitedly. Cassidy didn't need to turn her head to know that it was Laura.

"Who's that?" Jake asked.

"Don't worry," Cassidy assured him with a grin. Laura was bounding toward them with an excited smile. Cassidy waved, and saw that Alex was slowly trailing behind. He looked less than amused to have found Cassidy kissing a boy out in public.

"Oh, my gosh, how are you?! We didn't expect to see you here!" Laura gushed, hugging Cassidy enthusiastically.

"Hey!" Cassidy said. It might be unexpected, but she was happy to see her. Laura leaned in and put her lips an inch from her ear.

"Holy shit! You just had sex! I'm so happy for you! He's really cute!" she whispered frantically. Cassidy worked hard to keep her face neutral.

"You can tell?" Cassidy asked in a panicky whisper. Laura simply smiled.

"Yes! You're glowing, and I love it," she gushed in a low voice. Cassidy froze, unsure of how to react. Did she want everyone in the world to know what had just happened?

"Oh, sorry! Jake, this is my brother Alex and his girlfriend Laura. Guys, this is Jake," Cassidy introduced. Her stomach did a small flip. She hadn't told anyone in her family that she had a new boyfriend, and Alex was never the most welcoming – although his silent, begrudging tolerance was generally more appreciated than the teasing and tormenting that came from Matty, Eric, and Ben.

"It's so nice to meet you," Laura said enthusiastically, giving him a quick hug. Jake was clearly surprised, but recovered quickly.

"Nice to meet you," Jake smiled politely. Cassidy watched him and noticed his eyes kept flickering towards Alex, who was taking his time lighting a cigarette. Laura gave Alex a gentle nudge. He took a long drag before extending his right hand.

"Jake," Alex said with a nod.

"Alex," Jake shook his hand, a forced smile on his face. Cassidy bit the inside of her cheek. Why was Alex making this so awkward?

"What are you guys doing here?" Cassidy asked, desperate to make things feel less tense.

"Just out for a walk, it's such a nice night," Laura replied. "You?"

"I promised Cassidy some ice cream," Jake smiled. Cassidy grinned up at him.

"So, Jake," Alex began.

"We know absolutely nothing about you - tell us everything!" Laura interrupted cheerily. Cassidy was so thankful for her natural exuberance.

"Oh, there's not much to tell," Jake shrugged.

"I bet there is, especially if you caught our Cassidy's attention," Laura countered.

"Exactly how long have you known our Cassidy?" Alex asked pointedly, taking a long drag. Cassidy shot her brother an annoyed look. What was with him tonight?

"I met, or um, Cassidy and I met in early July at a baseball game, and then we ran into each other a few weeks later. I figured I better ask her out - what were the chances of running into each other a third time?" Jake said. Cassidy blushed.

"Oh wow," Laura smiled.

"Hmmm," Alex said. Cassidy knew he wanted to say

something, but she didn't really care. Jake was melting her heart more and more by the minute.

"It's been really great," Cassidy added glaring at Alex.

"What do you do, Jake?" Alex asked, flicking some ash on the ground.

"I teach stats at MU and work with their baseball team," Jake said.

"We went to college there!" Laura said, looking thrilled at the connection.

"Really? It's such a nice school," Jake smiled. Alex let out another hum, taking another drag. Cassidy bit her tongue hard. She needed a break.

"Hey, look at the time," she interjected, grabbing Jake's left wrist and pointing at his watch. Luckily, Jake picked up her cue.

"Oh, yeah, shit, I've got to get Cassidy home and I have an early class tomorrow morning," Jake said painfully. He wasn't the best liar, but Cassidy appreciated his efforts.

"No worries," Laura smiled.

"It was great to see you guys," Cassidy said.

"You, too," Laura said, giving Cassidy's arm a gentle squeeze. "Jake, it was great to meet you."

"It was," Jake said with a genuine smile. Cassidy glanced over at her brother who was busying himself with flicking more ash on the ground.

"Banker," she nodded at him.

"Banker," Alex returned the nod. Cassidy wanted to deck him. With a final wave, Cassidy entwined her hand in Jake's and dragged him down the street and back to his truck.

"Did I do something wrong?" Jake asked as they buckled their seatbelts.

"You? No, you were great," Cassidy said with a huff, resting her head on the seat behind her.

"It just, that felt... weird. I thought you and Alex got along," Jake said, turning the ignition and shifting into drive.

"We do. I have no idea what was with him tonight. Honestly, it really pissed me off," Cassidy sighed. They drove in silence for a few minutes. Cassidy was lost in her own thoughts, already planning to make an angry phone call to her brother.

"Laura seemed nice," Jake said, breaking the quiet. Cassidy smiled at him.

"She is. I hope you can meet them again when Alex is being normal."

"I'd love to meet your family," Jake replied. Cassidy's heart gave a thump.

"Really?"

"Of course. Do you want to meet mine?" Jake stuttered. The question brought with it a certain heaviness in the air.

"Um, um, yes," Cassidy smiled, completely caught off guard.

"You don't have to," Jake chuckled nervously.

"No, no - I definitely want to, but this conversation got serious quickly and I... I was surprised, that is all," Cassidy admitted.

"Oh, I mean, I just brought it up because we saw your brother, and-"

"No, no, I got it."

Jake's truck turned down Cassidy's street and then into the parking lot of her apartment complex.

"I had a good time tonight," Jake said as the car idled in front of the main entrance.

"Me too." Cassidy grinned before leaning over and placing

a soft kiss on his lips. "Thanks for the ice cream."

"Anytime," Jake smirked. Cassidy's cheeks burned as she smiled wide. She wanted to explode with joy. She waved to Jake and hopped out of the truck. She could hear the engine rumble as he drove off.

Cassidy showered and changed into an old T shirt and the shorts she used as pajamas. She paced back and forth in the living room, lightly swaying the beer bottle in her hand. Marissa was spending the night at Brandon's, so she didn't have anyone to help her sort through her feelings. She just had pure emotion. Ecstasy about the best sex of her life, joy about her time with Jake, annoyance about the weird interaction with Alex, and mix of surprise, confusion, and excitement that Jake had talked about meeting each other's families. Her mind was swirling. After another minute of pacing, Cassidy slammed her beer down on the end table, picked up the phone, and dialed Alex's number.

It only rang twice before there was an answer.

"Hello?" It was Laura.

"Laura, it's Cassidy. Is Alex there?" she asked brusquely.

"Oh, hi!" Laura had clearly been taken by surprise. "Sorry, he ran out."

"Out? You guys were just out," Cassidy grumbled. She wished she could be nicer to Laura at the moment, but she couldn't help herself.

"We got home and realized we were out of coffee for tomorrow, and he ran out to get some."

"Oh," Cassidy sighed.

"Are you calling to yell at your brother?" Laura asked playfully.

"I mean, come on, Laura, what the hell was his problem?"

"He was caught off guard."

"That's dumb."

"A little," Laura chuckled, "but turning the corner to see your little sister sucking face can definitely throw off your vibe."

"Ugh, Laura," Cassidy groaned.

"I was very happy to meet Jake," Laura said, changing the subject.

"Yeah? I mean, thanks for being nice to him; he appreciated it. We both did."

"It was very nice to see you happy like that," Laura said.

"What do you mean? Like what?"

"Like you're in love."

Cassidy swallowed. "I don't know if I'd go there quite yet," she said.

"I've never seen you look at a guy like that before," Laura pointed out.

"What? You've seen me in relationships before. I was with Kevin for two years. I loved him."

"You might have thought you did, but you never looked at him like that. Trust me, this guy is different. And I support anyone that can make you look that happy."

"Hmmm." Cassidy paused, not sure how to process her words.

"That may have been why your brother wasn't too keen," Laura explained.

"What? Why?"

"Cassidy, you were glowing!"

"You said it was because I had sex," Cassidy said, blushing again at the thought.

"That was part of it."

"I didn't think it was that obvious."

"It was to people who are looking."

"Alex would not have been looking for that on me," Cassidy pointed out.

"No, but he could see how much you cared for Jake and how much he adored you."

"That doesn't mean he can be a dick, and I called to tell him that."

"Look, just because it's taking him a moment doesn't mean that he won't come around. You need to give him more than a few minutes," Laura advised. Cassidy sighed. "But I'm already a huge supporter of Jake," Laura continued.

"Yeah?"

"Yeah. So start talking! I need to hear everything," Laura ordered playfully. Cassidy smiled against the receiver.

"Alright, what do you want to know?"

"Let's start with exactly what happened before you guys came downtown and go from there."

"Laura!"

"I'm practically your sister in law - an older sister at that. I have a right to know," Laura replied fondly. Cassidy felt her annoyance melt away. She never knew how Laura was able to do that. She always had such a calming presence, even over the phone.

"Well, I went over to his house for dinner…" Cassidy began retelling her evening. Laura hung onto every word. This was exactly what Cassidy needed: someone to talk to, someone she loved. She wrapped up her tale with Jake treating her to the ice cream he had promised, causing Laura to gush once more.

"I'm so happy for you!"

"I think I really am, too."

"You should be."

"Jake mentioned meeting each other's families."

"Wow."

"I know!"

"This is so perfect." Laura sighed dreamily.

"I'm trying not to get too ahead of myself," Cassidy said, biting her lip.

"Dive in, girl! Trust me, I think you'll come out swimming."

"Thanks." Cassidy felt a warmth flood through her body.

"Hey, Alex got back from the store a few minutes ago; I'm going to go hang with him."

"Oh, okay. Tell him I'm still a little mad at him."

"I will pass that along," Laura chuckled.

"Night, Laura. Thanks."

"Anytime. Night Cassidy."

Chapter 22

The breeze flowed through the open car windows, but Cassidy's hair was, thankfully, pulled back in a ponytail - otherwise it would have looked like a rat's nest by now. She smiled over at Jake as he steered them down the old streets of his hometown of Johnsonburg, about two hours southeast of Erie. It looked like a typical western Pennsylvania industrial town. proudly featuring its historical paper mill on every sign within the town's perimeter.

It had been almost two weeks since Jake first proposed the idea of meeting each other's families. When Jake's younger brother, Will, announced that he was coming home for a long weekend, Cassidy accepted Jake's invitation to join him on the visit. The drive was beautiful, and Cassidy enjoyed seeing a part of the state she had never been to before. She was intrigued to meet Jake's small family - just his mother and brother.

Two turns later, Jake slowed in front of a dark blue sided two-story house. The street was on a fairly steep hill, common for most of the western half of the state, and a large white staircase led from the sidewalk up to the pristine porch. Two rocking chairs sat to the right of the front door, and a small table set was on the opposite side. Cassidy smiled as she climbed out of the car. She imagined years of sitting on that porch and watching everything that happened on the street. It was a cozy thought.

"You ready?" Jake asked as he reached into the bed of his truck and untied both of their backpacks from the railing.

"I'm very excited!" Cassidy said as she took her backpack from him.

"I'd lower those expectations right now," Jake teased. Cassidy gave him a playful swat.

"Let me enjoy meeting your family."

"Okay." Jake let out a deep breath, as if steadying himself. Cassidy leaned up and gave him a light peck on the lips.

"It's going to be great," she assured him. They climbed the stairs to the porch and Cassidy resisted the urge to flop into one of the rocking chairs. Jake knocked on the front door before opening it and letting himself inside.

"Mom," he called out. Cassidy followed Jake closely, keenly looking over his shoulder to get a peek at the house. They walked into a small foyer. The walls were white and everything was trimmed with a dark wood that also encased the doorframes of the rooms around them. It was clear the house was older, but in the best way possible. Original features from the turn of the century were everywhere and Cassidy drank it all in.

"Jacob?" A female voice floated in from their right.

"Yeah, we're here," Jake called, setting his backpack on the wooden bench next to the door and motioning for Cassidy to do the same.

"You're here!" A middle-aged woman appeared in the entryway to what Cassidy assumed was the dining room. She gave Jake a kiss on the cheek, which he reciprocated.

"Mom, this is my girlfriend, Cassidy. Cassidy, this is my mom, Claire," he introduced. Claire was about two inches shorter than Cassidy. Her hair was dark with many strands of grey sprinkled throughout. Cassidy could tell her hair was long; it was wrapped into a large bun atop her head. She had the same green eyes as her eldest son, and while she was a petite woman, she had an air about her that said no one could mess with her - nor should they even try.

"Hi Mrs. Sullivan! Thank you so much for inviting me to your home," Cassidy said politely.

"Well, Jake said he wanted to bring home a girl he met at a baseball game, and naturally I was intrigued," Claire said flatly. Cassidy nodded and tried to ignore her lack of warmth. She remembered Jake saying she was a tough cookie.

"Yes," Cassidy smiled.

"Come on into the kitchen. I'm working on a loaf of bread and it needs more kneading." Claire gave a wave as she turned and headed to the right. They walked through a dining room that looked perfectly put-together and clearly had not been used in years, and into a bright kitchen. Dark orange counters ran along the perimeter of the room, and a large blue and silver metal table sat in the center. The style reminded Cassidy of something from a 1950s diner. The back wall, behind the large sink, was lined with windows that filled the room with light. There was a homey and well-used quality about this kitchen. Cassidy loved it.

"Cassidy, have you ever made bread?" Claire asked as

she walked over to the counter where a large bowl filled with dough and jars of flour were sitting in wait.

"No, ma'am," Cassidy replied honestly. "My mom has always been more of a Christmas cookie baker - or the occasional birthday cake baker, but that's about it."

"Well, time to learn," Claire said, motioning to the bowl. Cassidy looked up at Jake questioningly. He gave a defeated shrug and she walked over to join his mom at the counter.

"I'm ready!"

"Mom, she just got here," Jake said as he opened the fridge and helped himself to a can of Sprite. He turned and rested his back against the fridge as he cracked open the top.

"Oh, you boys," Claire sighed as she sprinkled flour on the counter and handed off the dough for Cassidy knead before turning to face her eldest. "You both come home and immediately want to rest!"

"Yeah, where is Will? I saw his car outside," Jake asked.

"He's in his room. Hopefully he's finally up."

"When did he get in?"

"The middle of the night," Claire scoffed. "He tells me he's leaving after his last class and will be here by 8:00PM. He then decides to go out with his friends first, and doesn't show up until 2:00AM! Scared the hell out of me, coming into the house. And now he thinks he can just sleep the day away."

"Excellent," Jake muttered in a bemused tone under his breath. Cassidy kept all her focus on the lump of dough she was kneading so she didn't laugh out loud and ruin her first impression with Claire. She made a mental note to giggle about this later with Jake.

"It was not excellent." Claire rolled her eyes.

"Then tell him to get up and make him help, rather than

subjecting my girlfriend to physical labor," Jake said, taking another sip of his Sprite.

"I'm learning something new," Cassidy interjected. While she appreciated Jake's concern, she knew she was earning points with Jake's mom. She was even kind of enjoying the process of kneading. It was a good workout.

"She is! Now keep that up," Claire instructed.

"Well, I'll go get his ass up," Jake said.

"Language," Claire scolded. Jake had taken a single step when, almost as if summoned, a loud creak from the staircase announced that Will was on his way.

"Look who's up," Jake drawled, resting his shoulder on the thick doorway between the kitchen and dining room. Cassidy did her best to turn to watch as she continued to knead.

"Look who's finally here," Will countered. While Will's voice was slightly deeper, Cassidy noticed how similar the brothers sounded. She suddenly wondered if outsiders thought that about her brothers, too. Cassidy herself thought they all sounded vastly different, but maybe that was just familiarity? Jake was patting Will on the shoulder as they entered the kitchen together. Cassidy nearly fell over. Jake and Will didn't just sound alike; they looked alike, as well. Will was maybe two inches taller than Jake and had slightly broader shoulders, but otherwise, they were identical: the same copper hair with gentle waves. The same green eyes, the same thin, but strong build. Their smiles even matched.

"Hey," Jake said to Will, patting him on the chest, "I want you to meet my girlfriend, Cassidy."

"Hi!" Cassidy smiled, abandoning the dough. Will extended his hand. Cassidy started to reach out, but quickly realized that her hands were completely coated in flour.

"Ah, sorry, I'm a mess," she said with a shrug.

"No worries," Will smirked before raising his forearm. Cassidy mirrored him and they bumped forearms in a non-traditional greeting.

"Nice to finally meet you," Cassidy chuckled.

"You, too."

"Jake told me that you're in law school," Cassidy said.

"Talk while you work the dough, please. It's not ready to proof yet," Claire directed.

"Mom," Jake protested, looking embarrassed. But Cassidy wasn't bothered. She was used to a strong-willed mother.

"I'm on it," Cassidy answered, returning to the half-kneaded dough.

"Yeah, final year."

"Where are you studying?" Cassidy asked curiously.

"Dickison."

"Oh, where's that?"

"Out by Harrisburg," Will explained. Cassidy nodded as she flipped the dough over with a thud.

"Have you been there the whole time?"

"No, no, I was at Penn State."

"You never told me that you and your brother were both there," Cassidy said to Jake.

"It's a big school," Jake shrugged.

"Yeah, I mean we only saw each other at baseball, really," Will added.

"Wait, what?" Cassidy asked in surprise. Jake never talked much about his brother, but she was shocked he'd never mentioned this before.

"I played catcher. Freshman year on JV, but I made varsity the last three," Will grinned.

221

"That's awesome! I played softball at Edinboro," Cassidy smiled.

"Oh, nice, what position?"

"Shortstop."

"I tried infield for a few years when I was a kid, but I covered for catcher one game when I was ten and loved it, never left," Will explained. Out of the corner of her eye, Cassidy noticed that Jake was looking a little left out and she wanted to bring him into the conversation.

"Jake and I met at a baseball game," Cassidy said, hoping to draw him into the conversation.

"Really?" Will asked.

"Jake, you didn't tell him?" Cassidy playfully scolded.

"Oh, um, well," Jake stuttered, clearly caught off guard.

"You suck, Jakey," Will smirked. Jake rolled his in annoyance and took a seat at the kitchen table.

"He does not!" Cassidy defended, giving the dough another hard shove.

"Well, I'm sorry for you, then," Will countered with an amused wink. Cassidy chuckled while Jake reached up and punched Will's arm with his left hand. If Claire was not standing in the room, Cassidy would have made another comment, but she figured best not to press her luck. Cassidy almost felt like she was back home.

"Boys!" Claire exclaimed. She pushed between them and came to stand next to Cassidy, peering over her shoulder.

"What do you think?" Cassidy asked.

"Not bad. Now shape it into a ball and put it in this metal bowl – I've already oiled the sides. It's going to proof for a couple of hours," Claire instructed. Cassidy nodded.

"So, Cassie," Will began.

"Cassidy," Jake corrected.

"Does everyone always call you Cassidy?" Will asked.

"Pretty much. Either that or Banker, but that was more in high school and college."

"Banker?"

"It's my last name." Cassidy explained, depositing the rounded dough into the bowl and making her way to the sink to wash her hands.

"My oldest brother always calls me Cassie, unless he's annoyed with me, but really, he's the only one. Kind of weird hearing it from anyone else," Cassidy said.

"Oldest? How many brothers do you have?" Will asked with a bemused look.

"Four." Cassidy turned off the faucet and dried her hands on the blue tea towel hanging from the dishwasher handle.

"Shut up!" Will exclaimed in disbelief. Cassidy was so used to this reaction that it had started to bore her.

"Yeah," she shrugged.

"Any sisters?" Will asked.

"No."

"Your parents are better than me - two was my limit," Claire chimed in. Cassidy chuckled. Will turned to Jake and gave his shoulder a playful shove.

"And you're still walking? I can see one brother maybe letting you date their sister, but not four," Will teased. Jake looked annoyed and took a long sip from his can of pop.

"I'll be perfectly fine. I just haven't met them yet," Jake said.

"Well let me know how that goes," Will chuckled. Cassidy rolled her eyes, then walked over and took a seat on Jake's lap.

"He'll be fine," she agreed. "And he has met one of them.

You met Alex," she reminded him.

"Oh, yeah," Jake nodded.

"Alex is…?" Will asked.

"My oldest brother," Cassidy explained.

"And how did that go?" Will asked suspiciously.

Jake hesitated.

"It was really quick; we just bumped into him downtown. It was like, a minute," Cassidy said quickly.

"So, he hates you?" Will asked Jake, smirking gleefully. Jake's mouth opened several times, but nothing came out. Finally, he sighed in defeat.

"Yeah, I think so," he admitted.

"Ha!" Will cheered.

"No, no, no!" Cassidy tried to interject, but she knew it was no use. The meeting had gone poorly and they hadn't addressed the subject since.

"Alright you three, out of my kitchen," Claire cut in, giving Cassidy a glare. She clearly did not appreciate her perching on her son's lap.

"Why?" Will asked.

"Because it's my kitchen and I have things to do. We're having a nice dinner tonight - this takes work," Claire said, shooing them with her hands. Cassidy climbed off of Jake and inched towards the entryway.

"Do you want help?" Jake offered.

"No, you get in my way," Claire said, giving Will a push.

"Hey!" Will whined, but he obediently followed Jake and Cassidy out of the kitchen.

Cassidy requested that Jake give her a full tour of his childhood home. Will followed them and did his absolute best to provide an embarrassing childhood story about Jake for every room they visited. Will was in the middle of a car-vomiting memory as they explored the half-finished basement that held had a pair of old sofas and a ping pong table - very clearly the boys' teenage hangout spot - when Jake, who was losing his patience with his brother, stuck his foot out and tripped him. Will, rather ungracefully, toppled onto one of the sofas before he rolled, or rather bounced, onto the floor. Jake instantly grabbed Cassidy's hand and pulled her along, dashing for the stairs before Will could get up and retaliate. Cassidy happily played along and sprinted after Jake. They ignored Claire yelling at them to stop running in the house, and quick time upstairs to Jake's old bedroom, closing the door behind them. They were laughing hysterically when they flopped down on his bed in the corner of the room.

"Jake," Cassidy scolded, still giggling, as her breathing returned to normal.

"He was annoying me. Besides, he's perfectly fine." He rolled to his side to face her.

"We came here to hang out with your family," Cassidy reminded him.

"And we're doing that. I just need a moment for just the two of us," Jake said with a grin as he leaned toward her.

Cassidy smiled as his lips gently brushed against hers. She kissed him back, soft and sweet, over and over again. Cassidy felt like she was floating. Jake had just brought his hand up to gently cup her cheek when Jake's bedroom door was violently flung open. They startled apart. Will was standing smugly in the doorway, smirking at them.

"Assholes," Will taunted.

"Get out," Jake groaned. Cassidy couldn't help but giggle again as Will turned to leave.

"Come on, let's go be social," Cassidy said, patting Jake's thigh as she sat up and hopped off the bed.

"What? No, why?" Jake whined. He clearly wanted to spend more time in bed.

"Because we're only here for twenty-four hours and you haven't seen your mom or brother in… what? Almost six months?" Cassidy asked, feeling a pang in her chest. She hurt at the thought of not seeing her family for such a long time. Even though they drove her crazy, they were her people.

"Ugh, fine," Jake groaned. He heaved himself off of the bed and followed Cassidy into the hallway.

"Will," Cassidy called out. "Come on, play a game with us."

"Game?" Will and Jake chorused.

"We should do something! Do you have a deck of cards?" Cassidy asked.

"Yeah, downstairs," Jake said.

"Perfect," she grinned. Will and Jake shrugged and followed her down the stairs.

Cassidy, Jake, and Will took over the large dining room table with their card game. Cassidy loved to play; it was a favorite holiday pastime among her and her siblings over the years. The trio played two hands of Rummy, followed by a spirited game of SlapJack that turned a little too violent between the brothers and caused Claire to emerge from the kitchen and angrily snap both of her sons with a dish towel. Cassidy quickly gathered up the cards to shuffle and start a new, less physical game.

"Wanna play poker?" Cassidy asked as she shuffled.

"I'm not losing all my money to you," Jake teased.

"How do you know I'll win?" Cassidy asked over the clack of the fanning cards.

"You have that air about you," Jake commented.

"We don't have to play for money," Will said with a smirk.

"I'm not playing strip poker, you dweeb," Cassidy chuckled.

"Shut up," Jake warned his brother under his breath.

"Your loss," Will winked. "We have the plastic chips, we can just play for those. That way, Jake can lose his pride instead of his money." Jake sighed.

"I'll play with the chips," Cassidy smiled. "Jake?"

"Yeah, why not," he agreed, standing to retrieve the chips from the closet in the foyer.

"Hey, Cass," Will began as Jake left the room.

"Hmmm?"

"When did you start playing ball?"

"Oh!" Cassidy was surprised at his question. "I started T-ball in Kindergarten, then moved up to softball in third grade. Played all through high school and college. You?"

"Same. Well, except I played baseball, and I stopped after I finished my undergrad at Penn State."

"Do you miss it?" Cassidy asked.

"Some days, but honestly, I'm so swamped with law school that I don't have time anyway. I wouldn't be able to enjoy it now. Or pass any of my classes," Will joked.

"I get that."

"Get what?" Jake asked, returning with the wooden box filled with poker chips.

"Being too busy now for playing baseball," Cassidy answered.

"Oh."

"Cass, you wanna deal?" Will asked.

"Sure."

"Cassidy," Jake corrected.

"It's okay," Cassidy smiled. She gave a final shuffle as Jake handed them each a stack of red, blue, green, and black chips.

"Did you play travel or go to tournaments?" Will asked as Cassidy dealt out the cards.

"Both," Cassidy replied, trying to keep a straight face as she spotted the three of a kind in her hand.

"Where was the furthest you traveled?" Will asked. He set two cards face down and nodded. Cassidy handed him two cards.

"Three," Jake said quietly.

"I think the furthest tournament was in Atlanta," Cassidy said, dealing Jake his card and taking two more for herself.

"Atlanta?" Will asked.

"Yeah, my freshman year of high school. It was a really good team that year, mostly seniors, and we got to go to Nationals!" Cassidy grinned, not only at the memory, but at her two new cards. They didn't give her the full house she was hoping for, but rather a four of a kind. Excellent!

"Did you win? Will asked, tossing a red chip in the center.

"Not even close," Cassidy laughed. Both she and Jake added a red chip of their own to the middle of the table.

"Really?" Will chuckled, adding two more chips to the pile.

"We were eliminated in the first round. The game was a bloodbath, to be honest," Cassidy shrugged, upping her bet to three blue chips.

"Damn." Jake matched Cassidy's chips. She winked at him, but he didn't meet her gaze.

228

"The trip was great, though. My oldest brother was a senior, so my family all came down to Georgia and we stayed a few extra days as a family vacation slash graduation trip for him. It was a good time. We loved downtown!"

"Nice," Will said, simply grabbing a handful of chips and plopping them in the center.

"Bullshit," Jake sighed at his movement.

"No shit," Will countered smugly.

"I'll call," Cassidy said, throwing in her own handful of chips and smirking at Will.

"Ugh, I fold," Jake dropped his cards face down on the table.

"So?" Cassidy asked Will, bouncing her eyebrows.

"Boom!" Will proudly laid down five red cards, all diamonds. "Flush!"

Cassidy hummed. "Good, but not great," she countered, setting down her hand which included four 10s. Jake let out an impressed low whistle.

"What?!" Will exclaimed.

"Read 'em and weep," Cassidy grinned, reaching forward and pulling the large pile of meaningless chips to her chest.

"Cheater!" Will teased.

"How?" Cassidy laughed.

"You dealt, obviously."

"Fine - you deal this round," Cassidy instructed, handing him the deck of cards.

"Fine." They played another hand of poker. This time, Cassidy only managed a lousy pair of fives, while Will had a full house. Jake folded early. A third game failed to materialize, as conversation took over and flowed naturally. Cassidy felt her heart soar. This visit was going so well. She hoped that she had made a good first impression with Claire, and she and Will were getting along effortlessly. The brothers and Cassidy sat and talked at the dining room table for well over an hour, swapping college dorm stories. Like Cassidy, Will had also had a weird roommate at the start of freshman year. They talked about late night practices, favorite drunk foods, and even high school prom themes. She and Will had so much in common; eventually Jake just sat back and let them get to know each other. The stories continued until Claire emerged from the kitchen asking for help to peel the potatoes.

Chapter 23

Cassidy emerged from the large, family bathroom after brushing her teeth and padded down the hallway to Jake's childhood bedroom. Claire wasn't thrilled about the idea of Cassidy and Jake sharing a bed. Cassidy wasn't surprised, knowing Lynne would have a similar reaction. She had volunteered to sleep on the couch, but Jake insisted she take his old room.

Jake was grabbing one of the pillows from his bed to use downstairs as Cassidy entered.

"Hey there," she smirked.

"Hey."

"Are you going to sneak back up later?" she asked in low voice, wrapping her arms around his middle.

"The stairs creak," Jake replied.

"Oh," Cassidy paused in thought. "Well, we could be quick now!"

"These walls are thin," Jake said flatly.

"Come on," Cassidy pleaded playfully. "We haven't had

231

sex in a while."

"We had sex this morning before we left," Jake pointed out.

Cassidy was feeling increasingly frustrated. "Jake," she said sweetly in a low voice, almost begging.

"Cassidy," Jake sighed. "Let's just go to bed. It's been a long day."

"Yeah, okay." Cassidy agreed reluctantly, remembering that he had done all of the driving.

"Night," Jake said, stepping out of her embrace.

"Aren't you going to kiss me?" Cassidy asked. She was getting confused. Jake leaned over quickly and gave her the briefest of pecks before turning and departing the room with his pillow. Cassidy stood frozen in place. What the hell was going on? She chewed on her bottom lip as she listened to him descend the stairs – they really did creak loudly. Disheartened, she shook her head and climbed into Jake's bed. It had been a great day, and she didn't want to spoil it by worrying about Jake being weird just now. With that, Cassidy snuggled into the pillow, smiling at the thought of a teenaged Jake lying in the same place, dreaming of his future. She quickly fell into a deep and blissful sleep.

Loud clangs of kitchen pans and the smell of something warm and sweet woke Cassidy the next morning. She stretched in the cozy, blue sheets of the bed, smiling to herself as she remembered where she was.

She rolled over and peeked at Jake's old, round alarm clock on the bedside table. It was 7:30. Cassidy let out a yawn and a final stretch before climbing out of the bed, knowing she should get up. She hated oversleeping when she was a guest. She had promised she would attend church with Claire and the boys - and whatever Claire was making right now smelled fantastic!

Cassidy quickly freshened up in the bathroom, put on a bra, brushed her hair and headed downstairs in her pajamas, looking a very cute and polished kind of disheveled.

The smell of breakfast cooking was stronger on the main floor. She could hear Claire singing along to the radio as Bobby Darrin crooned. Cassidy noticed that the large front door was open and assumed Jake had gone for a morning run since she hadn't seen him on the sofa. She shrugged it off and made her way to the kitchen at the back of the house.

"Good morning," Cassidy said with a smile.

"Oh, good morning," Claire replied, looking surprised to see her.

"It smells great," Cassidy commented as she came to sneak a peek the large frying pan filled with eggs and pancakes.

"It'll be done shortly."

"Do you need any help?"

"No," Claire replied. Cassidy could not help notice that she sounded a little short. She took a seat at the large table, wondering how to cut the tension.

"You know, Bobby Darrin was my oldest brother's first record. He bought it with his allowance and played it non-stop for weeks," Cassidy smiled.

"Well, who wouldn't like Bobby," Claire remarked as she flipped three pancakes in quick succession. She was softening, slightly.

"No one!"

Their moment was interrupted by the sounds of the front

screen door squeaking open and crashing closed.

"Jake?" Cassidy called out hopefully.

"Oh, hey, you're up," Jake commented as he entered the kitchen. Cassidy noticed he was in jeans and one of his white Penn State T shirts rather than his usual workout clothes.

"You went out?" Cassidy asked. Claire huffed behind her.

"Packing the truck," Jake replied shortly.

"Oh, already?"

"Yeah. Um, when you get a chance, do you want to get changed and bring your bag down?" Jake asked. Cassidy scrunched up her face.

"I want to eat this amazing breakfast your mom is making us, first."

"Fine, after that," Jake sighed. Cassidy noticed he looked fidgety.

"Well come on, the food is ready. Scarf it on down since you have to leave so quickly," Claire grumbled as she pulled plates out from the cabinet next to the stove.

"Mom, I'm sorry, it's just that I forgot I have a meeting with the baseball coach at the school tonight," Jake said. He patted his mom on the shoulder. Cassidy's head whipped around to stare at Jake. She knew damn well he didn't have a meeting that night. She couldn't figure out for the life of her what was going on with him. However, she knew that pointing this out in front of Claire would be catastrophic, and she would be walking back to Erie. She didn't push.

"Oh, shoot, was that this weekend?" Cassidy asked, playing along. She hoped it might buy her points with Jake's foul mood. The shock on Jake's face nearly doubled her over in laughter. She tucked it away to enjoy later.

"Yes, it's this weekend," Jake replied tentatively.

234

"Jacob, I know your job is important, and I'm happy you're doing so well, but you and your brother haven't been home at the same time in months, and now that we're finally all together, you bolt in less than twenty-four hours!" Claire huffed. Cassidy bit her lip and shoveled some eggs onto her plate. What the hell was going on?

"Mom, I'm sorry," Jake sighed. He grabbed a plate to start filling.

Breakfast was a delicious, though tense affair. Cassidy did her best to keep up the conversation, asking Claire about her ladies' book club, her Bible study group at the church, and her women's hunt club that had their first meeting of the season next week.

"Too bad Will missed this amazing food," Cassidy said as they finally cleared up their plates into the sink.

"He's always been my late sleeper."

"Cassidy, why don't you go get changed," Jake said abruptly.

"Oh, doesn't your mom need help with the dishes?"

"I'll help her," Jake said. There was no emotion in his voice. Cassidy desperately wanted to ask him what was going on, but bit her tongue. They had a two hour car ride ahead of them. She would have plenty of opportunity to grill him, and she planned to.

"Okay," Cassidy agreed and headed upstairs.

Less than thirty minutes later, Cassidy was dressed and packed up. She, Jake, Claire, and Will, who had been forcefully roused by his mother, were all standing on the front porch. No one was in a chipper mood.

"Thank you so much for having me," Cassidy smiled at Claire.

"I'm glad you could come, even for a short time," Claire nodded. Cassidy knew that was about the best she was going to get. It was unfortunate that this early departure is what Claire would focus on when thinking of her.

"I can't believe you're bailing," Will smirked. Jake rolled his eyes and the brothers shook hands. Jake had always told Cassidy that his family wasn't warm and fuzzy, but seeing it in action was something completely different. Jake moved his attention to his mom, apologizing once more and assuring her that it had been a great visit. Will moved over to Cassidy, a large grin plastered on his face.

"Did you orchestrate all this?" he asked in a low voice.

"Not at all! I'm not dumb enough to piss off your mom," Cassidy replied in a whisper. Will chuckled.

"Fair enough."

"I'm glad we met," Cassidy said with a smile.

"Me, too. And I'm glad Jake finally started dating a girl that isn't weird."

"Thanks, I guess?"

"It's a compliment."

"Well, come see your brother in Erie; we'll go to a game or something." Cassidy nudged his arm.

"That would be a lot of fun!" Will grinned.

"Get my number from Jake. Call anytime!"

"Definitely," Will said before embracing her in a big bear hug. Cassidy wasn't sure she had won Claire over on this visit, but she was thrilled to have befriended Will. At least two of the Sullivans liked her.

"Cassidy, time to go," Jake said firmly, grabbing her arm and pulling her out of the hug.

"Ooop," Cassidy grunted. "Bye!"

"Let's go," Jake sighed as he walked around the truck to the driver's side.

Jake and Cassidy gave a final wave as the truck rumbled down the street. They drove in silence, except for David Bowie serenading from the car stereo. But as soon as Jake merged onto Route 948, Cassidy let loose.

"So, what the hell?" Cassidy asked loudly as she shifted in her seat so she was facing Jake. He looked startled by her sudden outburst.

"What?" Jake asked. Cassidy glared at him.

"Don't what me - I want to know why you dragged us out of there!"

"I just, you know, wanted to beat traffic. If we'd stayed for church, we would have had to stay for lunch, and then my mom would have found something for Will and me to fix, and, well, we wouldn't get home until after dark, and we both have work tomorrow," Jake trailed off.

"Bullshit!"

"We're going home," Jake grumbled.

"Yeah, and we have a two-hour drive ahead of us. We're going to talk about this."

"There's nothing to talk about."

"There is," Cassidy insisted firmly. "You've been weird since last night, and then I wake up this morning and you're ready to leave all of a sudden!"

"I told you!"

"Yeah, and that was a lie," Cassidy argued.

"No."

"Yes! I think I deserve an explanation. I was so excited to meet your family. Your mom is a tough cookie, and I think she would have been happy if I had joined her for church this morning. Now she thinks I hate God, and I don't. I'm also a Lutheran – I thought we could bond over it.

"I didn't know you're a Lutheran?" Jake asked. Cassidy couldn't lie, she wasn't exactly a poster child for any faith.

"I'm not good about going anymore, but I go on Christmas and Easter. When I was a kid we were all at church every week."

Jake hummed.

"We're not here to argue about religion!" Cassidy said firmly.

"I'm not arguing religion, I just never knew," Jake countered.

Cassidy grunted. "Today was a really good opportunity for me to solidify a good impression with your mom. I want her to like me."

"She will!"

"She might, but right now, I'm not looking too favorable. I'm the bitch her son brought home and then turned tail and ditched her for."

"That's a little dramatic."

"Ugh," Cassidy groaned.

"Ugh," Jake groaned in mockery. Cassidy gritted her teeth. If he hadn't been driving, she would have hit him.

"Jake, you only get one chance at a first impression."

"It'll be fine," Jake said dismissively.

"At least Will and I got along. That'll give me some points. I guess this visit wasn't a total loss," Cassidy said. Jake muttered something under his breath.

"What was that?"

"Nothing."

"I think it was something,"

"Cassidy," Jake said in a warning tone.

"I don't understand why you have been in such a foul mood!"

"I'm not in a foul mood."

"Yesterday was great, and then you shut down last night."

"I did not shut down. I was tired."

"You, Will, and I had fun all day. I don't understand."

"Well, you wouldn't," Jake snapped.

"I seriously do not understand why you're defensive right now. Ugh, at least Will and I got along and had fun this weekend, otherwise it would have been a waste."

"Fuck Will."

"What?" Cassidy gasped in surprise.

"I'm serious, go fuck Will."

"Okay. I have so many questions right now." Cassidy's mind was spinning. Jake was normally so easy-going; why was he so angry? He had been the one to invite her.

"So do I."

"I thought you and Will got along? I know you said you weren't super close, but you seemed happy to see each other. Will was fun, we had a blast. What is going on?"

"Yeah, Will is the best," Jake said sarcastically.

"Better than you at the moment," Cassidy snipped back.

"Then date him."

"What?"

"You want to date him. I know you do. He's the one you like - you have everything in common."

"I don't want to date Will!"

"Oh come on! I saw you two together, the way you laughed, the way you looked at each other." Cassidy sat dumbfounded.

"Jake…"

"You're right. Maybe I should have let you two spend another day together. You could have gone back to Harrisburg with him instead."

"Where is this coming from?"

"Years and years of being the God's geeky older brother. I know how this works. Use me to get to him. Granted, you didn't know him ahead of time - this was just a nice surprise bonus for you."

"I don't want to date Will!!" Cassidy screamed.

"Oh please."

"I don't love Will! It's you that I love!" Cassidy spat. The words were out of her mouth before she could even process them. Jake swerved in shock, receiving a loud honk from the irritated Honda driver next to them.

"Shit," Jake said, regarding his swerve.

"Shit," Cassidy agreed, but more in shock at what she had just said.

"I'm sorry… what did you say?" Jake asked tentatively as they returned to their lane.

"I said I don't want to date your stupid brother."

"Oh," Jake said, sounding a little disappointed. Cassidy chewed her lip for a moment to muster up her courage.

"Because he's not the one I love," she added. Jake started to grin, though his focus was on the road in front of him. "It's you."

"Wow," Jake breathed.

"Wow? That's what you say after I bare my soul? Even after you yelled at me for flirting with your brother, which I did not do?! And, then—"

"I love you, too," Jake interjected, catching Cassidy completely off guard.

Cassidy was silent for a minute. "So, um, we just… said…"

"Yeah…"

"Pull over," Cassidy instructed.

"Why?"

"Because I don't want to almost die again," Cassidy sassed. Jake chuckled as he put on his blinker and slowed down. They rolled to a stop on the side of the road.

"What's up?" Jake asked as he set the parking break.

"What's up? Really?" Cassidy leaned over and pressed her lips to his for a few seconds. "I'm not having an 'I love you' moment without a kiss."

"Oh." Jake smiled before leaning in and connecting their lips once more. After a breathless moment, they pulled back and smiled at each other.

"So, we said it," Cassidy said.

"We did."

"This weekend wasn't a waste at all, then."

"No, I guess not."

"You should probably thank your brother," Cassidy smirked.

"Don't push it." Jake raised an eyebrow at her. Cassidy giggled to herself.

"But in all seriousness, that can't happen again."

"What can't?" Jake asked.

"You flying off the handle or getting all jealous or not trusting me," Cassidy told him firmly.

"Oh."

"Jake, I'm serious. I love you, but I need you to trust me and I need you to talk to me if you're feeling upset. I refuse to spend my time walking on eggshells and wondering if I'll set you off," she said honestly. Jake looked surprised and remorseful.

"I'm sorry, I didn't realize it was that bad."

"It was that bad."

"I'm sorry," Jake repeated. "Will just … ugh, I love him, but he knows how to get right under my skin. He always has."

"Trust me, I completely get strained and frustrating relationships with a brother. I do. It's okay to feel annoyed or sad, but just tell me next time. Trust me that I will take your side. Trust me that I'll take your feelings seriously."

"I do trust you, but I'm just not great at the whole trust thing," Jake admitted.

"I know you've had your trust broken. I've been there. It sucks. But you and I, we're different. This is our relationship. For this to work, we need to trust each other. Always. Even when it's hard."

"You're right."

"I know," Cassidy teased. Jake grinned at her and placed a gentle peck on her lips.

"I do love you."

"I love you, too, Jake,"

"I am really sorry I upset you today."

"It's okay. But I think you need to call your mom and say sorry to her, too."

"I will. I promise."

"Well, let's get back home," she said.

"Oh, you didn't want to…?" Jake trailed off.

"I'm not having sex in the cab of a truck on the side of the highway, Jake."

"Just thought I'd ask, you're usually the more adventurous one," he teased.

"We'll adventure when we're not on four wheels."

"Have it your way," Jake chuckled, shifting the truck back into gear and merging on the highway. Cassidy couldn't help but smile as she watched him.

"I love you," she said as she settled back in her seat and crossed her legs.

"I love you, too."

Chapter 24

The next two weeks passed by fairly uneventfully for Cassidy. She was seeing Jake at least three times a week. And he had kept his promise, they spent a lot of time talking and he trusted her with a lot more of his emotions. Outside, the temperatures dropped as they entered the fall. Snow was just around the corner in Erie. Fall was always lovely, but short in northwest Pennsylvania; snow fell anywhere from late October to mid-April.

Work had become the part of her life that she dreaded the most. She had always enjoyed her job well enough, but now it was stressful. Two more people had been let go, and all perks, including free coffee and good toilet paper, had been taken away. Cassidy was stuck crunching the same numbers over and over with Mr. Jelif and never seeing any relief. She hated that this burden had been placed on her. While logically, she knew this meant that she would likely keep her job the longest, the stress was doing her head in. Her nails were bitten down to the quick.

Both Jake and Marissa were fantastic distractions for her,

and Cassidy knew she wouldn't be hanging on without them – she would have quit on her own. In fact, she had been toying with the possibility for a few days now.

It was a Wednesday - a normal October Wednesday - when Cassidy walked into work and got the shock of her life.

"Cassidy," Gladys wailed as she walked in. She was in tears, and Cassidy rushed over to the large reception desk where Gladys sat.

"Oh my god, what happened?"

"I had six months left until retirement," Gladys sniffled. Cassidy suddenly noticed that she was filling a box with her possessions.

"No!" Cassidy gasped in horror.

"I was so close. I've worked my whole life, I just wanted to make it 67 for full social security so I could retire and relax. Six months! My birthday is in six damn months and they gave me the axe. I've been here for decades," Gladys choked out as she added another framed picture of her family to her box.

"What happened?" Cassidy asked. Her heart and mind were racing. Was she responsible for Gladys's departure? She had told Mr. Jelif to cut back, and she knew layoffs had to happen - but not Gladys! Not the support staff who earn much less than the accountants.

"Mr. Jelif called me into his office at the end of the day yesterday. He said he was happy with my work, but that they don't have the money to keep me so I had to be let go," Gladys sniffled. "I was so shocked! I couldn't even plead my case, I just ran out in tears. When I got home, there was a message on my machine that said I could come in this morning to clear out my desk."

"Oh, Gladys," Cassidy said softly. Her heart hurt. Gladys

was the first person she had met there. The first face she saw when coming in for the interview. The first person to greet her on her first day. She knew all the best stories and had gossip on everyone. Cassidy adored the woman.

"No one will hire me for a lousy six months of work, especially at my age. I'll just have to take social security out early. I tried so hard to wait so I could get all the money I had earned."

"You're damn right you earned it," Cassidy agreed firmly. A man in his late thirties came in the front door.

"Cassidy, this is my son, Richard," Gladys introduced. Cassidy and Richard nodded at each other. "He wanted to drive me today. Didn't think I should be driving a car in my state."

"I'm glad he did," Cassidy said, "although you shouldn't be driving home feeling sad - you should have a party!"

"Damn straight," Richard interjected. His eyes were dark with anger, and frankly, Cassidy couldn't blame him. If she ever had to go pick up her mom after she unjustly lost her job, Cassidy would be throwing fists.

"I think I've got everything," Gladys said, looking around at the now sad, bare reception station.

"Is there anyone else you want to say goodbye to? I can bring them out here so you don't have to go in," Cassidy offered.

"No, I've said my goodbyes. I'm glad I got to see you, though."

"It was wonderful working with you these last three years," Cassidy said, giving the older woman a big hug, which she reciprocated warmly.

"Oh darling, you were a joy. You've got big things in your

future. Don't let small places hold you back," Gladys smiled. Cassidy wiped away a few escaped tears.

"The company directory is here," Cassidy said, picking up a thin, spiral bound book. "Do you need any numbers?"

"No, I've got who I want. But you keep it. My address is in there. Send me a letter sometime," Gladys grinned.

"Definitely will do."

"And don't let Devon get away with any of his garbage. My only regret is I never got to tell him to go pound sand. I was saving that for my retirement party," Gladys said. Cassidy was torn between laughing and crying.

"I can get him and you can tell him now?"

"Nah, that baton has been passed to you."

"I will definitely add it to my to-do list," Cassidy smirked.

"Goodbye, Cassidy Banker."

"Goodbye, Gladys."

Cassidy watched as Gladys followed Richard, carrying the box of her things, out the door and onto the street. She swallowed hard to bite back a blood-curdling scream.

After collecting herself, she continued into the main office, which was glum and awkwardly silent. All eyes shifted to Cassidy. They all knew she had been saying goodbye. Cassidy wished Gladys could have seen the sadness in everyone's eyes. She was going to be incredibly missed.

"Damn," the grating, deep voice of Devon exclaimed as he walked over to her. "Can't believe they fired the old lady. We're all chopped liver, apparently."

"Go pound sand, Devon," Cassidy snapped, not interested in debating the company's bleak future with him. She smiled proudly to herself as she arrived her desk. She knew she'd done Gladys proud.

Chapter 25

Cassidy climbed out of her car as soon as she pulled into her parents' driveway. She grabbed her dress from the back seat and headed into the house.

"Hi!" Cassidy called as she let herself inside.

"Hi, sweetie," Lynne yelled back from the direction of the living room. Cassidy headed down the hall and into the living room. Lynne was sitting on the brown sofa and working on her cross-stitch.

"I brought my dress for you to hem," Cassidy said, holding up the purple dress.

"Oh, good. Set it on that chair for me, I'll get to it later."

"Thanks, I appreciate it," Cassidy smiled, hanging her dress over the chair.

"What are you up to today?" Lynne asked, concentrating on her stitching.

"Not much. I'm going to pick up a couple of subs from the pizza shop in town to bring home for Marissa and me later today," Cassidy replied.

"Mmm, sounds good."

"You?" Cassidy asked, leaning casually against the wall.

"Waiting for your dad to get home from his Booster Club meeting, then we're going over to the Richardsons for a dinner party," Lynne smiled.

"You and dad are going to a dinner party? When did you guys get so swanky?" Cassidy teased.

"It's amazing how easy life gets when the kids are out of the house," Lynne winked.

"You're hilarious, mom." Cassidy rolled her eyes.

"That reminds me, you will go to Eric's wedding, right? I need your RSVP," Lynne said.

"I'll send it in as soon as I get my invitation," Cassidy said pointedly.

"Oh, you're on ours. It's in the kitchen on the counter," Lynne said nodding in the direction of the kitchen.

Cassidy scrunched up her face. "What?" she grumbled.

"It's not a big deal, Cassidy," Lynne shrugged.

"How is it not a big deal that he can't even bother to send out invitations?" Cassidy huffed as she turned to the kitchen.

"Cassidy," Lynne sighed, setting down her cross-stitch to follow her daughter. "There are a lot of us, and they needed to save on postage." Cassidy let out a loud snort as she started digging through the pile of mail on the kitchen counter.

"First of all, that's bullshit; stamps are cheap. And secondly, Alex already told me that he and Laura got theirs." Papers were flying across the counter now.

"Would you stop making such a mess? It's right here," Lynne said, pulling out the invitation and handing it to Cassidy. Cassidy studied the blue and white floral invitation. It was lovely. She slowly turned the card over, still nestled in

249

the lip of the envelope and she saw the address line:

To: Art and Lynne Banker, and family

And family?

"What is this?" Cassidy asked.

"It's the envelope. I need to throw that out," Lynne said. She reached to take the envelope, but Cassidy pulled it back before she could grab it.

"And family?" Cassidy pushed firmly.

"Yes. You are family," Lynne replied. She was clearly already bored with her daughter's inquiry.

"But it's just that. I am and family?"

"Um, I'm not sure," Lynne lied.

"Mom, I already know that Alex got his own," Cassidy pointed out.

"I'm pretty sure it covers you and Ben," Lynne relented. Cassidy pulled a face. "I doubt Eric even knows Ben's address at school, and Ben doesn't care. He's just going to show up. Be like Ben."

"You must be joking," Cassidy said with wide eyes.

"Cassidy, do we really have to go over this again? Eric's wedding is not about you," Lynne said firmly.

"I know! I just wanted my own damn invitation. I'm already not a bridesmaid. Is a piece of paper too much to ask? Or just maybe my actual name listed on the envelope?" Cassidy clenched her jaw and threw her hands up in frustration.

"Do you want a copy of the invitation? I'll get you one," Lynne offered.

"No, that's not the point."

"Cassidy, you're being incredibly difficult and I don't know what to tell you. You'll have to talk to Eric," Lynne said. Cassidy felt something click inside of her. That was exactly what she was going to do.

"You're right. I'll go see Eric - right now!" Cassidy exclaimed.

"You will not!"

"Yes, I will. I'm allowed to go visit my brother," Cassidy insisted as she separated the invitation from the envelope, dropping the card on the counter and keeping the envelope for herself. Evidence.

"You are more than allowed to visit any of your brothers, but right now you are angry. Not to mention, you just drove all the way out here," Lynne pointed out. "Stay and calm down before getting back on the road."

"I have no intention of calming down. I want to be pissed when I get there," Cassidy huffed.

"Cassidy!"

"Thank you for your help with my dress, Mom, and I'm sorry to leave so quickly. I love you," Cassidy said as she headed for the front door.

"Cassidy!" Lynne called once more, but Cassidy closed the door behind her before another word could be said. Deep down, Cassidy felt horrible. She knew it was rude to walk out on her mother. However, at that moment, rage was driving her.

She quickly turned the ignition in her Chevy and backed out of her family's driveway. The entire drive back to the city was a blur. Cassidy wasn't even sure how she made it to her brother's - the car must have known the way. She spent the whole drive formulating arguments and rants in her head. She was ready for a fight.

Cassidy reached the city limits and pulled onto a street lined with small, white houses. She parked in front of the house her twin shared with his friend, Derek, and stomped toward the front door, envelope clutched in her right hand.

Almost the moment she firmly knocked on the door, it swung open, revealing Derek, his black hair disheveled and still in pajama pants and a white tee. He had clearly not been awake long.

"Cassidy?" Derek said, looking surprised.

"Is Eric here?" Cassidy demanded.

"Um, yeah."

"Thanks," Cassidy said, pushing past him into the house.

"Hey, wait! What are you doing?" Derek asked, watching her stomp down the hall.

"Eric!" Cassidy called.

"What the hell are you doing here?" Eric asked, coming out of the kitchen. He looked less than impressed.

"We need to talk," Cassidy said, her mouth in a thin line. Eric stared at her for a long moment before giving a defeated sigh and leading her back to the kitchen. Derek disappeared back into the living room.

"Alright, what do you want?" Eric asked, resting his back on the edge of the thick, white counter. He took a sip of coffee from the mug he was holding.

"I'd like to talk to you about this!" Cassidy said, holding up the envelope.

"An envelope?"

"Yes. I stopped at mom and dad's this morning and mom asked me if I was going to your wedding. I told her I hadn't received my invite yet, and she tells me that I'm on theirs. I go to look and I find this envelope that lists mom, dad, and family," Cassidy enunciated.

Eric simply stared at her, looking quite bored with another one of his sister's rants.

252

"And family!" Cassidy reiterated. "Not only do I not get an invitation; I don't even get my name on the lousy envelope?!"

"You stormed in here because you need your name written on an envelope?" Eric asked, unfazed.

"It's not just that my name isn't on the damn envelope. I don't get to be a bridesmaid, I don't get an invitation - I am being completely squeezed out of this wedding!" Cassidy whined, throwing her arms in the air.

"Oh, for fuck's sake, Cassidy!" Eric groaned.

"Finally, you're noticing me."

"Cassidy! How many goddamn times do you have to be told?! This wedding is not about you!" Eric said firmly.

"I know! I'm not asking it to be about me, I'm just asking to be invited like a human adult. I am your sister, in case you forgot."

"No! You're not just asking to be invited; you're pissed that attention is on me," Eric argued.

"What the hell is that supposed to mean?"

Eric pushed himself off the counter, set his mug down, and began to pace. He was practically shaking. "You take over everything!" he suddenly yelled.

"Stop being dramatic."

"You are dramatic," Eric returned. "It's always been about you. You ignore anyone that doesn't give you all the attention. You ignore me."

"Oh, come off it," Cassidy scoffed.

"Yes, you do. You always have."

"What? When?"

"We started school and you made friends and left," Eric said.

"Oh, for fuck's sake."

"You did. You've been popular since kindergarten, and you just went off your own way. You got into softball and got more and more popular. Your life was your friends and parties and the entire world being about you!" Eric said. He was looking flushed as he ran his hand through his hair in frustration. Cassidy scrunched up her face.

"You're full of it; you don't even acknowledge me," Cassidy countered.

"You never acknowledged me. You never have!"

"Eric…"

"No! You're going to listen to me for once! You've always had all the attention. You're the only girl: extra attention! You're good at softball: extra attention! You're popular: extra attention! You complain that I don't tell people you're my twin - well when the hell was the last time you did? All through school, half of your friends didn't even know I was your brother, let alone your twin, but all of mine knew about you. The world has always been all about you and you've lapped up every moment. You always said you weren't included by our brothers, but you always were. You made the choice to spend time with your friends over us. But you'd snap your fingers or shed and a tear, and boom, the whole family is all over you. Oh, poor little Cassidy, life is so hard for her! No! It never was! It never will be! There's a reason I went to college two hours away. For once in my whole life, I didn't have to sit in the shadow of my perfect twin sister. I got to make a life for myself! And guess what? It was amazing! I've never experienced that before. I got a job back here because I missed the family. But I've worked hard to build a life that doesn't revolve around you!" Eric ranted in a full explosion of emotion that had been bubbling just below the surface finally found a release.

Cassidy stood in shock. She suddenly felt like she was going to throw up. Eric took a few breaths before continuing.

"And then I met Ellie. I have a chance to have a life of my own forever. A life that's mine! Out of your shadow. But, no, you've been miserable since I announced our engagement. And yes, before you ask, of course I told her you were my twin. On our first date, actually. When was the last time you told anyone you had a twin?" Eric asked forcefully.

Cassidy swallowed hard. She couldn't remember the last person she'd told. She had told Jake, right? She felt angry and sad, with a large pang of guilt, all at once. Her heart was racing and her stomach was doing flips. Their entire relationship was rushing through her mind and there was a lot of reevaluation she needed to do. So much that it hurt.

"Ellie wanted you to be in her bridal party. Before we were even engaged, she mentioned it. She wanted to get to know you. Don't blame her. I'm the one that told her not to," Eric told her.

"Why?" Cassidy was having trouble processing everything.

"Why?" Eric repeated. "Because you always make everything about you. All the shopping and events with the girls? You would complain every step of the way. You would go out of your way to tell horrific stories about me, about all of us, to put the spotlight on how great you are. You wouldn't shut up until everyone loved you and the entire day became about you. And while I can handle you ruining my day, I won't let you do that to Ellie. I love her and I won't put her through your bullshit."

Cassidy felt like she had been punched in the gut. She could feel Eric's eyes on her, but she couldn't make eye contact.

"Even right now, this moment is about you," Eric said. Cassidy looked up at him in surprise.

"What?"

"You're thinking about who to run to because I was mean to you," Eric said, starting to pace again. "Alex is the logical option. The ultimate big brother. He'll protect you from your evil twin. He'll coddle you and make everything okay. He may even call me and tell me to stop being a dick. Matty is also a good choice. He won't baby you, but he'll cheer you up quickly and make you laugh. And if you can get him riled up enough, you two can come up with a plan to ruin the reception. He'd like a chance to make a big scene. Of course, there's also Ben. Not the obvious choice, but a good one for you. He absolutely worships you, as you expect him to, so it's easy for you to turn him against me. Your finest accomplishment. I don't think you'd go to mom and dad, though. You've been trying your hardest with them for months, and they won't give in to you. I'm shocked they haven't tried to force me to add you to the wedding party, but I do appreciate that they've taken my side for once. Thus black balling them in your books."

"What?" Cassidy repeated. Her stomach was turning painfully, and her throat was tightening. She could feel a sob looming. Eric had read her like a book.

"What?" Eric repeated, stopping his pacing right in front of her.

"Ben does not worship me," Cassidy said quietly.

"Wow, you're even too full of yourself to see your biggest fan," Eric huffed.

"What are you talking about?"

"Ben adores you. He always has. Don't you remember those years in elementary school when he desperately tried to play

256

baseball, even though he was always the worst player on the team? He saw his beloved big sister play, and he would have done anything to be like you. Thankfully, he finally stopped. Hand-eye coordination is not his strong suit; soccer is much better for him. But he played because of you. He always stole your old jerseys to wear. Always waited up for you when you were out on dates or out at parties. The second you got into Edinboro, he said he was going there, too. He was desperate to go, to be just like you. Alex, Matty, and I talked him out of it. We told him Mercyhurst would be better for him; he'd like being in the city more. But that was a lie. The real reason we convinced him to switch was so he wouldn't learn the hard way that you weren't going to give him the time of day if he went there. You would have broken him. And MU worked out great for him. He's having fun, he's creating his own life, and Alex is just a mile away if he needs someone," Eric explained.

Cassidy stood completely frozen for a long moment. She wanted to cry, scream, throw up, kick something. Possibly all at the same time. But she refused to do it there. She swallowed hard once more. She had come to tear Eric to shreds, and he had ripped her to pieces. And the worst part was, it was all true. Eric was right. There was a heavy rock in the pit of her stomach.

"And you're right," he continued, "the invitation envelope thing was me. And that was petty. I just get so exhausted by your bullshit sometimes, Cassidy." His fists were clenched. This had clearly taken a lot out of him, as well.

"You should hate me," Cassidy said in a small voice.

"I should. But the really annoying thing is, I don't. I'm just frustrated as fuck and I want one day to myself. That's it. So, you're still invited to the wedding. I will get you a proper invitation in the mail this afternoon. One that is just for you, with your name on it and everything. All I ask is that you not act like a selfish dick. Just for one day," Eric said with a large sigh. Cassidy let out a shaky breath.

"Okay. Um, I'll let myself out." Cassidy glanced up at Eric once more. His jaw was clenched and he was holding back tears. He looked almost as wrecked as she was.

"Bye," Eric said quietly.

Cassidy turned and walked quickly back to her car. She drove in a frozen trance for a mile or so, but then the floodgates broke loose, and she started to cry. Cassidy ran Eric's words over and over in her head. She continued to think back over the years. She detested that he was making sense. Her heart hurt. She had so much to think about. She was rarely wrong. She hated that she was feeling very wrong. And for so many years. It was painful.

How she made it back to her apartment parking lot was a mystery, her eyes were filled with tears the whole way and her mind had most definitely not been on the road. After she parked, she took a few minutes to settle herself. She didn't want to walk through the lobby and up the staircase giving people a reason to stare.

Her stomach hurt. Her heart hurt. She could feel a headache coming on. Finally her tears stopped, and she wiped her nose with the back of her arm. It was gross. She gave a hearty sniffle and exited the car.

Cassidy's hands were shaking as she put the key into her apartment door and let herself in. Once inside, she dropped her purse and keys ungracefully onto the floor.

"Yes! Food time! Subs! Subs! Subs!" Marissa cheered from the living room. Cassidy felt another pang. She'd forgotten lunch. Shit.

"I'm sorry, I didn't get them," Cassidy replied glumly as she made her way to the living room.

"What? Why not? Oh, my god!" Marissa said as Cassidy came into the room.

"Um, we can order something, get it delivered," Cassidy said with a shrug.

"Fuck the subs, what happened? Are you alright?" Marissa asked frantically. She grabbed Cassidy's arm and pulled her down next to her on the sofa.

"It's all my fault," Cassidy whimpered. Her breathing was choppy.

"What's your fault?" Marissa asked.

"Eric. Our relationship. My relationships with everyone," Cassidy said, tears starting to fall.

"What do you mean?"

"Eric didn't push me away. I pushed him. I'm the bad guy. And worse, I'm the bad guy who played the victim. My entire life!" Cassidy enunciated. Marissa looked confused.

"You just came up with this theory this morning?"

"No. I went to my mom's to get my dress hemmed and we started talking about Eric's wedding. Naturally, I lost it. Even more when I learned I wasn't getting my own invitation, I was just tacked on to theirs. I went crazy. I think I blacked out I was so mad. I just stormed out to confront Eric, and when I got there he went off on me," Cassidy explained. Her voice shook and tears slid down her face.

"He went off on you? But you have been excluded from everything," Marissa pointed out. Cassidy shook her head.

"No. I deserved it. He brought up how I've pushed him away over the years. And he was right. I mean, completely right. I had these blinders on and I didn't even see him. Or anyone, for that matter," Cassidy choked.

"I feel like I'm still a bit lost."

"I did this," Cassidy said firmly, staring directly at Marissa. "All of it. I have sabotaged every bit of my relationship with him, and the worst part is, I've blamed him. I've played the victim. I've bragged about being the victim. When in reality, I, I, I'm the bully."

Marissa looked at her for a long moment. There was a harsh silence in the apartment.

"Are you saying you lied?" Marissa asked carefully. Cassidy simply shrugged.

"I'm saying I learned a long time ago how to get attention and make people like me, and I've done it by standing on others," Cassidy said, wiping her eyes.

Marissa made a clucking noise. "That sounds awfully dramatic."

"See, I'm doing it again," Cassidy huffed.

"Doing what?"

"I made this about me," Cassidy said.

"But it is about you; it always is!" Marissa said. Cassidy's eyes widened and Marissa bit her lip, realizing what she had just said.

"You said - "

"No! I didn't mean it like that, it was a slip of the tongue," Marissa said, trying to recover.

"But you must've seen it. You know me better than anyone," Cassidy insisted.

"I do know you better than anyone, and I know you're not evil," Marissa said.

"Wait, who said anything about evil?" Cassidy questioned.

"I said not evil. You're just not close with your twin."

"Be honest. Have I pushed him away?" Cassidy asked desperately. Marissa sighed.

"I don't know what happened between you two growing up. In the six years I've known you, you and Eric have never been close. I never saw it as pushing him away, but you have avoided him. I only have one sister, so I'm not an expert on sibling relationships. I just assumed yours wasn't working. I mean, you and Alex are buddies, so something works," Marissa told her honestly.

Cassidy thought for a long moment. "I try with Alex, though. I just never tried with Eric. I don't know why. I mean, then more I think about it... I can't remember the last time I wished him happy birthday. And we share the same one!"

"Look, you need to take some time to reflect before making any big decisions. You have a lot to process, I am here to talk whenever you need it, but I don't know the right answers either," Marissa said honestly. Cassidy smiled at her.

"Thanks."

"Anytime," Marissa said. "Now, you sit here and try to feel less miserable, or more miserable, or whatever you're supposed to feel right now. I'll go down the street to the shitty sub shop and get us some lunch."

"There's cash in my purse; lunch was to be my treat today," Cassidy sniffled.

"No, no, you can save that and bring me the good subs the next time you're out - and don't get detoured next time," Marissa said, wagging a finger at her playfully. Cassidy let out a snotty chuckle as Marissa slipped on her shoes and left to get lunch.

Cassidy grabbed some tissues out of the box on the coffee

table and just let herself cry. She had a lot to think about, but at the moment, all she could do was cry.

Chapter 26

It was late Sunday morning. Cassidy was in her living room perched on the large, blue chair, staring at the phone. She had spent a long time on the phone with Jake last night. He had been a good sounding board, and seemed to understand her stress. He was supportive, but definitely understood Eric's side more than hers. However, that was beneficial to helping Cassidy truly understand. There was a long road in front of the twins, but that door had finally been opened. And Cassidy was very grateful to have Jake to help her navigate it. He seemed to be honored to be brought along on the journey.

Cassidy was attempting to bolster herself to pick the phone up and dial. It had been a long, sleepless night for her, and she knew what she had to do - hell, what she actually wanted to do.

She took a deep breath, grabbed the receiver and dialed. The phone rang four times before someone picked it up.

"Hello?" She had been hoping Eric would answer, but damn, it hurt to hear his voice.

"Uh, hi Eric. It's Cassidy," she said nervously. There was

a long pause.

"Hi," he finally replied. Cassidy took another deep breath to steady herself.

"So, um, after our talk yesterday, I've, I've had a lot to think about. And, um, I wanted to say that… that, um, well, you're right," Cassidy stuttered. She bit her lip and closed her eyes anxiously as the words came out.

"Oh," was all Eric said.

"Yeah, um, so, I was just wondering if you would like to meet me for a drink sometime soon. Like, in the city, and we can talk like civil human beings - you know, like actual siblings," Cassidy stammered.

Another long pause.

"Oh, I, um," Eric started.

"I mean, I get if this is too soon, and, I um, just wanted to-"

"Yeah, let's meet for a drink," Eric interrupted. Cassidy felt like a weight has been lifted off her shoulders.

"Great! When works for you?" she asked.

"Tonight?" he proposed.

"Yeah. Yeah, tonight works."

"Cool, cool," Eric replied quietly.

"Um, where?" Cassidy asked, chewing on her lip.

"How about that new place downtown… off Third?" Eric suggested.

"Sure. I haven't been there yet, but I've heard good things," Cassidy agreed.

"Great. Meet at 8:30?"

"See you there," Cassidy said before returning the phone to the receiver and letting out a long breath. She was meeting her brother for a drink. Why the hell did she feel so nervous? Cassidy quickly shook the feeling off and hopped off the chair to go for a run. She had to get her head right.

Cassidy exited the parking garage and started the two-block walk to the bar. The cold, fall night breeze felt ominous. She made it to the large, silver door of the bar in just a few minutes and hurried inside to warm up.

"Welcome. How many?" the bored-looking hostess asked from her stool by the door. She was chewing gum with her mouth open.

"I'm meeting someone," Cassidy replied, scanning the large wood and silver room in search of her twin. The bar seats were completely filled and over half of the tables and booths were occupied. In the sea of slicked-back hair and sports jackets, she didn't stand a chance of spotting him quickly.

"I don't think anyone has come in waiting," the hostess said with an unhelpful shrug.

"Cassidy?" a familiar voice came from behind her. Cassidy spun around to see Eric smirking behind her. He was wearing a dark grey Members Only jacket and jeans. His hair was gelled back.

"Hey!" Cassidy turned and smiled at him.

"Is this who you're meeting?" the bored hostess asked. Cassidy resisted rolling her eyes.

"Yes, table for two."

"Follow me." The hostess hopped off her stool and led them about a third of the way back to a high-top table. Eric and Cassidy thanked her and climbed onto their seats.

"Sooo," Cassidy said tentatively as they were seated.

"Sooo," Eric shrugged.

"I'm glad we're doing this."

"Um, sure."

"Look, Eric, please. I'm trying here. We've literally never done this before so, you've got to give me a moment to get used to it."

"Do you think we're the only twins that can't handle meeting for a casual drink?" Eric asked with a smirk. Cassidy couldn't help but let out a small giggle. She was happy the tension had started to break.

"Probably."

"Hey! I'm Kelly, I'll be your waitress." A perky, dark haired teenager suddenly appeared at their table.

"Hi," Cassidy smiled at her.

"Do yinz need menus or do you know what you want?"

"Oh, I'll just have a Miller Light," Cassidy said.

"Corona," Eric nodded.

"No food?" Kelly asked. Both Cassidy and Eric shook their heads. "Kay, be right back."

"She's nice," Cassidy commented lamely. She just needed to break the awkward silence.

"Yeah."

"So how's work?"

"It's good," Eric nodded. "Yours?"

"Um, kind of shitty right now," Cassidy admitted.

"Really?" Eric looked surprised.

"Oh yeah."

"Haven't heard you say anything at dinners."

"Well, you know…"

"You want to be the perfect one," Eric interjected. Cassidy winced.

"You know how mom gets. She's just so frantic and she

obsesses over anything wrong…" Cassidy trailed off.

"Here yinz go," Kelly said in a sing song voice as she delivered their drinks to them.

"Thanks," the twins said in unison.

"If you change your mind about food or need refills, I'll be around." Kelly smiled before bounding over to her next table.

"Cassidy," Eric began before taking a sip, "you should tell the family if work is going badly."

"I'm telling you right now," Cassidy countered.

Eric let out an annoyed sigh. "I wish you would talk to us."

"What? I talk all the time!"

"About nonsense. You're too standoffish," Eric accused. Cassidy half choked on her drink.

"I'm standoffish with you, but I'm actively working on that, hence this exact moment."

"Did you tell Alex?"

"No, and I'm starting to regret that I told you."

"I get it. You were always secretive, being the only girl, but we're adults now."

"I'm not secretive," Cassidy said slowly, realizing how false that statement was as it passed her lips.

"How long has work been bad?" Eric asked.

"A little over a month," Cassidy admitted, not making eye contact.

"You could have said something the other week at dinner."

"I don't get why this is such a big deal! You just want to enjoy that things are sucky for me."

"Is that honestly what you think of me? That I'm anxiously watching and waiting for you to fail?" Eric looked a tad offended.

"Um, I mean," Cassidy stuttered; it sounded harsher when

he said it out loud than it did in her head.

"Oh come on. Stop playing the little girl victim," Eric grumbled.

"I'm, I'm-" but even Cassidy couldn't finish that sentence. "I'll work on it," she said, finally, trying to ignore Eric's smile.

"Why is work shitty?" he asked seriously.

"The company's running out of money and we're downsizing."

"I'm sorry. I know that's happening a lot of places, but it sucks that it's happening for you."

"Thanks," Cassidy replied tentatively. Maybe this wasn't so scary.

"Are you going to stay or look for somewhere else?"

"Right now, I'm staying. My boss has me helping with the number crunching, which kind of means I'm safe until the end…. But it also means I'm kind of the hatchet man."

"You have to fire people?"

"No, but I'm the one that has to say that we don't have enough money for everybody. I'm trying to make other suggestions, but we've already lost coffee, snacks, three accountants, and the secretary. The writing is on the wall."

"You should really start looking. You don't want to have to scramble when it finally collapses," Eric pointed out.

"I'm trying not to think about it."

"Unfortunately, you have to."

"Ugh, this is depressing," Cassidy said, shaking her head. "How's Ellie?"

"Oh," Eric looked surprised. "She's good! School is back in session, so she's busy."

"What grade does she teach again?"

"First."

"Aww, the littles," Cassidy cooed. Eric chuckled. "Does that mean she wants a lot of littles herself? Or has she already had her fill of them?"

"Well, you just dive right in there, don't you?"

"We have never conversed before as adults. I'm not going to get it perfect the first time around," Cassidy said playfully. Eric chuckled and rolled his eyes.

"She does want kids - we want kids - but we don't have any specific plans. Although I guess you can never fully plan."

"If you could, we wouldn't have Ben," Cassidy said.

Eric laughed. "No, we wouldn't."

"But we love him anyway."

"To Ben," Eric said mockingly, holding his beer up for a toast.

"Ben," Cassidy agreed clinking her glass against his bottle. They both chuckled as they drank.

"What about you?" Eric asked as their giggles subsided.

"Do I want kids?" Cassidy asked.

"I was going to ask if you were dating one person, or four, but sure, the kid question is fine."

"You're so funny," Cassidy said sarcastically. "I mean, ideally I would like to have a kid or two at some point. I think I would be a good mom."

"Yeah."

"But, um, I am dating someone - just one."

"Really?"

"Yes. I'm surprised Alex didn't say anything."

"He didn't. I guess that is why he's your go-to," Eric said off-handedly.

"I'm not going to apologize that Alex and I get along."

"I wasn't asking you to."

"But you should know, I didn't tell Alex a thing. Jake and I went for a walk downtown one night and we just happened to run into him and Laura. Complete accident."

"Hmm," Eric hummed in thought.

"I really haven't told anyone because I wanted to see where things were going first."

"How is it going?"

"Good," Cassidy replied, blushing slightly. "Really good."

"Do the rest of us get to meet him?" Eric asked.

"Uh, yeah, yeah, we'll, find a time," Cassidy stumbled. Eric started to laugh.

"You act like introducing a boyfriend to the family is equivalent to walking to the gallows."

"No, no, it's not!"

"Feels like it is. We're going to be perfectly civil. Everyone was very nice meeting Ellie - well, except for you."

"I wasn't mean to her, just not... super warm and fuzzy. Again, adding it to the working on it pile."

"Fair enough."

"But I want to make sure that the timing is right. He's from a really small family and we're... kind of big."

"Ellie's in the same boat. Hey, maybe they can be friends! I mean, Laura is practically one of us at this point, so she's too much of an insider."

"I love Laura," Cassidy said defensively.

"So do I!"

"Gah, I remember meeting her. I was what, a junior in high school when they started dating?" Cassidy mused.

"I know, I'm the same age." Eric stared at her looking quite bemused.

"I know."

"Anyway, what did Alex think of... what's his name? Your boyfriend?"

"Jake."

"Yes, Jake."

"Well... Laura liked him. She said I was glowing," Cassidy smiled.

"Glowing? Oh, my god, are you pregnant?" Eric hissed.

"No!"

"Thank God. I had to ask."

"Fine, but no, I am not pregnant."

"Okay, so Laura said you glowed, but not with child," Eric confirmed. Cassidy rolled her eyes. "And Alex?"

"Alex... um, he, was just...."

"Ohhh!" Eric gasped, a grin starting to appear. "Alex hates him, doesn't he?"

"Um."

"So, what happened?" Eric asked, looking positively giddy for gossip.

"You could be less excited about this, Mr. please tell us about your failing job, we're here for you," Cassidy said mockingly.

"I'm sorry. But I am wondering why they didn't get along. Alex is usually easy going."

"I know!"

"Is that why you don't want to bring him home?"

"Kind of. And Jake didn't do anything, Alex was just cranky and miserable with him. Laura likes him though."

"Hmmm."

"She does! We talked on the phone later that night. And Alex and I aren't fighting. We got along fine at dinner the other week."

271

"Did you talk about Jake?"

"Obviously not."

"Obviously."

"Wait, how long did you date Ellie before you brought her home?"

"We're not talking about me," Eric countered.

"We should be. You guys were together for what, almost a year before you dragged her around."

"So?"

"So, Jake and I have only been together since July! I have plenty of time," Cassidy said, taking another drink.

"Ah yes, bring him over at the holidays; that won't be stressful at all," Eric said sarcastically.

"Shit," Cassidy sighed as Eric chuckled.

"Just bring him over, sooner rather than later. You'll feel better about it," Eric advised.

"New topic!"

"We don't have very many," Eric smirked.

"Um, well… Are you planning to bring Ellie to First Friday dinners when you're married?"

"Oh!" Eric seemed surprised by the question. "I hadn't given it much thought. I guess if she would like to come, she can, but she generally uses that time to meet up with her sister."

"Does she just have the one sister?" Cassidy asked, suddenly realizing she knew nothing about her future sister-in-law.

"Yeah, Kara. She's a year older."

"Is she nice?"

"More welcoming than you've been to Ellie," Eric said pointedly. Cassidy bit her tongue at the repeated jab. "But I don't know her super well. I mean I see her at least once a month, but we don't have a ton of conversation."

"Blending families is hard."

"Yeah."

"You know," Cassidy began after a long moment, "I really would be happy to see Ellie - you know, to get to know her a bit."

"Really?"

"Yeah. I mean, I'm not making any promises, but I think if I … try, we could get along, at least a bit."

"First you will promise me that you won't hijack that whole wedding," Eric said firmly.

"Really? That's what you think of me?"

"That is what I know of you," he enunciated carefully.

"That's not fair!"

"Well."

"Eric," Cassidy sighed. "Can't you see I'm trying? I would appreciate a bit of grace here."

Eric paused. "You're right, I'm sorry."

"Forgiven." The twins smiled at each other. The peaceful moment was broken by their bouncy teenage waitress reappearing at the table.

"Yinz want another drink?" Kelly asked. Cassidy and Eric looked at one another.

"Yeah," Cassidy nodded, watching her brother.

"Yep, me too," Eric nodded with a smile.

"Sure thing. Hey, can I ask something? Are you two related or something? You really look alike," Kelly said looking between the two. Cassidy and Eric both chuckled. It had been a very long time since they had been compared.

"We're siblings," Eric said.

"Twins," Cassidy added with a smile.

"Oh wow, yep, definitely see that," Kelly said emphatically.

"That's cool you guys are adults and still hang out, so nice! Well, I'll go get those drinks for you."

"Well," Cassidy chuckled as soon as Kelly was out of ear shot.

"Oh, Kelly," Eric said with a playful sigh.

"She thinks we're friends!"

"I think that proves that we are excellent actors," Eric quipped. Cassidy laughed.

"To the theater careers we missed out on!" Cassidy raised her mostly empty glass.

"Damn straight," Eric agreed, clinking his bottle against hers before they both downed the contents.

"Can I ask you something important?" Cassidy said, leaning forward slightly.

"Hmm?"

"How have we been here for an entire drink and not discussed mom's new hair cut?"

"Oh, my god," Eric gasped. "It's terrible!"

"What is that woman thinking?"

"Absolutely no thought could have gone into that decision," Eric said.

They stayed for another couple of rounds. Cassidy and Eric talked far into the night, about everything and nothing at all. There really could be a relationship there. And both twins were thrilled.

END OF PART ONE

Bonus Content

Do you share a birthday with any of the characters? Stop by Jane's Instagram @janeneagwrites to let her know!

January
19th: Cassidy & Eric

February
11th: Ellie

March
1st: Art

30th: Laura

May
6th: Jake

June
1st: Brandon

August
15th: Ben

October
20th: Lynne

November
5th: Marissa

27th: Alex

December
2nd: Matty

Acknowledgements

This book has been a labor of love. Just shy of two years from writing the first sentence to the release date. The support I have received along the way and the overwhelming cheers at completion have meant the world and honestly brought me to tears. My writer friends, Shanice, Danielle, and Tori – the ones that have helped me craft my unique voice and supported my storytelling for many, many years. My editor, Elyssa – you took my "baby" and helped me sand the edges and gave me so much confidence in the world I created. My beta readers: Shanice, Bethany, Ally, Joni, Brittannie, and Rachel – you all put in the time (a lot of time) and effort to give feedback and encouragement. The Writers Way crew that listened to me, cheered me on and picked me up when I hit blocks. My cover designer, Bec, who crafted the coolest slew of covers and helped make one perfect for my book. And to Megan who took all these pieces and made them book shaped and perfect.

I love writing stories, but they have always been for me. I'm sharing this piece of my soul with the world, and it is scary. I couldn't do it without the cheering section behind me. You all mean so much, even if I haven't mentioned you by name.

Cassidy and I will be back in 2026 with the rest of her tale and I hope she comes to mean as much to my readers as she does to me. She's not perfect, she makes mistakes, but she keeps going. As do I.

- *Jane Neagley*

Follow Jane on instagram @janeneagwrites or online at www.janeneagwrites.com.